Soccer Star

Also by Gregory Saur

Royal Pains and Angels in the Outhouse

Otherworld: Orcish Delight

Stuck in the Past (with Jack Irish)

Panterror! The Epic Babysitting Adventures of Rachel Pugsley

The Pond Scum Gang

Diving Catch

Soccer Star

by

Gregory Saur

Saur
&
Saur

Saur & Saur
Published by Saur & Saur

Soccer Star

First Paperback Printing
2019

Printed in the United States of America

ISBN-13 (pb): 978-1-949317-13-8

To soccer stars everywhere. May you always use your power for good.

"**W**hat do you see when you see the Christmas star shining above the stable?" Brittany lazily asked her brother.

"Easy," muttered Mason. "It looks like a soccer ball being blasted by the greatest right-footed striker in the universe."

Brittany sat up with a jerk. It was Sunday morning before church and the two were sitting on the couch dressed in their uncomfortable church clothes, while waiting for their ride.

"Are you crazy?" she demanded. "You think the Christmas star is a *soccer ball?*"

"Yeah, why not?" Mason asked almost belligerently. He tugged at his white-collared shirt and stared at his sister seriously. "I mean, if He created everything good in the universe, He must've created soccer, too. Stands to reason." His eyes gleamed with sudden conviction, as if he wasn't the boy who never paid a lick of attention during Sunday school. Instead, he looked like a prophet. "I bet all the stars in the sky were kicked there by angels."

A deranged prophet, Brittany decided.

"There are no such things as soccer stars," she scoffed as she smoothed down her worn dress. Her brother was soccer crazy. Christmas had nothing to do with the stupid game.

As if reading her mind, Mason lifted his eyebrows and grinned at her. "You wanna bet?"

SOCCER STAR

Prologue
Part I

"**B**ro, you're going to get us in so much trouble," Zeon Slaydon grumbled to his little brother. "This place is rubbish when it comes to having fun."

Shio, four years junior to Zeon, had all the youthful enthusiasm that had fled Zeon since reaching his teenage years.

"Relax, Ze," he said with a grin, speaking with a lazy Californian American accent. "I have everything under control."

"That's when it all hits the fan," muttered his brother. Zeon shook his head and plunged his hands into the pockets of his tight black jeans. They barely fit and he had to settle with just hiding the tips of his fingers.

With a black leather jacket and dark aviator shades, he looked nothing like the son of a millionaire former-soccer-star-turned-fashion-model. Instead, he looked more like a depressed teenager going through a gloomy phase.

At the moment, he stood next to his little brother but stared past him at the window of a clothing store selling chains for belts. The music blaring from this store was the opposite of Christmas. If anything, it sounded like Christmas dying a horrible death.

"You worry too much," Shio told him cheerfully.

"Whatever, Shio," he growled. "Just don't get the coppers on us."

"Why not?" Shio asked daringly. "They'd be on our side. We could use more players. I bet they get bored standing around this place doing nothing."

"Don't bet on it," grunted his brother. "I'm going to the bench and pretend I don't know you."

"Come on, Ze, you can be keeper."

"Not on your life," Zeon scowled. "Dad would never approve. He'd have a heart attack if any of us stood in front of a goal not trying to score."

Shio chuckled at just the thought of that. Their father told them they were born strikers and had no place near the goal, unless they meant to put the ball in the back of the net. "Be defense, then."

"Right."

The boys were standing in a large open space, just beyond the food court, of the Devon McCourt Mall near their home in Rosewater, California. Whoever Devon McCourt was, he must have hated fun.

Everything in the mall was bland and drab. Around them were stores selling clothes, shoes, mobile devices, and a lot of other "rubbish." There were no stores with toys, books, movies, or, worst of all, soccer gear.

The last one really set Shio off. In England, where their parents were from and where they frequently visited, you could find a football (in America it was called a soccer ball) everywhere you went. Not just England, but pretty much all of Europe had footballs in every direction. Shio couldn't understand, or stand, the thought that this mall, so close to his home, had no use for English football.

"Dad and Mum should be coming soon," Zeon said reasonably, and perhaps hopefully. "They asked me to keep you out of trouble, remember."

"Just keep the ball out of the goal and you'll have no trouble," Shio said, as he dumped his backpack on the hard floor and bent over to open it.

His brother groaned. "You're daft! You really mean this, don't you?" He glanced hastily around and was relieved to see nobody watching them. Yet. "Why do you have to be such a bleeding idiot?" Looking at the back view of his brother, he drew back his foot as if about to kick. "I should punt your backside for this."

"Try this instead." Shio withdrew a small soccer ball and rolled it between his legs to his brother.

Zeon made to kick it at his brother's bent-over form, but at the last moment stopped the ball with his foot and kept it there. He sighed. "No way. This ball isn't moving."

Shio stood and turned on his brother. "Don't be so posh," he said, slipping into his normal English accent. "Playing football is a lot better than just standing around like scenery."

Zeon sighed. His brother was right.

They didn't go out much by themselves. Almost never. Too many people recognized them from the internet and gossip TV shows. Their father, Michal Slaydon, had starred on the pitch with Liverpool and England, as well as clothing advertisements, while their mother had played professional tennis before dropping out to become a clothing model. Ever since the two stars had married eighteen years earlier, the media in every country they went to couldn't get enough of them. They went berserk trying to fit in as much Slaydon coverage as possible.

Zeon and Shio's parents did their best to keep their family out of the limelight. It made it difficult to raise five children in a normal way—even outings to the mall required careful planning. Planning that was about to all go out the window.

"Mum will never let us come here alone again," Zeon said, almost pleadingly. "They trust us, you know."

"Then you should trust me," Shio said reasonably.

Zeon sighed, saying, "I'm not daft." It was Christmastime and the mall's loudspeakers now played some lovey-dovey pop song by a teenage singer about finding love in the snow. He idly wondered if he'd met the singer—probably had once or twice. Having famous parents had its perks, but also its downfalls. Life was full of peaks and valleys, his dad always said. Just as long as there was a soccer ball to kick, it would all turn out all right … right?

One good thing about the USA, few people watched soccer, or cared much for it—not like English fans. Still, with social media and television, there were plenty who recognized the Slaydon name and family faces. And like the English, the Americans loved their gossip.

That morning, when their father mentioned having to stop at the mall to discuss donating items from their clothing line for a Christmas auction, Shio casually asked if he could come. Their mother, Natasha Slaydon, had been against it, but Zeon mentioned wanting to buy a new CD and promised to keep an eye on Shio. Their mother told him to buy the CD on the internet and just download it, but she knew Zeon enjoyed collecting the physical CDs of all his music. He always said it meant more in his hand and he liked the cover art. She finally relented and Operation Devon McCourt commenced. Christopher and Maria, the youngest at nine and seven respectively, would stay at home with Teresa Manning, the hired tutor and nanny. The oldest, Marcus, had gone to Sweden for a ski trip with his girlfriend's family.

For the mall trip, the boys took a separate car from their parents, just in case the paparazzi, that army of camera-wielding maniacs, spotted them. They left from the back entrance of the house as their parents left from the front. Their grandfather drove them and dropped them off at one of the mall's side entrances, precisely as Mr. and Mrs. Slaydon stepped onto the curb from the parking lot. Their parents both wore long coats, ball caps, and sunglasses as disguises from the public. As they neared, the boys and parents barely exchanged nods before entering the mall.

In Europe, security would have been even tighter. The Slaydon parents wanted their children to grow up as normally as possible. At the same time, their greatest fear was a kidnapping, or worse. While they gave some freedom to their kids, they never left the house without a plan.

Their grandfather then went to park the car and wait. He never noticed the third car that had followed and parked some distance away. Some plans were better than other plans.

That had all happened an hour ago. Their parents were still meeting with some organizer. Zeon hadn't been able to find a store selling the new CD he wanted, and Shio hadn't been able to find anything fun to do. Both were grouchy as a result. Zeon handled his disappointment with gloom. Shio decided to make his own fun.

"Pass the ball, Ze," Shio said, backing up a few steps, dancing on the toes of his yellow Adidas sneakers. He wore black and white athletic pants and a red jersey from his club soccer team. Everything about him—his looks, his clothes—spoke loud and clear, "I'm a soccer star!"

Zeon sighed. He used to play soccer, but just for fun. Shio, on the other hand, lived for the game.

"Look," he said. "Just take a seat and wait for Mum and Dad. There's no place for a game, Shio."

They were in the middle of a large, tiled, square room, boxed in by stores on three sides, with the fourth being an opening that led to the main thoroughfare and food court. Benches for weary shoppers were flanked on either side of them, facing each other. Where they stood, a cluster of potted palm trees grew beneath a skylight.

It was late afternoon on a Thursday, but people still roamed the stores. Christmas was just over a week away. Intent on holiday shopping, nobody seemed to notice the two boys.

"The benches are the goals," Shio said, shrugging his slight shoulders. "Palm trees mark out-of-bounds." He grinned. "If we start something, there can be two fields."

"You're off your trolley," Zeon growled at him. Still, he rolled the ball to his brother. "Go have a gas. I'm going to the bench and act like I've never seen you before." He was just about to do it, too.

In truth, the boys did not look very much like brothers. Zeon stood a head taller than Shio but was stockier, taking after his father. Zeon had a lighter complexion and a round face. His chestnut eyes slanted down away from his pug nose and he had a small mouth above his rounded chin. Standing next to his father, he looked almost like a younger brother. At fifteen, he was starting to fill out as a man.

Shio was almost like his counterexample. With a darker complexion and slighter build, he took more after their mother. His eyes, a dark brown like his mother's eyes, were almost black, slanted down toward the nose, and shaped like almonds. A sharp chin, wide mouth with thin lips, and big ears sticking out from his thin face, gave him the unfortunate nickname of Elf during the holidays.

Not long before, at a holiday party after Thanksgiving, his mother had actually dressed as an elf queen and he went as her elf servant. Their father went as a knight in shining armor while Zeon and Marcus, their older brother at seventeen, were his squires. Their younger siblings were lucky enough to be too young to attend that one. Still, the family was the hit of the party and Shio had come home with lipstick all over his cheeks. Zeon claimed all "his" lipstick didn't miss.

In any case, as Zeon had learned over and over, life with Shio was never dull. No matter how hard he wished it could be sometimes.

Prologue
Part II

Just as Zeon started for the bench, it happened, just like always.

"Um, excuse me," said a shy young female voice, "but you're Marcus Slaydon, aren't you?"

"It's really you! And that's your brother, Shio," said another high voice, this one hyper.

All the Slaydon boys had brown hair clipped close on the sides. Marcus's and Zeon's hair was slightly darker and spiked in the front. Shio preferred his swept to the side so it looked like waves of milk chocolate caught in a hurricane. He stood out, while his older brothers were hopelessly mistaken as each other.

Zeon inwardly groaned. He turned to mumble a negative, when Shio—his good looks, athletic body, and small brain— stepped smoothly in front of his brother.

"Hiya!" he said cheerfully. Then he quickly slipped into his American accent. Having been all over the world, he'd developed several accents and was rarely too shy to use them.

"My name is Keanu Kissmigh and this is my friend Bode Lishous," he said, smiling.

Two girls, both about fourteen, stared at him. Neither knew what to say for a moment.

"Uh," said the girl who had spoken first, "I, I think you're Shio Slaydon, you know, Michal Slaydon's son."

"And you're Marcus," the other girl blurted, looking at Zeon. "I've seen you before."

"Really?" Zeon asked dumbly. "I mean, I don't recognize you."

The girl at least had the grace to blush. "I mean on the TV and, er, on the internet."

Shio shook his head. "Bode is my best friend, but he's, um, well, he's not all there. You'll have to excuse him. Are you sisters?"

The girls looked at each other and giggled, shaking their heads. One was taller with dark hair and the other a little more compact with dots of acne surrounding her petite nose.

Zeon shoved his brother away, sending him stumbling to the side.

"Ignore, um—"

"Keanu," Shio said helpfully, rubbing his shoulder.

"He's, uh, my—"

"Brother," Shio said. "I already said we were brothers."

Zeon felt his face go hot. "He's a real pest, is what he is."

"I love your accent," said the first girl—the taller one—to Zeon. She giggled again. "It's really cute."

"Thanks," said Shio, "you have a nice accent too."

"Is he always like that?" asked the second girl. She rubbed the pimples self-consciously, but her eyes never left Zeon's face.

Zeon gulped. "Uh, yeah," he mumbled. "But look, uh, we're not, we're not who you think we are." He laughed hollowly. "Lots of people think that though."

The first girl looked crestfallen. "Really? Oh, we're so sorry. You two really look like—well, I'm so, so sorry."

"Are you sure?" the second girl demanded, not giving up. "You look exactly like Marcus."

"I'm definitely not Marcus," Zeon said, a bit sharply. "Look, we were about—"

"To challenge you two in a game," Shio said, again stepping in front of his brother.

"No, we were about to meet our parents. Bye!" Zeon grabbed Shio's shoulders from behind and dragged him back. After a few steps, he physically turned Shio around and put his arm firmly around his back.

"What about my ball and bag?" Shio hissed.

"Hopefully those girls will take it all with them," Zeon muttered.

"You didn't even let me finish," Shio complained.

"What do you mean?"

"Keanu Kissmigh. I was going to say Keanu Kissmigh—"

"Quiet!" Zeon said, shoving his free hand over Shio's mouth. He glanced back. "They're still watching us!"

They reached the other side of the large space and were in front of a jewelry store.

Shio jerked from his brother's arm and bent down to tie his shoe. "Relax, Ze," he said. "I don't think they even care about us."

"What do you mean?" Zeon muttered. He stared intently inside the store at a display of diamond rings. "They were on us like flies."

"All they wanted was Marcus." Shio looked up and fluttered his eyelashes. "Oh, Marcus, I love your accent. It's so cute!"

Grunting, Zeon threw a knee into Shio's side, sending the smaller boy crashing into the tile.

"Oops," he muttered without apology.

Shio glared from where he lay on his side and kicked his brother's shin.

Zeon hopped back in pain. "Ouch, you maniac!"

A tall man dressed in black pants and a crisp white shirt and tie charged from the back of the jewelry store. "Hey, you kids better scram!" he said sharply. "We don't want your kind hanging around here!"

Zeon quickly yanked Shio to his feet and the brothers hastily retreated from the store. Thankfully, the two girls had vanished and they were able to return to their former spot. Shio quickly went to his ball and flicked it up with his feet, easily keeping it in the air.

Zeon slumped to a seat on the edge of a bucket holding one of the palm trees. "Life is the pits," he said. He rubbed his shin. "And you kick like a horse with a gas problem."

Shio deftly kept the ball up, tapping it with his feet and thighs so it didn't hit the floor. At the same time, he kept in one spot. "You started it," he said.

"Did not!"

"You're right," Shio said. "Marcus did."

Zeon got up in a huff and stomped to the bench away from Shio and farthest from the jewelry store. Leaning against the armrest, he scowled at his younger brother as he rested his head on his hand.

His mind started to drift and his thoughts went back to the girls ... why did everyone only think about Marcus and Shio? What about him?

Shio ignored his brother as he kept count of how many hits of the ball he had without allowing it to hit the floor. He'd just hit two hundred when he became aware he wasn't alone. All at once, he caught the ball neatly on top of his right foot and brought it to the ground, letting it rest at his feet.

"Hiya," he said, turning to his right.

A boy about his age, wearing a wistful expression, had been watching for a while.

"You're good," the boy said.

Shio shrugged. "You fancy a go? I mean, you want to try?"

"Um, sure," the boy said. "My mom is in Lillard's buying a dress. She could be in there for days."

Shio passed the ball to the boy and soon the boys were chatting while sending the ball between their feet. Two touches became one and soon the boys were lost in a game of pass as they weaved their way between benches, the cluster of palm trees, and the occasional shopper. Most ignored the boys, but there were a few hard stares.

Zeon was scarcely aware of their laughter as he sank deeper into his thoughts when, all of a sudden, he felt a presence next to him.

Jerking upright, he turned and saw a man dressed in a black trench coat reading a newspaper. He'd sat so quietly that Zeon had never noticed him. The man put down the paper when he saw Zeon's reaction.

"Sorry if I startled you," he said without emotion. He ran a large pink tongue over his unshaven lip as if tasting something good. Then flipping the paper closed, he smacked it on his lap and turned his head to Zeon. "Surprised to see me?"

Zeon grunted and dropped his gaze. "I should have smelled you, Luke," he said. The man reeked of cheap cologne. Zeon had smelled it so often he'd gotten used to it. "Why are you here?" His fright quickly turned to annoyance, but at the same time he seemed slightly nervous.

Luke Benchie always made him feel just a tad uncomfortable. He rarely ever spoke, except when spoken to, and he always smelled like he bathed in cologne. Shio and Christopher joked that he drank the stuff for tea. Eight years ago, he'd been hired as a driver for the family, for when they needed an extra driver, or wanted to get around town without being noticed. Otherwise, he ran errands and did the shopping when the Slaydons couldn't, or didn't want to leave the house to face the paparazzi.

Average in height, he had black thinning hair and a plain face. Unremarkable in name, looks, and personality, Luke served loyally and without complaint. Zeon's parents trusted him with picking up the children when needed and he did his job well. It was just that he never seemed comfortable around the Slaydons.

Once Zeon had asked his mum about it, and she'd explained that he came from a poor family who practically worshipped Liverpool and cheered Michal Slaydon like a hero. "Working for us," she'd told him, "is like you one day working for Iron Man. It just seems like a dream to him."

Luke cleared his throat, bringing Zeon out of his thoughts.

"Your father texted me that they would be late. He wished to make sure you and young Shio were being taken care of."

Zeon grunted and gestured at where Shio neatly chested down a high pass from a strange boy. "See for yourself. We're all about to be arrested."

"Yes," Luke said, his eyes narrowing. "I've been watching. Shio has your father's skill. He's quite good." Luke sounded more interested than impressed … and not alarmed at all.

Zeon smiled wryly and crossed his arms. "What he got in looks he got double in skill. That's what Mum says."

"Does she really?" Luke turned to Zeon and smiled. "That is something to be noted. You don't seem to mind that much. Do you?"

"About not being a brilliant footballer?" Zeon laughed. "I don't care. I see what Dad and Mum have to go through and I want nothing to do with it. I'd rather be something different."

"Like what?"

Zeon squirmed under Luke's gaze. This had to be the longest conversation he'd ever had with the driver. "Don't really know yet," he said sullenly. "Maybe a doctor or something." Then he grinned. "But Shio? He's different. He's going to be like Dad. He'll be playing pro one day. You'll see."

"Oh, you never know," Luke said absentmindedly. "The thing is, Zeon, to plan and always be open to change. You may not know yet what you want to do in life, but that will come. Life finds a way of bringing you to where you're intended to be. You just need to be ready for it."

"Like it brought you to be our driver?" Zeon asked, dubiously. "Is that what you wanted?"

Luke smiled and sat back. "Actually, yes," he said mildly. "It's a dream come true. You have no idea where I come from."

Feeling chagrin, Zeon grunted an apology and reached into his pocket for his phone. From a poor family now working for his childhood idol. Of course Luke would be happy. Zeon shook out his legs as he slumped back with the phone in front of him. As he was about to enter his password, he heard a cry of alarm.

Then a soccer ball sailed from nowhere, smacking his lap, right between his legs.

"Ooo!" he groaned, doubling over from sudden pain.

"Oops!" Shio cried from the palm trees. "That was supposed to curve more. Nice stop, Ze."

His eyes bugging out, Zeon croaked an answer before dropping to his knees, still bent over in agony.

Luke put a hand on his shoulder. "Are you okay, Zeon?" he asked, sounding concerned. "I'm afraid I didn't see it until the last second."

"Just … fine," he croaked. "Worry about Shio," he gasped. "I'm going … to get … him."

With great effort, he staggered to his feet.

Luke muttered something and quickly started reading his newspaper. "I don't step between quarreling siblings …"

Shio stared timidly from behind a palm tree. "Really, Ze. I was aiming for the spot next to you. I only meant to startle you. That's it."

The boy who'd been playing pass backed away slowly. He looked scared.

Zeon could only imagine what his own face looked like. Then, he turned his murderous gaze on the soccer ball that had settled a few feet away. As he stepped toward it, an outraged squeal came from the store behind him.

Whirling, he saw a middle-aged woman charging him with two large shopping bags in her hands.

Terrified and thinking she meant to barge him over, he flinched back and fell into Luke's lap, tearing the paper.

The woman didn't even look his way.

"Georgie Adams!" she seethed. "I heard there were boys fooling around out here and I was sure it wasn't my son! Now get over here right this minute!"

Shio scrunched his eyes and twisted his mouth in a frown. "We were just playing," he said.

The woman had never stopped moving. She glared at him. "Young man, I don't know who your parents are, but if you were my boy, you'd be very sorry right now. Now I suggest you find them before security finds you. This is no playground!"

Shoppers stopped to stare. Zeon saw the man from the jewelry store step out and lean against the wall. A smirk played across his smug face.

Zeon swallowed as he slowly slid away from Luke and took a seat on the bench.

Poor Georgie Adams gulped and ducked his head. He quickly met his mother and took one of her bags. "Sorry, Mom," he muttered.

"Embarrassing me in front of everyone!" thundered the woman, as she kept a brisk pace toward the mall's thoroughfare. "I've never been so ashamed! I told everyone it couldn't be my son. Not him! He wouldn't dare do such a thing as playing *soccer* in the mall."

Georgie left, his head bent low. He never looked back. The woman's voice seemed to take forever to fade.

"Nice one, Shio," Zeon said as his little brother trudged sheepishly to the bench.

Shio carried his backpack listlessly next to him. Both acted oblivious to the shoppers around them. Most had quickly resumed their activities, but a few still lingered, drawn to public trouble like flies to a trashcan. Both boys had grown up surrounded by camera-mad paparazzi and fans. Only Luke acted uncomfortable with the attention.

"Look, boys," he said nervously. "Why don't I take you home now? Zeon, we can stop on the way to buy your CD."

"How did you know I didn't get it?" Zeon asked, frowning.

"Easy. You're not carrying a bag or listening to it."

"I'd rather wait for Dad and Mum," Shio said, flopping in the small space between Luke and his brother. He sighed sadly. "It was still a good idea," he said.

Zeon grunted. "You know, Shio. If you want mates, just ask Dad. He'll find some for you."

"I just wish I could go out and find my own, like everyone else." Shio kicked the tile sadly. "Why can't we go out by ourselves and play football with nobody caring?"

Zeon snorted, "Because this is a mall, not a pitch." He tried putting an arm around his brother's shoulders, but Shio shook it off.

"You know what I mean," he growled.

Zeon shook his head sadly. "Shio, Shio," he said, "don't you understand? You're a Slaydon. You can't and won't ever be normal. Get used to it."

Luke huffed, as he gathered his torn paper in a ball as quietly and discreetly as he could. "Shio, if you're done," he said stiffly, "and I do think you're done, please put your ball away before anything else happens." He clapped a hand on the boy's knee. "I think I see a security officer coming this way."

Shio jumped up as if shocked and grabbed his ball. He then quickly moved behind the bench and hastily started stuffing it back into his backpack, ducking out of view.

This did not stop the guard from marching straight to the bench.

Thankfully, the guard did not come alone.

"There you guys are," said a soft British voice with a hint of humor. "Where's Shio gone off to?"

"Dad!" Shio sprang from behind the bench. Standing behind the guard, still dressed in his hat and glasses, Michal Slaydon grinned widely.

"I figured they would be here, sir," the guard said, grinning. "It's not often we get a call about soccer hooligans hitting shoppers with balls."

"It was just me," Zeon said hastily. "I mean, Shio just hit me. We didn't cause any trouble. Really."

"Is that right?" Michal Slaydon squeezed his lips tightly. "I was just in the process of closing a charity deal when I heard somebody screaming about seeing two Slaydon boys in the mall. I stepped out to see what the matter was and found two highly excited girls with cell phones. Yes, your pictures were there, all right." He grinned mischievously. "They didn't even recognize me, but were set on calling their friends. I judge we have about thirty seconds to get out of here before a teenage mob of hysterical girls comes crashing down on us."

Shio leapt onto the back of the bench and dropped his backpack in Zeon's lap. Then, he threw himself on his dad's back.

"Ooof! Shio, you need to warn an old man before you do that, mate," his father said, pretending to stagger. He reached back and gave a light smack to the back of Shio's pants. "No more football until we get to the pitch. You hear?"

"Let's go, Dad," Zeon said, sounding tired. "I hear screaming approaching."

A babble of voices was definitely approaching.

Michal Slaydon nodded. "I already texted Granddad to meet us outside of Lillard's. He should be waiting with his engine running."

The group started from the bench toward the large store behind them.

"What about Mum?" Shio asked, still hanging onto his dad's back.

"Finishing the deal," his dad replied. "We're giving this guy rights to sell our clothes and in exchange he's agreeing to donate to our Holiday Charity Ball next Sunday."

"Mr. Slaydon, perhaps I should take the boys," Luke said. "You can stay with your wife."

"That's okay, Luke. I'm glad to get out of those business meetings. Granddad will drive us. Why don't you stick around and do some holiday shopping?"

Luke almost sounded desperate. "But you called. I thought you needed me."

"Sorry about that, Luke. You know how Granddad hates being seen in public. I just wanted to make sure the boys didn't burn the place down."

"Never a dull moment in the lives of the Slaydon family," Zeon said without humor.

"Pardon me," said another voice. The jewelry store employee had followed them to the entrance of Lillard's. "But are you, are you Michal Slaydon? The soccer star?"

Michal Slaydon stopped and turned slowly.

"He's probably the one who called security," Zeon mumbled.

"Yes, I'm Michal Slaydon. And these are two of my boys. I'm very sorry to inform you, but no, I'm not buying in your shop today. Perhaps for New Year's. Cheers."

"Is, is there anything I can do to help?" the man said desperately, wiping sweat from his brow. "I mean, please let your boys know they're welcome anytime. Even if they do bring a soccer ball."

"Distract the crowd behind us," Michal Slaydon said, already turning around. "That would be brilliant."

When the throng arrived, many holding out cell phones ready to snap pictures, they were met by an amused security guard and one beaming jewelry store employee.

"Ladies! And gentlemen! Please stop right there!" cried the man, smoothing down his white shirt.

"Where are the Slaydons?" cried a woman loudly. "We thought they were here!"

The man held up both his hands and then motioned to his shop. "They are! Well, they were. They may have left, but if you're interested, you may view the watch Michal Slaydon has his eye on, or the diamond broach Natasha Slaydon wants. Come right this way ..."

The Slaydon family had escaped danger that day. A new day would arrive.

The Kickoff

Chapter 1

"So, do we kill him today?" the voice asked casually, almost as if bored. It was early Friday morning, hours before sunrise.

The woman blinked and dropped her gaze. Even from the shadows she could feel the cold eyes staring at her. Watching for her reaction. She swallowed. Across from her, the man sounded as cool as a glass of lemonade on a hot summer's day. Did death mean so little to him?

The woman tried to hide her shock by brushing her blouse free of imaginary crumbs. Then she looked up. They were in her apartment at her kitchen table. She was *not* going to be intimated.

As if reading her mind, the man slouched lazily back in his seat and calmly fingered an unlit cigarette as he continued to stare, always just beyond the light from the single bulb hanging over their heads. It hung like an all-seeing eye, blaring down without blinking or flinching.

She knew better. Beneath his cool exterior, the man was frightened. Or was he?

"You know what he said," she replied, trying to sound casual but firm. "We wait until he tells us. Not until then, and only *if* he tells us."

Her companion grunted and pushed himself forward so his face hit the glaring light straight on. He never flinched. Placing his elbows firmly on the table between them, he pressed his knuckles into his chin, squashing the cigarette. "You know he's crazy, right? Stark mad."

The woman glared, her eyes flickering with real anger. "Don't say that!" she snapped. "He's going to make us rich."

"Or dead."

"Whatever," the woman muttered.

They'd only known each other for a few months, brought together by a daring scheme from a mutual acquaintance. It was a scheme that promised to make all of them very rich. Or very dead. The mutual acquaintance happened to be the man she loved. And who loved her in return. He wouldn't put her in real harm's way. Everything would go as planned.

"Nobody is going to die," she said carefully. "Not us. And not him. Not the package. It's a straight case of kidnapping and ransom. That's it. Happens all the time all around the world."

The man in front of her snorted in disbelief. Then he chuckled harshly. "Is that what he told you? Really?"

"I love him!" the woman said, almost pleading. "We're doing this together, don't you get it?"

The man threw up his hands as if surrendering. "Okay, okay. I get it! We'll do it your way. We grab the package and zoom away in our getaway car. Then we wait for the five million to be wired to our bank accounts and off we go to a new country and new future! You go with lover boy and I go with greenbacks." He laughed bitterly. "Sounds like a fairy tale."

The woman swallowed her anger, mixed, she had to admit, with a dose of fear. "It's no fairy tale. We've planned this for months and he had it planned for years. Everything will work out. We're not going to let him down."

The man raised his eyebrows. "You sound like you mean it."

"I do." She met the cold, mocking eyes and dropped her voice.

"Right." The man sighed. "You just said he planned this for years and that we planned for months ... well, as I understand it, he already changed his plans. At least a dozen times."

"You know what I mean," she said icily. "He planned what to do when the opportunity arrived. The opportunity has arrived for the right one at the right time. This is it. We're not going to let him down."

"Huh," the man said.

"Huh?"

"The tough woman act. It's all the rage now in Hollywood, isn't it?"

"This is no act."

The man suddenly grinned, "We'll see when the time comes."

"It has already come."

"So you say."

"Look. I don't really know you, but I do know one thing. *He* helped you and *he* helped me. You know where we were when he found us."

The man lost his humor. For a long moment he stared frostily into her eyes, but she didn't look away this time. His piercing gaze held no warmth. His eyes were large, dark marbles with a glint of cold green. It was like gazing into the eyes of a cobra just before it bit you on the nose.

"You agreed to this and so did I," he said, almost in a purr. "But let's get one thing straight. This is about more than money. This is about cold-blooded revenge." His voice grew rough and twisted. The woman's heart started beating rapidly and she had to force herself not to shudder or drop her gaze. "He was wronged and so was I. Kicked out by society like garbage. Yes, he pulled me from the gutter. Saved me from the streets, sure. But you? You're just a privileged, spoiled rich girl who stayed out too late and met the wrong guy. You think you're doing this for love? For him? I don't care. I'm doing this for the eight years of my life that was crushed and kicked out from under me. The eight years I wished I was dead, or worse, that I had never been born. And if I kill one rich punk to make it all worth it, then I will. With pleasure. Got it?"

The woman kept her lips tight and never broke her gaze. Then she glanced down at her watch. "It's time," she said. "We have to meet the, er, package."

The man stretched as he stood. "I'll grab my coat. Do you want to stop for coffee?"

Shio woke up with a start. For a moment he lay still. Downstairs he could hear the arguing, still going on. The muffled shouts of his parents sounded like distant bombshells from an old war movie. Unfortunately, these were hitting not only too close to home, but *in* his home. This one had started during dinner that night and had yet to let up, except for a short, tense bedtime routine. But now that the kids were supposedly safely tucked in, the barrage of yelling began again.

He rolled over on his bed with a sigh. His parents didn't fight very much, but when they did it was like World War III had broken out. Marcus told him it was because they were both such big stars that they couldn't stand to lose. Shio didn't care much about why, just as long as he didn't lose his parents. Too many kids in California were victims of divorce and he didn't want to join the club.

A loud crash shook the floor. For a moment Shio tensed, but then he relaxed. His parents yelled and sometimes broke things, all accidents of course, but they never went beyond that. He was used to their carrying on and knew there was nothing he could do about it. Stepping between his parents when angry was like stepping between a bull and a tiger. Just as long as they made up ...

He vaguely wondered if he and his dad were still flying to New York that morning. They were supposed to leave at dawn to make it to New York by night. His mum and siblings would fly out the next week to meet them. For a moment he stared in the thick blackness wondering what lay out there. Would his parents cancel the trip?

Then he noticed a dark shadow entering his room. He froze and his heartbeat quickened. Ever since he could remember, his dad and mum drilled him and his siblings about the danger of kidnapping. Being children of celebrities made them targets. He was just about to call out when the shadow spoke.

"I'm scared," said a small voice. Instantly, Shio went limp with relief. His little brother, Christopher, slept in the next room but often sought the comfort of an older brother when he couldn't sleep. A small whimper told Shio that he'd brought their sister with him.

Groaning, Shio slid out of his covers and shivered in the cool air. He reached over to his bed stand and clicked on the light. The three Slaydon children blinked at each other in their pajamas.

"Well," Shio growled, brushing tousled hair from his brow. "You coming up?"

They needed no second invitation. The two youngest Slaydon children ran and leapt on his bed, quickly moving to either side of their older brother.

"Why didn't you go to Zeon's room?" Shio asked, more out of curiosity than annoyance. He actually welcomed their presence. Lately, it seemed as if their family was slipping away and it felt nice to be needed.

"He snores," Maria said, sniveling. "He sounds like a monster."

Shio shivered as their dad's angry voice reverberated from the floor. The real monster was below them.

A little while later, their grandfather poked his head in, drawn by the light. Seeing the children huddled together, he shook his head. "It's a bit late to be up, isn't it? But no worry, I'll join you. Sometimes it can be hard to sleep." The shouting continued below. "For everyone."

Shio quickly made room for his grandfather, more than happy to see him.

Even at his old age, their grandfather moved easily as he slid next to Shio on the now crowded bed. Christopher and Maria instantly crawled over Shio to sit on their grandfather's lap. Shio leaned against his shoulder, happy to have him like a pillar of support.

Granddad Rubinov was their mother's father and had first come to England from Russia as a small boy when his parents fled Communist persecution. He'd returned to his native land as a young tennis pro, having learned the game in his adopted country. Shio didn't know much about his life there, since Granddad rarely spoke of it, but he knew his grandmother died giving birth to his mother. He also knew Granddad Rubinov, though crushed, had put aside his grief and spent the next several years raising his daughter as best he could, which meant she played a lot of tennis.

By the time Shio's mother was a teenager, she was a star on the court and a fashion queen off the court. Her looks made her more famous than her serve and she started pulling away from the game. This hurt her father, who had served as her tennis coach.

Then she'd met a soccer star during a Wimbledon tournament and had fallen in love. Michal Slaydon was just making his mark for Liverpool then and had asked the right people to meet the model tennis star in person. The two had hit if off immediately. When they married, Granddad Rubinov returned to Russia.

Then the kids started coming and Granddad was invited to babysit when their parents traveled for their professions. Natasha Slaydon had put away her tennis racket, but had started her own clothing line and was busy with charities and modeling. By the time Shio came around, Granddad Rubinov was a permanent fixture in the Slaydon household.

He was a man who'd seen a lot of hardships but never let it dry up his soul, making him the perfect substitute parent. Now in his sixties, he kept his lithe, athletic form from his tennis days, mostly, he claimed, from chasing after the boys. His once thick dark hair had thinned and grown stark white, sticking out around his head like a lion's mane. Dark eyes flashed from his wrinkled face, weathered by the scorching sun of many tennis matches, half hidden behind a clipped goatee. He almost always wore a fierce look and rarely smiled, constantly looking as if he had tasted something bitter. However, the kids knew beneath his rough exterior was a gentle soul who would do anything to protect them.

The only problem, he couldn't protect them from hearing the loud shouting from beneath their feet. Maria's lip trembled.

Immediately, Granddad's eyes softened and he made shushing noises. "Just thunder in the dark," he said. "That's all your parents do. They make bangs, but then it goes away. Come now. Let's have a story."

Soon, he had the children caught up in a funny tale about a snobby prince who married an apple tree to claim he bore good fruit. Christopher and Marie didn't get it as their eyes struggled to stay open, but Shio gave his grandfather a smile. Just as the finale neared, when the good fruit turned rotten, a sharp knocking sounded at the door.

Shio jumped and Granddad went tense. "Who's there?" he said. The muffled yelling had died down and Maria and Christopher had drifted to sleep. Shio had just begun drifting off but now his eyes were wide open.

The door swung open and Luke stepped in with Tom Blazer right behind him. Tom Blazer, tall and bald, had played with Michal Slaydon at Liverpool and remained his closest friend. He lived down the block and served as advisor and manager to the Slaydon family. Both men wore suits in the late hour and both looked grim.

"I think we need to get the kids in bed, except for you, Shio," Luke said, his lips barely parting they were so tight.

"What's going on?" Shio asked, sliding off his bed, not caring that he wore his soccer pajamas in front of the grown men.

"There's been … a problem," Luke said.

"What problem?" Granddad demanded.

"It's time for you to leave, Shio," Tom said bluntly. "There's been a leak about an argument here and there's a crowd of media forming outside the house. Your dad is coming with me to the airport. Mr. Rubinov, Luke will drive us, but we're hoping you could take Shio by the back way."

The Slaydons lived in a mansion on five acres of land surrounded by a wall with multiple ways out. The front drive had a double gate at the end, but in the back was a small lane that led to a hidden door in the wall. Used in emergencies to slip out quietly, it opened to a small road lined with trees on either side that twisted and turned, before meeting up with the main road just outside the neighborhood where the Slaydon family lived. Only some of their neighbors, mostly celebrities themselves, knew about it.

"Of course," Granddad said, with a grunt. He wore a bathrobe and slippers. "Let me get dressed first." He gently put down Maria in Shio's bed and lay Christopher next to her. Neither one stirred. They would sleep there that night.

"You get dressed too, Shio," Tom said. He rubbed his unshaven jaw, blocking the door so Granddad couldn't leave. "I don't know who tipped them off, but this could be big. Those bloodsuckers out there have been waiting for something like this for a long time. To find out Mike's going to New York without Natasha ... I almost wonder if it would be better if Shio was to be seen with him. You know, to show that the family isn't kicking him out."

Granddad shook his head. "You don't use the children as pawns in a game," he said gruffly. "Shio comes with me. This trip has been planned like this already. We won't let gossip mongers run our lives."

"Right," Tom muttered, giving a tight grin. He winked at Shio. "Isn't it great to be famous?"

Shio, feeling sick to his stomach, hurried out and ran for the bathroom, suddenly needing to go badly. He felt eyes watching him. It was not a good feeling.

Chapter 2

A little while later, Shio leaned back in the backseat of the Slaydon silver BMW, dressed in his soccer warm-up pants and a long-sleeved T-shirt. Even in mid-December, Southern California proved more cool than cold. Later, in New York, he would have to find a coat.

The door opened on his left and a young woman smiled at him as she slid in next to him. She took the middle seat, placing her bag next to her.

"Hello, Shio," she said. "I hope you don't mind me riding with you, but Tom thought it would be best. You know, if I went with your, er, father … well, people wouldn't understand."

Shio shrugged and looked away.

Teresa Manning worked as his private tutor and traveled with the family to make sure he and his siblings didn't fall behind their studies. She came from New York and had been recommended by Luke, her then and still current boyfriend.

In her mid-thirties, she looked much younger and had a pretty face. With curly dark hair tied in a ponytail, no makeup and wearing jeans and a sweater, she still looked attractive. She was flying to

New York, but not as an employee. She'd asked just a day before to visit her family for Christmas and had been given permission.

Schoolwork was put on hold for the holidays, something Shio was very happy about. Teresa wasn't a bad teacher, but she laughed too much and tried too hard to be his friend. Worse, she knew nothing about sports, especially soccer.

Granddad, having packed the bags in the trunk, slid behind the wheel and they were off. Shio's dad had already left to face the cameras and microphones. Even behind darkened windows, in the backseat of a luxury sedan, he would be mobbed with questions and flashes.

Shio hated that part of being a celebrity. But he still wished he was at his dad's side to face it down. He mentioned this aloud and Teresa giggled nervously.

"They wouldn't understand," she said. "They always think the worst. The media is like this country. They think they own the world and everyone around them is their personal puppet. When things don't go the way they want, they jerk the strings and try to get everything back in line." Then she sat back and closed her eyes.

Shio stared out the window into the dark. Then the radio flipped on to the international news.

"Granddad," he groaned, "do you have to play the radio? It's not even music!"

"Of course I do, my boy. How else is an old man supposed to learn about what's happening in the world?"

"Use your phone," Shio grumbled.

"I'm an old man, Shio. Phones to me are things used to call people from long distances. I don't know why your father lets you boys have one when you do everything on it *but* call people."

"I promise. I'll call you when we get there." He fingered his flip phone. All the Slaydon children carried one—just in case they needed to call in an emergency … or play a game.

"Call me what, I wonder," Granddad grumbled. "Young people always come up with funny names for people like me. Yesterday some punk called me a 'fogey.' What is that?"

They'd left their street and headed to the highway. It was a little after four in the morning, but traffic was far from light. Shio still saw crowds of people hanging out just outside of restaurants and bars.

"What are they doing?" he asked, yawning. The voice on the radio was talking about another shooting.

Blue flashing lights lit up a parking lot as they drove by. Several police cars were parked in front of an all-night diner.

Granddad grunted. "Beware the world, Shio. It's so mixed up it doesn't know what it's doing. Those people out there and those poor people from the radio, they are lost. Just like Teresa. They don't know how to think, only react."

Shio glanced over at Teresa, but she looked to be asleep. He sighed. "What do you mean?" he asked tiredly, wishing he could be sleeping too. "I mean, what's wrong with Teresa?" He knew his granddad would tell him anyway. He was constantly lecturing his grandchildren on the "ways of the world" and how to avoid falling in the "wrong places."

"The world tells you there is no right or wrong. People are free to do whatever they wish, no fear of consequences." Shio's granddad sniffed. "Good and bad are myths. They are only found in fairy tales. Then somebody does something stupid, like what you heard on the radio, and what happens? Outrage. Condemnation. Suddenly it is horrible. But that is a reaction. Not thinking."

His granddad paused for a breath. He was only warming up. "Thinking leads to understanding what is right and what is wrong. When people take away those two things, it leads to judgment and hate. Everyone becomes their own judge and executor of the law. When it does not go their way, they start to hate. It's horrible.

"I tell you this, Shio, because Zeon mentioned to me that you wish to find more friends. Well, then you must always do what is right. That way you will know a real friend when you find one. Do right and meet people like yourself. Those are your true friends, Shio. The people who go out of their way to treat you with respect and not with judgment—good or bad."

"I just want to find mates to play football with," Shio grumbled. Silently, he called Zeon a bad name for blabbing about his problems.

Just then Teresa's head lolled to the left and she slumped down on his shoulder. Annoyed, Shio pushed her away and leaned against the door. He watched as the bright lights faded into the rear and they pulled onto the highway.

"I'm tired of everywhere I go people treating me like some new toy to scream about and take pictures of."

Granddad nodded in the mirror. "Those are people who don't believe in right or wrong. They care nothing about your right to privacy and can't be your friends. Don't worry, Shio. Not everyone is like that."

"Yes, but I'll never meet those people."

They drove in silence after that and Shio had just drifted off when they reached their destination.

The sun had yet to show itself when Granddad stopped the car at the drop-off area in front of the airport.

Michal Slaydon, wearing a dark cap pulled down low and faded leather jacket stood next to Tom on the sidewalk waiting for them.

He grinned when Shio jumped from the car and threw himself in his arms. Lifting up his son, Michal Slaydon nodded his thanks at Granddad.

"We lost the cameras on the way here," he said when Granddad asked. "But they'll find us quick enough. Tom saw a group inside already."

"So we better get a move on," Tom said, grunting as he pulled out Shio's and Teresa's bags from the trunk.

Teresa emerged from the other side of the car blinking away her sleep. "Hello, Mr. Slaydon," she said, yawning. She pulled out her phone. "Need to text my parents that I'm about to fly out," she said absently.

"Don't forget," Tom told her, "you're flying coach. We'll be in first class. As of now you're on vacation so you're on your own."

"Of course. Thank you." Teresa gave him a smile as she took her belongings. She then waved goodbye to the Slaydons before disappearing into the airport.

"Now let's reach first class before the media mob finds us," Tom said.

"We should have taken a private jet," Shio mumbled as he hopped down from his father. He slung his travel bag over his shoulder.

"Private jets just aren't this much fun," Michal Slaydon said, smiling. Then his eyes narrowed. "Speaking of which, I hope you don't have a football in that bag."

Granddad watched them go into the airport and sighed. Someday he would have to get over his hatred of flying. After flying between Russia and England and then from England to America so many times, he couldn't bear the thought of lifting his body off the ground in one of those metal capsules. No more. He'd just started the car and was about to put it in gear and pull away when he heard a tap on his window.

Rolling it down, he peered into a face that had given up on right and wrong.

"Sorry, gramps," said a rough voice, "but you need to lighten up."

A black box was shoved in his face and he saw a bright blue spark jump out, just before everything exploded.

A terrible pain seared through his head and he felt himself fly back, only to be violently stopped by his seat belt. Bright white flashed through his vision and his body stopped working. Dimly he was aware of rough hands removing his seat belt and his body being shoved to the side.

Barely conscious, he could only moan. He had to warn … warn … he couldn't remember who … or what … A terrible fear filled his rapidly beating chest. Not only couldn't he move, he couldn't even remember who he was.

"Relax, gramps," said the voice somewhere above him. "You'll recover. Maybe."

All Granddad could remember before everything went black was the man had worn a uniform. Then he knew no more as the car lurched forward.

Chapter
3

After one of the worst days of her life, it was another school day for Brittany Tiff and her brother Mason.

School had never liked Brittany. Neither did most of the kids in school. At best, they ignored her. At worst, they called her names like Stink Fish or Char-Broiled. The only good news, sixth grade was nearly halfway over and winter break would start later that day.

It was a cold winter's morning on a Friday, the week before Christmas. Her breath wafted before her like smoke and she snuggled in her worn coat. With no scarf, she had to bear the cold wind blowing in her face. She bore a lot these days.

Mason was still gobbling down his breakfast when she'd left to trudge to the bus stop at the end of their street. She didn't mind, but was happy to be alone. She needed the time to gather her thoughts and prepare for a final day of ridicule.

The day before, she'd tried out for the school's junior basketball club against her better judgment. Having no friends while being sister to one of the best athletes in school was not easy.

"Come on, sis," Mason had encouraged. "Don't listen to all the haters. Just find a sport you like and start playing. You'll find friends that way. I did."

"You don't get it," she'd shot back. "I'm not you! I don't like any sports! Besides, Mom can never bring me to practices."

"That's why you go out for school basketball club. You can take the activity bus."

"Then why don't *you* go out for the team!" she'd shouted at him.

Always reasonable, Mason had gently shaken his head. "Sis, you know I'm a soccer player. Soccer is my life."

"I know it, but nobody else thinks so. Everyone says you should play basketball."

Mason's face had clouded then. Just because of their skin color people liked to judge them. That, and because their mother was poor. Poor kids like him should only play basketball.

"Nobody knows nothing!" he'd nearly shouted. "Go out for basketball and that's it! Now I have to go to soccer practice with Ben." He'd stomped away without looking back.

That had been yesterday just after school. Both had returned home later that night looking miserable.

Brittany had wasted two hours of her life running up and down a gym chasing a basketball while enduring cruel remarks of girls wondering what she was doing there.

One girl asked her plainly if she was being taped for *America's Funniest Videos.* Other girls spoke about "stink fish" and wondered if she'd gotten lost. Why else would she be there?

Afterwards, Brittany didn't bother going to the locker room to change. She ran straight for the bus and sat in the back, not saying a word the entire ride home.

Mason didn't have such a great time at his practice, either. His team, the Sharks, had qualified for the town's annual holiday tournament but faced the top-tiered team, Burnhurst United.

In the town of Burnhurst, upstate New York, soccer rivaled football as the biggest sport in the area, and Burnhurst United was its top travel team. That was the team Mason longed to play for but never could. Unfortunately, it required not just a tryout, something he thought he could make, but also a lot of money to pay for uniforms and travel expenses. The team went all over the state and even outside the state to play top teams.

Money was something the Tiff family never had enough of. Their father had died before Brittany was three. A year older, Mason barely remembered the tall, broad-shouldered man who never seemed to stop smiling. All he had left were the pictures.

One picture, his favorite, had his dad in a soccer uniform and standing on a ball. He'd played semipro soccer, worked as a mailman, and served in the Army National Guard, while being a great husband and father. A drunk driver had stolen it all away one terrible night when he was returning from an Army exercise.

Now their mom worked two jobs to support the family and they barely made ends meet. Mason's soccer dreams rested with the Sharks, the local recreation team you just had to sign up for to play. His best friend gave him rides, so he at least got to play the game, but it was nothing like playing for United.

The Sharks had just enough talent to squeak into second place in the recreation league standings. That qualified them as the last team to make the Burnhurst Holiday Tournament, sponsored by the United team.

The recreation teams were said to be invited to promote diversity and community building, but really they were invited to give the top tournament teams a tune-up before the real competition started.

The winner of the tournament received an invitation to a national tournament in Orlando later that spring. In the eight years of the tournament's existence, not one recreation team had ever won a game. Usually they lost by five or more goals.

So at practice that night it had been no surprise when most of the Sharks had the attitude of why bother?

"We shouldn't even show up," grumbled Craig Anderson, one of the so-called best players on the team.

Mason thought him a "so-called best player" because the best part of Craig's playing was his mouth. He ran decently, but he always tried to dribble and wanted to score. In the ten games they'd played, he played center forward and only managed two goals, mostly by luck rather than by skill.

"Don't even say that," Mason snarled when he heard him. "This is our chance to show those United show-offs we can play soccer too!"

"Can we?" asked Ben Morales, Mason's best friend.

That stung. Ben and Mason often talked of playing in high school one day and both were huge Manchester City fans. Ben always had Mason over when they played on television.

Small and burly, built like a bowling ball, Ben didn't run fast, but he played stout defense and proved almost impossible to knock off the ball. He had surprisingly quick feet and pushing him felt like pushing a brick wall. Unfortunately, he tended to shy away from contact.

"I mean," he said hastily, when seeing Mason's glare, "we only got second place after the Jets forfeited from lack of players." He brushed a shock of dark hair out of his eyes. "We haven't exactly earned our way to play United."

Mason sighed, knowing his friend was right. That was the problem with rec soccer. Kids could quit as they pleased without a second thought. There was no commitment. And if a player did prove to be really good, a travel team would snatch him, or her, up at any time … unless, of course, that him or her couldn't afford it.

He glanced at Shelly Perkins across from him. He wondered why a team hadn't taken her yet.

Shelly noticed his look and sneered at him. Mason quickly looked away.

On the first day of practice, Mason had groaned loudly to Ben that their team had too many girls.

Besides Shelly, the girls included Rebecca Richer and Shawna Martinez. Neither Rebecca nor Shawna had ever played the game and they acted like it. If they kicked the ball during a game it was a cause for celebration.

Shelly, on the other hand, was new to the school that year, but had starred on her old soccer team. She played forward like a freight train late for a stop.

In almost no time, she proved to be one of the best players not only on the team but in the entire rec league. Unfortunately, she'd heard Mason's remark on that first practice and had never forgiven him.

Both were good players and the only two Sharks who really understood how to make runs and break down a defense with quick, short passes. They just never passed to each other. Shelly made it clear that she didn't like Mason, and Mason had given up trying to patch things up … not that he'd ever really tried. He actually wished a team would take her away.

Just then, Coach Smith arrived with his son Brandon in tow and a bag of balls.

The players were gathered on the side of the field before practice. A travel team was finishing up their practice in front of them. Of course it had to be United.

Once he realized that, Mason's heart dropped.

Out on the field, he watched as Tommy Sandhurst, the best player in school, passed the ball to Mark Claxton and quickly made a run to open space. Two defenders instantly converged on the ball. Mark never stopped the ball but faked a dribble to his left before suddenly sweeping his left foot back and using his heel to send the ball right in the path of Tommy. The defenders were caught off guard and Tommy easily dribbled away.

"Did Marco Reese ever show up, coach?" Craig asked glumly, watching the same play.

"No, son," grunted Coach Smith. His eyes never left the field and his face looked slightly gray. "He did not."

Marco Reese had signed up way before the season began and was supposed to have moved to the area in October from outside the country.

At the start of the season, Coach Smith promised him to be top quality and their ace in the hole. "No other team wanted him, but I knew foreign kids played this game like breathing air," he'd gushed to his team after they'd lost their first game. "Once he shows up, we'll be the top team, I guarantee it." Marco Reese had never shown up.

Now it was more of a sad joke when players asked if he had come … like he was a mystical savior who would rise from the ashes.

For a moment, the entire Sharks team watched the United practice with gloomy faces.

All the United players seemed taller, stronger, and smoother. Their movements flowed easily across the field, like they were choreographed.

"We have no chance," a Sharks player said with firm conviction. This was Alec Burgess, a tall blond kid who read more books in his life than he'd talked to people. His parents made him play to get him out of the house. Otherwise he would sit in his room and read. Currently, he was big into fantasy with knights and dragons. Fantasy with soccer, and winning, wasn't in his league.

Next to him, a slight kid named Daniel scratched his floppy auburn hair and grunted in agreement. He had the speed to play forward, but lacked the size and strength. At the moment, he also lacked the desire.

Their coach made no comment. Coach Smith had entered the season with a friendly attitude, just wanting everyone to get their chance to have fun. But as the season wore on, he slowly emerged as a clueless father going through the motions of teaching soccer to say he coached his son.

Brandon, for his part, was a decent player and the team's best goalkeeper. But his father only knew the basic drills better suited for children just learning the game.

That was not going to work against United.

When United finished, going ten minutes over, they exited the field carrying their travel bags and gear.

Shelly boldly stepped out on the field to meet them.

"Hurry up and get off the field," she said frostily. "You guys already stole ten minutes of our practice!"

Most of the players ignored her, but Mark and Tommy made sure to step close to her.

"What girls' team are you?" Mark asked, raising an eyebrow.

Like Mason, both Tommy and Mark were seventh graders at Henry Knox Middle School. Tommy was in Mason's gym class, but he only saw Mark in the halls. What he saw of him made him think of Mark as a stuck-up snob. Always talking and always surrounded by popular kids, he had slicked-back black hair and a handsome face only marred by a mouth marked with cruelty. He was the one who started calling his sister "Stink Fish."

Shelly twisted her mouth. "The team you're going to play this Sunday in the tournament," she shot back.

Mason inwardly cringed. He couldn't budge his body. He so badly wanted to be on United. Why didn't Shelly just leave them alone?

He groaned when Tommy and Mark stopped short. Both pretended to look worried.

"Is that right?" Tommy said. "I mean, we have a game on Sunday?"

"Yeah," Mark chimed in. "I thought we only had a practice against some loser team. Wait … you must be the Sharks!"

Tommy laughed. "More like the Minnows." Then he saw Mason. "Hey, Mason!" he called out loudly. "You're in the wrong place and wrong sport. Basketball tryouts are at the school!"

"Who is that?" Mark asked.

"Ah, he's okay," Tommy said as they resumed their walking. "He's in our class, but he's no soccer player. Rec soccer is a joke."

"Hey, get a move on!" shouted the United coach. Tall, slim, and fit like a soccer player, he trotted from the other side of the field carrying a heavy bag of balls like it was a bag of balloons. "If I beat any of you to the parking lot you owe me ten laps next practice!"

Tommy and Mark immediately started jogging with all the other United players.

The coach, wearing a United warm-up suit stopped by the Sharks players. He put down his bag and grimaced.

"Sorry if any of my players made a nuisance of themselves," he said.

"Ah, no, no, not at all," Coach Smith said nervously. "You must be Reilly Thompson."

"That's me." The United coach smiled and offered a hand. Reilly Thompson barely looked at the Sharks players as he shook with Coach Smith. "See you on Sunday … that is, if you make it."

"Oh, ah, we'll be there," replied the coach, not convincingly.

"We'll be there, all right!" Shelly said loudly. "You can bet on it!" She had turned from where she'd stopped on the field. "Tell your stars to look out for number 11!"

"Good luck, Coach," Coach Thompson murmured, still not looking at Shelly. Then he grabbed his bag and hustled after his players.

Shelly glared at Mason, who had yet to move. "Great job, big mouth," she said. "Thanks for backing me up!" Then she ran onto the field.

The practice went downhill from there.

Mason had shared all the details with Brittany later that night, leaving nothing out—not even the part where Shelly had rocketed a supposed pass right into his gut from ten feet away. He'd almost stopped breathing for a full minute.

Then he listened in silence when Brittany told him what happened to her. He shook his head at hearing about her humiliation.

Brother and sister always shared before bed. Their mom worked a late shift at a diner, right after working as a clerk in a downtown clothing store—one of the few remaining ones that hadn't folded.

Their mom rarely had time to stop in to see her kids before leaving for her second job. When she did, she was too tired to do much. This meant Brittany and Mason had to take care of each other … especially through the bad times, which was all the time these days.

And so, on this Friday morning, Brittany was not in the best of moods. Even with the sun out and the cold, crisp air filling her lungs, she only felt gloomy and full of bitterness.

Then she saw her neighbor, Melissa Kramer, sauntering from her house at the corner. Melissa used to be Brittany's best friend back in the third grade. Back then they had shared sleepovers, birthday parties, and many afternoons playing together. That was before Brittany was labeled "Stink Fish" and "Char-Broiled."

Even in the stiff cold breeze, Brittany felt her face grow warm at the memory of Melissa calling her Char-Broiled on the bus back in September. She looked down at her dark brown skin and seethed. That was when she knew they were no longer friends and never could be friends again.

Later that same day, she'd found her mom on a rare day off and couldn't hold back her tears.

"Why, Momma?" she'd asked through sobs. "Why are people so mean?"

Her mom had gathered her in her arms and put her firmly on her lap. "Hush, baby," she'd said. "You just cry it out. People are mean because they're blinded. They don't see all of you."

"They see enough to call me names! And smell enough! I can't help it if I smell sometimes!"

"Oh, baby, I'm so sorry. Those people … they're blinded by hate, ignorance, and just plain meanness. Whatever you do, don't you become like them. Don't hate them back, you hear?"

"What do I do, then?"

"You just remember who you are and do nothing back. The more they hate the more they look ugly. If that's what they want, you let them. The time will come when they see they're wrong. Until then, they're lost causes. You just be you. Be loving, kind, and caring. That's the only way you can fight against such evil."

"I can't!"

"Yes, you can. You're my daughter and I love you. I'll always love you."

Ever since, Brittany had ignored Melissa and pretty much everyone else in her school. She spent most of her time volunteering at her church and for Sunday school with the little kids—the ones too innocent to hate.

On this day, Brittany couldn't ignore Melissa, because for the first time in months, Melissa wanted to talk. Something inside her was bursting to get out and she couldn't hold it a second longer.

"Brittany, guess what!" she said excitedly as Brittany reached the bus stop. "You wouldn't believe it, but Shio Slaydon is coming to New York today!"

Brittany scrunched up her face, but then took a deep breath. She had to be kind. "Who's that?" she asked neutrally.

Melissa put both hands on her head as if Brittany had just smacked her with a frying pan. "Are you, like, crazy?" she practically shrieked. "Shio Slaydon? You don't know who Shio is?"

Brittany shrugged helplessly.

"Well," she said, "who is she?"

Melissa about blew up. "Are you crazy! Look!"

She dropped her backpack to the ground and quickly bent to open it.

Brittany sighed. Melissa and she were just two very different people now. Melissa wore a bright white coat and new jeans clinging to her long, slim legs. Tufts of golden blond hair were just visible from under her hood. Everything about her, her milky white skin, and even her pink and purple backpack, said rich and dainty.

Brittany looked down at her faded tattered green coat, a hand-me-down from her mother. Her own backpack came from her brother. Everything about her said drab and too poor.

She looked back behind her and saw Mason finally leaving the house, still munching on toast. Their house even looked dumpy. Once painted white, its siding looked more grayish now and was chipping. Though two stories, it felt small and cramped inside with only three small bedrooms.

Melissa's house also had two stories, but was much bigger and made of brick with a dark blue roof. Even though an only child, Melissa had her choice of three rooms to sleep in, all twice the size of Brittany's tiny room. Sometimes she wondered how they were ever once friends.

Melissa jerked up, snapping Brittany's attention back to the matter at hand.

"This is Shio Slaydon," Melissa said in triumph. She shoved a school binder in Brittany's face, almost bopping her in the nose. "He's, like, the cutest boy in the world."

Brittany raised her eyebrows and stepped back. A magazine cutout of a boy about her age, or even younger, smiled at her with smooth tanned skin and dazzling white teeth.

"Oh," she said. "It isn't a girl. He, uh, looks nice."

Melissa almost fell over. "Don't you know who he is? Like, don't you know anything?" She almost sounded upset.

Brittany had about had enough.

"I already told you. No!"

"Everyone knows who he is! Well, maybe everyone who matters."

Brittany's face burned. "I don't have cable TV," she mumbled defensively. "I don't watch anything."

"So?" shot back Melissa. She turned to Mason, who had just arrived. He stared with wide eyes at the girls as he continued eating toast. He never stopped eating these days.

"What's up?" he asked, still chewing a mouthful.

"You know who Shio Slaydon is, right?" Melissa asked him.

Mason swallowed. "Is that Michal's Slaydon's son? Of course I do. His dad played for Liverpool. He was one of the best soccer strikers in the world. Why?"

Brittany inwardly groaned as Melissa whirled to her with victory dancing in her eyes.

"See?" shouted the blond girl in triumph.

"I don't care about soccer!" Brittany said defensively. "It's just a stupid game."

"You just don't know anything," Melissa said. "Shio's mom is Natasha Rubinov—she used to be, like, only one of the best tennis players in the world! And now she has her own clothing line!" Melissa's eyes, lined with green eye shadow goop, suddenly went soft and—goopy. "Shio got his face from his mother. I mean, his eyes and mouth. But his gorgeous hair is from his dad. I'm telling you, he, like, got all the best features from his parents, making him the perfect hunk."

Brittany rolled her eyes. The "hunk" was a little skinny kid who probably thought girls had cooties.

Melissa went on about how the Slaydons had five kids, all gorgeous, but none as great as Shio.

Exasperated, Mason asked why all the talk about the Slaydons.

So Brittany got to hear all over again how Shio Slaydon would be in New York that day. Apparently they were having a Christmas Charity Ball later that week, but there was some trouble.

"Nothing too bad, of course," Melissa explained. "Shio's parents might be splitting up, so this could be the last ball for a while. You see, they have this charity ball every year, each year at someplace different. This year it will be in New York, just three hours from here! Like, I so wish I could be there!"

"Me too," Brittany muttered. Ordinarily she hated going to school, but now she searched longingly for the bus.

Mason lost interest when nothing soccer related was mentioned. He pulled out a pair of headphones and was just starting to listen to music when Ben came trotting from his house across from the Tiff house.

"Glad I made it," he huffed. "What did I miss?"

"Nothing," Brittany said sharply, before Melissa could launch into *another* gushing monologue about the great Shio Slaydon and his perfect parents going through a divorce.

Thankfully, Mason and Ben fell into conversation about soccer, leaving Brittany to be Melissa's ears. The girl loved to talk.

She pulled down her hood and smoothed down her perfectly straight hair held up by a headband. All her stray tufts were put back in order.

"I hate jackets," she said distractedly, having pulled out a hand mirror. She checked herself out critically. "They make me look like a marshmallow."

Brittany snorted.

Taller than Brittany by two inches, Melissa had a long, graceful neck and was skinny as a rail. She reminded Brittany of a bird—a graceful swan, but with one problem. She also had a bird brain. It was too small and narrow to think outside her private little world where everything revolved around her.

"How do you know so much about the Slaydons?" Brittany heard herself ask. "What are you? A stalker?"

Melissa's blue eyes blinked rapidly and she snapped her mirror shut, returning it to her coat pocket. "I, like, have cable TV. You know, something your family can't afford. People care about the Slaydons and report on their lives all the time."

Brittany shrugged away her hurt at the insult. "Sounds terrible. I bet they hate it."

"They love it! They do interviews all the time. Shio might even be a fashion model next!"

Brittany made a face. She knew she was just being spiteful and should stop. But she couldn't. After the day before and now listening to Melissa drone on about some stupid English celebrity family famous for being good looking and for playing soccer and tennis, she couldn't handle it. Melissa cared more about the Slaydons, people she'd never meet in a million years, than her, somebody she'd once shared a friendship with.

"What sort of name is Shio?" she asked. "Sounds like a dog's name."

"It's Russian, stupid. His grandfather from his mom's side is from Russia. I bet you didn't know that he went to the Olympics in Russia!"

"Wow. Too bad I don't care."

"That's because you know he won't ever care about you."

Brittany looked at the picture on the binder again. "What is he? Ten or eleven? I'm pretty sure he won't care about you either."

"What do you know?" said Melissa hotly. "At least he doesn't look charbroiled and have messed up hair!"

Brittany's throat tightened. "Don't say that," she said dangerously. "Call me names, but don't make fun of my skin color."

Melissa suddenly looked frightened and hastily stuffed her binder back in her bag. "I didn't mean anything," she muttered. "But you do have messed up hair."

Ben and Mason had stopped talking.

Mason stepped next to his sister. He wasn't the tallest boy in the school, but he was stocky and all muscle. When he stared at you, you knew it. He did so now at Melissa. "Everything okay, sis?" he asked coolly.

"Yeah, great," Brittany mumbled.

"I said I was sorry," Melissa said, turning her back on them. "You don't have to be so sensitive."

Thankfully, the bus rumbled into view and Brittany gathered her bag and her nerves. Another day of school … but then it would be winter break—a break from people and attitudes like Melissa's.

Once the bus doors swung open, Melissa practically leapt on the bus. She immediately found a "saved" seat in the midst of the popular crowd. Several girls greeted her by name but quickly fell silent as Melissa launched into the news about Shio.

Brittany put her head down as she followed in her wake. Nobody looked at her.

Mason slid into a seat with Ben near the front. Brittany, left standing alone, searched for the nearest empty seat. She thankfully found one near the back just as the bus lurched forward, nearly knocking her to the ground.

Her sagging spirits were given a slight lift when she did sit and she heard a girl whisper to a friend two seats in front of her. "Hey, who's Shio Slaydon?"

"No idea," was the reply. "Sounds like a dog's name."

Chapter 4

On Friday afternoon, the airport was packed with returning business travelers, mixed with tourists and visitors for the holiday season. On this particular Friday, it was also packed with photographers and more than one news reporter.

"Michal Slaydon, former soccer star, fashion model, and international celebrity, is rumored to be in New York on his own with his young son," reported a sparkly woman in a bright red dress. She stood in front of the baggage claim staring into a camera like it was a bowl of frozen ice cream ready to be licked clean. Her smile never melted.

"He's here," she continued brightly, "to prepare another Slaydon treat to the world—a charity holiday bash open to invitees only. The only question is, where is his equally famous and alluring wife, Natasha Slaydon? Rumors have it there has been a tiff in the family and she's staying in California with the other children. Hopefully with his arrival, that just reportedly happened, we'll get the answer."

A crowd of photographers clogged the area near the reporter. Security had already pushed them back and in the process had attracted a gaggle of curious onlookers. Perhaps not surprisingly, many young women had gathered also, many wearing Slaydon soccer jerseys. Some holding signs. One said, "DUMP HER. MARRY ME!"

In a private room, just under the baggage claim, Michal Slaydon grinned wryly and ruffled his son's hair.

"Sorry, mate," he said without humor. "Welcome to New York, yeah?"

"Yeah," Shio said, not smiling.

The two were sitting side by side on top of a small table in a mostly bare room with bright white walls and tiled floor.

Two hard chairs and a single lamp kept them company. They'd been whisked straight to the room soon after landing, when word reached them about a mob forming to meet them.

Michal Slaydon sighed. He was not a big man and, like Shio, had a slight build. He'd signed with the Liverpool youth team at the age of fourteen and played for a Liverpool team for sixteen years. Only when his famous quick dribble and lethal right foot started to betray him did he sign with an American club in New York. There, he'd played four more years before hanging up his boots for good. In his last two years playing, his American team had won the league trophy. Many wanted him to continue playing, but his growing family needed him. And he needed the rest.

Unfortunately, after three World Cups, ten Champion League appearances, and countless other major football (or soccer) tournaments, there were not many places in the world he could go without attracting attention. Of course, his famous wife did not help matters when it came to a private life.

Michal Slaydon didn't mind the attention too much—he knew it came with the territory, and to be honest, he loved performing under bright lights. He enjoyed people watching him, especially when they were supporters. In the good times they loved him and it was fantastic. Five times he led the English League in scoring and once he'd been named World Footballer of the year. But in the bad times, like in the World Cup quarterfinals when he'd sailed a penalty over the bar that knocked England out, they wanted him executed.

When he'd missed the kick, it was the darkest time of his pro career. The media led the way with questions about his focus and commitment to his country. Some asked how he felt about single-handedly destroying his country's chances of glory. Then they turned vicious, wondering if his wife and family provided too many distractions. After all, he had so many kids (three at that point), obviously he wasn't training *that* hard.

The media started attacking his wife with words and questions. The worst came when the anger carried over to the streets and the English fans. People he didn't know yelled at him. Death threats were sent. Once, his mobile phone number was leaked and nasty messages poured in nonstop. He still felt nervous answering his phone.

Only his club—manager, players, and loyal Liverpool fans—kept him from losing it on the field. Rallying around their best player, they'd won the league that year. Off the field, it was his family that really kept him from going mad.

That was the problem. He wanted to protect his family, something difficult to do when cameras constantly followed his and their every move. Even during vacation, his boys had to suffer cameras spying on them swimming in pools or relaxing on the beach.

At least in America they had *some* privacy. In America, soccer (or *real* football) wasn't a big deal. If he blew a kick in New York, it would be jeered on the field, but that was it. For the most part, his family was not quite as recognizable. Except for fashion shoots and team functions, they stayed out of the news. Until now.

Somehow, rumors had leaked about his and his wife's terrible row—an argument that reportedly sent him packing to New York while his wife remained in California.

The Slaydon Arc had never betrayed him.

Michal Slaydon sighed and rubbed his unshaven jaw. The "Slaydon Arc" was a tight network of trusted family and friends. Only those who could be counted on with secrecy were allowed in the arc. The arc served as a shield that protected the family from the prying outside world. He couldn't imagine who had left the arc to leak news about the argument.

The worst part, it had already been decided that he would go first to New York to visit some of his mates from his old team before the charity ball. Now he didn't know what to do. After retirement from soccer, he and his wife settled on living in California—not just for the weather, but living amongst celebrities gave their children the best chance of growing up in a "normal way." Amongst kids of movie stars and other star athletes, their kids wouldn't be singled out. Now with Shio at his side, he didn't know if he could protect him. The media could eat his boy alive and not care an ounce.

Shio rested his head on his shoulder. "How much longer, Dad?" he asked.

Michal Slaydon grinned as he looked down. He wrapped a strong arm around his son's back and pulled him tighter.

"You know your mum loves us," he said. "We'll be fine. All right? We're just waiting until things settle down."

Shio grunted. "We're still going to kick the ball around, right?"

Michal Slaydon chuckled. "You're my son, all right."

He'd promised on the plane the two would find a field and a ball that night. Sure, he had the slim build of his mother, but Shio also had the fierce fire of his father. Of all the kids, he was most likely to follow in his father's footsteps. He'd already signed a contract with Manchester City's youth team that would start in two more years.

In his young life, Shio had already played with and against some of the best players in the world, all over the world. With his mum's quickness and lateral movement and his dad's speed and accurate foot, he would be a dangerous midfielder or striker for any team around his age.

But what made his father most sure that his middle son would grow up to play was Shio's absolute love of the game. When he played football, his whole mind went with him. He didn't just play the game. He *lived* the game. Just like his father.

The other boys played well, but they didn't have the same desire. To them, it was just a game. Marcus had seen too much of what the media and angry fans did to his father to ever want to put himself in that position. Zeon actually liked tennis better.

Christopher was only five and was more into Ninja Turtles. Of course Maria, his only daughter, wanted to be like her dad, but only seven, she acted too nice to steal the ball from other players.

This was all fine to Michal Slaydon. He loved his children and would support them in anything they did. He just couldn't help but feel a deep pride whenever he saw Shio with the ball at his feet.

"We'll have to see, Shio," he finally said. "Our plans might have changed, I'm afraid."

"I wish we lived a normal life," Shio mumbled. "It's not fair. You and Mum can't even have a row without causing a circus."

His father sighed. "I understand … Being famous has its ups and downs, yeah?" He gave a sideways grin. "You remember seeing me at the last airport, right?"

Shio shrugged himself out of his father's arm and hopped off the table. For a moment, his smooth face grimaced in a scowl. His dark almond eyes were almost black and he looked so much like his mother that Michal hid a grin.

In the last airport, they'd come across a huge wall mural of Michal Slaydon lying down without a shirt and sporting loose-fitting jeans, showing a lot of boxer shorts. Sweat glistened from his abs and he held a bottle of Slaydon cologne. At the time, Shio had found it funny. Now he bit his bottom lip.

"Most dads and mums aren't on airport walls," he said.

Michal Slaydon's smile fell. "No, I suppose not. But remember, most dads and mums don't take their kids to World Cup finals with kings and queens."

Shio's dark face cracked in a small smile. "Or wear perfume on the tele."

"That's your mum. I wear cologne. Expensive stuff too. Stuff you can't afford."

"Or stomach."

"That's it, you little bugger. You come here!" Michal Slaydon leapt off the table and went after his son.

When the door opened moments later, Michal Slaydon had Shio in a headlock and was rubbing his hand across his nose. Both were laughing at the time. Quickly they stood.

"Are we interrupting?" Tom Blazer asked after a short moment of awkward silence. He let go of the doorknob and straightened his tie. One eyebrow lifted. "I understand this room is used to interrogate terrorists. Is that what we need to do now?"

Michal Slaydon grunted and put both hands on Shio's shoulders. "Only if you have something to confess, Tom."

Both men stared at each other.

Then, sighing, Tom walked in, followed by a beefy red-faced security guard. Sweat stains marked the armpits of the guard and he wiped his face with the back of his sleeve.

"Look," the guard said in a thick heavy voice, "we already apologized for the accommodations. This was the closest place to bring you safely. But if you want—"

"Hold on," Michal Slaydon said hastily. "I want to apologize for anything this man has said to embarrass me, my family, and the crown. I assure you. We usually don't let him off the leash."

For a moment, Michal Slaydon and Tom Blazer glared at each other while the security guard watched nervously. Shio then stepped on his father's foot and ran at the tall man.

"Finally, you're back!" he cried, leaping up.

The tall man deftly caught him under the arms and lifted him up easily. "Hey, taking care of your father's messes for twenty years is good training, but it's never easy, little guy."

"Put my son down before I have this man taser your cheeky grin off your ugly face," Michal Slaydon snarled. Then he broke into a wide smile and went to give the man a hug.

For a moment, Shio was squashed between them. Then he was dropped down and shoved to the side.

Shio looked ready to jump back in, but his father grabbed him by the shoulders and pulled him back.

"Careful, Shio," he said. "I don't know the last time he had his rabies shot."

Tom snarled and made a biting sound while snapping his teeth.

Tom Blazer had played midfield while Michal Slaydon starred as striker. Between them, they had the most goals in team history.

The two served as best men for each other's weddings. Both their wives agreed that neither had grown up yet.

The security guard, face gleaming with sweat, had a hand on his belt somewhere between his taser and gun.

Finally having mercy, Michal Slaydon laughed and dragged Shio back to the table, where he took a seat on the edge of the table with his boy on his lap. "Okay, Tom. Tell me the good news."

Tom sighed and did his best to look sad. "I don't have rabies," he said. Then he perked up. "Now the bad news." He turned to the security guard. "Sorry, Bob, but I think you can tell your boss we won't be staying long."

"It's Tony," the guard said, wiping his nose. He grunted. "Look, I understand things are crazy right now, but we're going to do our best to get you out of here safely. We just didn't expect things to get so, well, we just weren't prepared. But, believe me, we're no strangers to people of your caliber, Mr. Slaydon, coming in here. We can get you through an army of reporters, no problem."

For the first time, the guard looked comfortable. He puffed himself up and smacked the sides of his belt with both hands. "My team and I once got to escort that singer Jay—"

Michal Slaydon raised his hand and shook his head. "Thank you, Officer," he said, "but I don't intend on ducking the press. I intend to face them."

The guard looked crestfallen. "You mean you don't want us to get you out—"

"Not me," Michal Slaydon said firmly. "I learned if you don't face the lights now, they'll light you up later with a story they made up themselves. I'd rather give the facts now, while I still can. But I would like for my son to get out of here safely before that happens. Tom, that was supposed to be your job."

"That's the bad news," Tom said cheerfully. "I did just that. You can't fire me for incompetence. Mike, you remember Teresa, right? She's still at the airport renting a car. I spoke to her and she agreed to smuggle young Shio from the airport and over to her parents' place for a few hours before taking him to the hotel. That way, you can cool things down here and meet up there."

Michal Slaydon bit his lip. He slapped Shio's knee. "That sound good to you?" he asked.

Shio shrugged. "I guess."

"We haven't met her parents," Michal Slaydon said, mostly to himself. "I do understand they checked out, of course." He looked pointedly at Tom.

Tom nodded. Part of his duties was to oversee background checks on all close employees of the Slaydon family. That was how Luke had gotten the job as driver for the family in the first place. During the background check, Tom discovered that Luke's father had passed away, but had been a huge Liverpool supporter, particularly of Michal Slaydon. Luke's father had died in a Liverpool Slaydon jersey and had asked to be buried facing Anfield Stadium. With Liverpool, you never walked alone and Luke had gotten the job.

"Her father is a retired doctor and her mother taught preschool," Tom said, as if reciting facts. "They have two dogs and one other grown daughter who lives out west." He winked at Shio. "Teresa also mentioned a big backyard with plenty of room for soccer."

Shio slid from his father's lap and grinned shyly. "Sounds good to me." He slipped a hand in his pocket and pulled out his phone. "I can text you when I get there."

"And I have the GPS coordinates of their home in my phone," Tom said smugly. "You have to admit, for a right middy I know how to get things done."

Michal Slaydon nodded. "Sounds good," he said absently. "I'll, uh, call your mum to let her know the plan." He pulled out his own phone and then looked questioningly at Tom. "And how do you plan to get Shio to Teresa?"

The security guard perked up and looked ready to suggest a full-scale procedure when Tom reached behind and pulled out a cap from under his coat.

"Camouflage," he said. "How else can you easily travel through a New York airport without being noticed?" he asked.

The guard's shoulders sagged. "You make him a Yankees fan," he said with disappointment. "Wait here and I'll grab a hoodie to go with it."

Tom jammed the dark blue New York Yankees cap on Shio's head.

Michal Slaydon just shook his head. "Cheers," he said.

Chapter
5

Moments later, a young boy slipped out of the side room with a tall man in a blue suit close behind. A dejected security guard followed after, speaking dejectedly into the walkie-talkie on his shoulder.

The boy wore black athletic pants, sneakers, and a gray Yankees hoodie that hung close to his skinny knees. His hood was pulled up over a Yankees ball cap, sunk low on his brow. Few people gave them a second glance.

As they bypassed security and headed toward the main entrance of the airport, they heard a loud commotion from the baggage claim area.

"Michal Slaydon is coming!" cried a voice. "I see him!"

Quickly, the man pushed the boy through the terminal. With a hard gaze, he kept moving. The boy looked bored but allowed himself to be herded forward.

The security guard paused and watched with admiration as travelers cleared the path all the way to the automatic doors.

Outside the airport, the man led the boy straight to a dark blue Toyota Corolla.

"This is your ride, Shio," Tom said quietly. He looked around until satisfied nobody was watching. Then, he hastily opened the back door and pushed the boy in. "All your bags will go with your father, right?"

Shio waved a hand in response and the door closed. Tom nodded at the driver and waved them on. He stood watching until the car disappeared down a hill. Michal Slaydon never got a text from his son saying he'd reached the house. A much different text would be sent instead.

Granddad awoke curled up in the back seat of the BMW, covered in grimy sweat and smelling of vomit. He'd thrown up sometime during the night. Or was it night? He had no idea what time it was or where he was, or pretty much of anything.

Pain pulsed in his head and he groaned mightily as he gingerly sat up. Blinking blearily, he saw faded light filtering through the windows. Dark shadows of trees were in all directions.

He fumbled for the door latch and soon stumbled free from the car. Falling to his knees, he breathed the fresh air in deeply. After a long moment, things started to make sense. He'd just dropped off Shio at the airport with his father ... somebody knocked on his car door ... and then terrible pain.

Shio ... Michal Slaydon ... They were in terrible danger!

He lurched to his feet and had to catch the back of the car as everything started to swim. That was when he looked down and saw the note pinned to his shirt.

Pulling it free, he sank to the ground, leaning against the back tire. They'd parked the car on a dirt road in the middle of a forest. Looking up, he couldn't even see the sky.

Closing his eyes, he fumbled in his pocket and was surprised to find his wallet still there. And his cell phone. Natasha insisted he have one, just in case of an emergency. An emergency like one of the children being kidnapped ...

The note gave a warning. Shio would be safe as long as nobody contacted the police. If that happened, as soon as it happened, Shio would die.

Typed in large font, it had no signature or any other marking. It caused Granddad Rubio to shake with fear and rage.

He'd fled communism to the land of the free. And this is where he ended up. With a quivering hand, he dialed the number of Michal Slaydon.

Shio stared at the window, struggling to keep his eyes opened. The time difference between New York and California was quickly catching up to him. It was three hours earlier here, but he hadn't gotten much sleep the night before.

Teresa snapped on a classical radio station and glanced in the rearview mirror.

"Everything good, Shio?" she asked, sounding oddly nervous. "I mean, my parents never met you or any of your family before. I hope you don't mind."

If she felt the effects of rising early and the time difference, it didn't show. Her eyes were wide open and couldn't stop moving. They switched from the road to the mirror to the radio and back to the road. Her hands gripped the wheel tightly.

"I tell them all about you, you know," she said. "They're really excited to meet you."

Shio blew out his breath. "Yeah, it should be brilliant." Leaning his head against the window, he gazed listlessly at the New York skyline in the distance. The sounds of violins lulled him to sleep.

He woke with a start sometime later. Drool covered the side of his face and he hastily wiped it away. He'd been out for a while. The car had stopped and he sat alone in the backseat.

Blinking rapidly, he looked around and saw Teresa standing outside the car with a strange man and a woman. Night had almost fallen, but they were no longer in the city. The car sat on the shoulder of a two-lane road running between a thick section of trees on one side and a sharp drop on the other. The car sat parked just at the edge of the drop.

Puzzled, he opened the door and stepped out.

"Where are we?" he asked groggily. "Where's the city?"

Teresa turned on him and for a moment looked frightened. Then she grinned and gestured at the woman. "Oh, Shio! You're awake! I'm afraid we have some car problems. This is my sister and, er, her boyfriend—"

"Jon," said the man, cutting in. He grinned to reveal crooked teeth that looked more frightening than friendly. His head had the shape of a football with not enough air, round but slightly misshapen. Shio immediately didn't like him. Towering several inches over six feet, he had thick arms and legs hidden by bulky jeans and a heavy plaid shirt. One of the arms now extended and offered a large meaty hand.

Shio shook the hand limply, still not understanding quite what was going on. "Where's the house?" he asked, rapidly becoming fully awake. He couldn't see the familiar New York skyline anywhere.

"We're almost there, sweetie," Teresa's sister said, smiling much too wide. She didn't sound right either. Taller and wider than Teresa, her voice came out deep and rough. Calling him "sweetie" sounded as natural as a center forward calling an opposing goalie "honey." Her face was covered in brown freckles that made her face appear constantly dirty. "Jon and I came out to pick you two up. Teresa just called about the engine trouble."

"My sister is Mandy, by the way," Teresa said quickly. She licked her lips nervously. "Uh, don't worry," she rushed on. "I called your father and explained everything. He knows all about it."

Shio instantly dropped his hands to his pockets but couldn't find his phone.

"Oh, I have your phone," Teresa continued, seeing his stricken face. She sounded like a noisy engine rattling on. "I'll give it to you when we reach the house. We have to go—it, uh, might snow soon. And it's getting cold. Come on, Shio!"

Shio was about to argue when Jon took him firmly by the arm. In his clothes, he looked like a lumberjack found in stories. His grip felt like a lumberjack's too.

"Come on," he said flatly. "I don't want to carry you." He smiled, but without humor.

Shio shivered as he was guided to a beat-up car parked in front of the Corolla. The color of a burnt orange, the car had New York plates and more scratches and dents than Mandy had freckles. It also smelled bad—a sour smell of sweat and old socks.

"Get in the back with Mandy," Jon said brusquely, one hand still on Shio's shoulder. The other hand had the back door open. "Teresa will sit in the front with me."

Shio felt his heart beat hard as he complied. Nothing about this felt right. He couldn't wait to get to the house and call his dad. He would demand to go to the hotel immediately.

The others entered without talking and soon the car pulled away from the rental.

They traveled down the road for miles without passing another car. Nobody spoke. Shio only saw barren trees against the falling sun. Hope seemed to be fading as fear grew inside his chest. Something was awfully wrong.

Suddenly, Jon jerked the wheel and they turned down a narrow lane almost hidden from the main road. Passing a small copse of trees, they reached a row of old, rundown houses. They looked more like shacks, or houses ready for retirement. Most sagged with age and hadn't seen fresh paint in over a decade. All the yards were overgrown with brown weeds and littered with junk. Old tires, rusted cars, and piles of bricks served as lazy lawn ornaments. Only a few of the houses had lights on.

Shio wanted to say something, but Mandy pressed against his side and jabbed an elbow into his ribs. He just licked his lips and wondered what was happening to him. He didn't believe his dad agreed to any of this.

Jon hit the brakes in front of an unlit single-story house at the end of the lane, just where it turned into a small circle at the base of a large barren hill overlooking the sad collection of dwellings.

"Used to be a farm community," Jon grunted from behind the wheel as he switched off the engine.

"Is this where your parents live?" Shio asked doubtfully, ignoring Mandy's elbow. He'd seen enough and just wanted the miserable trip to be over. At the same time, this did not look like a friendly place to stop.

Teresa laughed from the front, sounding almost like she was crying. "Oh, no," she said. "This is Jon's place. We have to pick something up first. We'll go to my parents' place right after."

"Come on in," Jon said, almost like a threat. It was more of a demand than an offer.

Shio had little choice as Mandy opened the door and pulled on his arm. Unlike her sister, she was built like an ox. Her eyes were the same as Teresa's, only harder. Otherwise, both her face and body were more blocky and compact. Except for the eyes, she looked more like Jon than Teresa. Both would've made great defenders in soccer.

As he stumbled from the car, he saw the door of the house open. A man stepped out and waved.

"About time," the man said lazily. "I had time for a nap. You just woke me." He grinned when seeing Shio but spoke to the others.

"I see you got the package without trouble. Michelle, I am very impressed."

"Shut it, Jack," Teresa's sister spat. "The name is Mandy!"

The man laughed lightly. A few inches shorter than Jon, and much smaller in the shoulders and trunk, the man had an air of menace about him that caused Shio to shudder. Short dark hair was clipped close to his square, grizzled face. Emerald green eyes gleamed with intelligence and viciousness. He reminded Shio of a cougar he'd seen at a zoo once. Intelligent and dangerous, no matter his size.

"Call yourself what you like, *Mandy*. But if we're caught, your family will identify you no matter what. Right, Teresa?"

Teresa blushed and Mandy, or Michelle, jumped between them. "Leave my sister alone," she growled. "She's one of us."

"We shall see about that," the man said matter-of-factly. Then he moved from the door. "Well, what are you waiting for? For the cops to come? Get inside!"

Every instinct told Shio to run and not go inside the house. Mandy's grip told him otherwise. With Jon and Teresa following just behind, he entered the house after Jack.

With all his travels with his dad and mum, he'd never felt afraid or awkward in the presence of adults … until now. Teresa wouldn't look at him and the others didn't seem to do anything but look at him. He didn't think they wanted his autograph.

Once inside, Shio was led down a narrow hall before being shoved into a small room full of musty furniture. Jack had switched on a light when he'd entered, but the light proved dim.

"Shoes off," Jon said gruffly.

Shio arched his back and shivered. Inside felt damper and colder than outside. Looking around, he saw faded and torn wallpaper. Mandy had left his side and flicked on an uncovered lamp on a scarred stand. For a moment, he blinked in the glaring light.

"Shoes off, or I pull them off," growled Jon, jabbing Shio sharply in the back.

Swallowing, the boy bent down and complied. A stained carpet covered the floor. Worn with holes, it looked dirtier than a mud pit. Shio grimaced when his unprotected feet touched the filthy surface. His shoes probably cost more than the entire house.

"Trust me," Jon said, kicking away the shoes. "It'll be better this way. Now take a seat." He roughly shoved Shio farther into the room, toward a worn couch by the lamp.

Mandy sat in a worn cushioned chair across the room. The room was otherwise empty.

Jon leaned against the entrance and leered down at Shio. "You look a little sick, kid," he said.

Shio dropped his gaze to the old carpet. He felt his knees trembling. A terrible feeling settled in the pit of his stomach. Teresa sat next to him and took his hand. Her eyes pleaded with him desperately to understand.

"Look, Shio," she said softly, "it's going to be okay. Nobody is going to hurt you. This will all go away soon."

Jack laughed sharply. "Don't lie to the boy." He'd disappeared in the back of the house and now returned carrying a short metal rod about two feet in length. Two short metal prongs stuck out from the end. "We all may get hurt in this. So it had better be worth it."

Teresa shuddered and dropped Shio's hand.

"Where's my phone?" Shio said evenly. His voice came out small and soft, but hid any fear. His gaze went to Teresa. "I want to call Dad now." She didn't look at him.

"Nice accent, kid," Jack said with a harsh laugh. "You sound all prim and proper. Too bad you won't be calling him anymore." He moved into the room and stood over Shio. "You know, originally we planned to get Marcus, the first born. But when he took off with his foreign girl we were stuck with Zeon, your snobby brother. Too bad for you, we discovered something." Jack bent down and grinned evilly at Shio. His teeth had a yellow stain in the light. The boy sat grimly and refused to flinch. "You play soccer like your father. He adores you because of it. So that makes you the perfect one."

"The perfect one for what?" Shio asked, surprised his voice came out steady. A terrible fear gripped him.

"The plan for a better future!" Jack boomed. "You're to become the symbol to start the revolution!"

Shio wrinkled his nose. Jack's breath smelled of cheap beer. The man was absolute crazy. He flicked his gaze around the room. There were two windows, both to his left and both covered in shades. Otherwise the only exit was to get through Jack and then past Mandy and Jon. Escape looked impossible. His bottom lip started to quiver.

Mandy spoke up from her chair. "Relax," she said, looking at him. "You're not going to get hurt if you cooperate. Jack just likes to be dramatic." She sounded bored.

"Speaking of getting hurt," Jack said pleasantly, holding up the rod. "Do you know what this is?" he asked Shio, but looked around the room for an answer. "It was once a cattle prod." He pressed something on the rod and a dark blue line of electricity sparked at the ends of the metal prongs. It sounded like a bug zapper meeting a fly.

Shio flinched. Next to him, Teresa gasped.

"I know, right?" Jack said. "I had it modified. Now it shoots enough electricity to knock down an elephant." He stood over Shio and leered. "It's meant for you."

"*NO!*" shouted Teresa. She grabbed Shio and pulled him to her. "You never said anything about this!"

"Relax!" Jon barked. "You know we have to do it. He has seen all our faces. I worked on the modifications. It should knock the boy for such a loop he won't remember any of this, at least not for a long time."

Mandy got up from her seat. "Did he know about this?" she demanded, glaring at Jack.

"Of course," Jack said smoothly. "Your beau is the one who suggested it. He knew about my past and Jon's electrical genius. Now, it was meant for an older person, but I'm sure it wouldn't harm a child. Well, not too badly."

Teresa stood, pulling Shio up with her. Her arms were wrapped protectively around his chest. "You can't do this!" she said. "The family trusted me!"

"That's their mistake," Jack said, grinning at her. "Isn't it? Trust is such a fickle thing." His voice grew hard. "Now move away from the boy."

"Do it, Teresa," Mandy said tersely. "You agreed to be a part of this, so don't back out now. Without you, we never could have gotten this far."

Jack turned on her and chuckled. "Funny, those were the exact words I planned to say to you."

"Well you don't have to," snarled Mandy. "Let's get going. It's getting late." She didn't look at her sister or the frightened boy.

Teresa trembled. Shio could feel her heart beating. Or it could have been his own. He stared up as Jack took a step toward him, the prod pointing straight at his face.

Jack's face had the maniac expression of a man drunk with power. Only his eyes held deep hatred as they locked with Shio's.

Shio's mouth went dry. Every instinct told him to run, but not a single muscle obeyed. He'd never felt so afraid. *Where is Dad?*

"Let's see," Jack said, pausing in front of Shio, still waving the prod menacingly. "Take off the hat. And that ridiculous hoodie. You're no Yankee."

"J-just do it," Teresa said to Shio through tight lips. She dropped her arms from around him. "They're just bluffing."

Shio didn't think so, but he pulled off the cap, dropping it to the couch. Then he shrugged off the hoodie, holding it in front of him. He swallowed once more.

Jack leered down at him. "That's bet—"

All at once, Shio threw the hoodie at the man's face and raced for the nearest window. Seeing the cruel pleasure in the man's face spurred his body into action.

Chaos immediately erupted.

"Stop him!" shouted Mandy.

Jon yelled, but crashed into Mandy, causing both to stagger.

Teresa screamed and tumbled onto the couch.

Shio slammed into the window and tore aside the shades. Heavy glass blocked his way. He tried yanking it open but his fingers couldn't lift it even an inch.

Jack had roared when the hoodie flew at him. It took a moment for him to knock it aside with the cattle prod. Then he lunged after Shio. As he reached the boy, he turned on the prod to full power and whacked him hard on the arm.

A flash and sizzle sparked and then the boy went flying hard into the window before bouncing back and crashing down on the worn carpet. His body jerked slightly and then went limp. His young face had twisted into pain, but slowly relaxed.

When everything settled, Shio lay sprawled on his stomach like the picture of death.

For a moment, nobody spoke. Smoke and the acrid smell of burnt cloth filled the air. Then Jon whooped and jumped up. "I knew it would work!" he cried. "Oh, man, did you see that!"

Teresa sobbed from the couch. "How could you?" she wailed.

"Shut your mouth!" Jack snapped. "Both of you! Go see if the kid is still alive!"

Mandy moved to stand near Jack. Her face was like stone, but her eyes watched approvingly as Teresa got up from the couch with jelly legs. She made her way unevenly to Shio's prone body and knelt next to it to feel for a pulse. "He-he's still breathing," she said, sounding relieved.

"Good," grunted Jack. "Now we have to change his clothes and get out of here. Pronto."

Teresa stared up at him. "Why?" she asked. Tears filled her eyes. "What are you planning?"

"What am I planning?" Jack asked her, as if speaking to a child. "I'm planning on making it through this alive. We don't want anybody to recognize his clothes, do we? I have sweatpants and a shirt in the back room. We burn his stuff and vanish. Jon will take care of the rental, right?"

"I'm on it," Jon said. He sounded happy and excited, like he was on a grand adventure.

"Teresa will do it," Mandy said suddenly. "She'll change his clothes."

"But—" Teresa made to protest, but her sister stopped her with a cold look.

"You work for him. You're like his nanny, so you do it! Jack and I will clean up around here. When you're done, carry him out of here and we'll wait for Jon to return with the car. That is, unless you want to go with Jon?" The last question held a menacing threat that caused Teresa to shake her head.

"No," she whispered. "I'll do it." Without another word, she rolled the limp body over. Then, grabbing Shio under the arms, she lifted him up and dragged him past her sister and Jack. Jack laughed when he waved the prod in her direction, causing her to flinch.

"Take a right," he told her. "In the back room on the left you'll find the clothes. Hurry up. And if you're thinking of doing something foolish, there're no windows back there. That used to be the room used to store supplies. We'll wait here until you're back."

Minutes later, Teresa returned with Shio's limp form draped over her downtrodden shoulders. He now wore baggy sweatpants and a generic shirt. She dumped him on the couch and immediately fell into a ball at his feet and started shaking in silent sobs.

Jack and Mandy stood in the front of the room watching. Jack turned to Mandy with real admiration in his eyes.

"I think I underestimated you," he said. "You do have what it takes to pull this off."

Mandy shrugged. "We're all in this together. Teresa had to know that. Now she can't back out."

"So we all live," Jack said, rubbing his jaw. "Well, we'll see what happens next."

Mandy glared at him. "What happens next is that we load him in the car and then drive far, far away from here. Then we wait for the word."

"The word?" Jack asked, tilting his head. "What word is that?"

Mandy only growled that she heard Jon returning. Sure enough, the sound of a car pulling up came from in front of the house.

"Let's do this," Mandy said.

Jack plucked Shio from the couch and threw him over his shoulder, relieving Teresa of the duty. The younger woman seemed on the verge of a breakdown. He carried the unconscious body while whistling a jaunty tune.

Walking to the car with his free hand still clutching the cattle prod, Jack waited for Mandy to open the back door. She watched with distaste as he slapped the back of the boy's thighs with the prod.

"You sleep tight, you hear?" he said before laughing.

Then he dumped in the package, splaying the boy's body across the backseat. Wiping his hands clean, he stepped back to allow Mandy to arrange the kid so he curled into a ball and could be covered with a towel.

"Bad news, I'm afraid," he said nonchalantly. "But I won't be going with you. The boss asked me to stay here and wait for him. We're the ones who have to arrange for the money."

Mandy shot him a look. "That wasn't part of the plan."

"Plan?" Jack asked. "What plan? It has already changed more times than I can count. Look, there's not enough room in Jon's junk heap for all of us without looking suspicious. The boss said that if you can be trusted, you're in charge. Well, you can be trusted. He should meet me next week and that's when we decide how and when to return the package. After we're all paid off, of course."

"What about me?" Teresa asked, wiping away tears as she left the house.

Jack snorted. "Oh, you're going. After all, you're the boy's nanny."

Mandy licked her lips, but then nodded. "Fine. Get in the car, Teresa. Sit in front with Jon. I'll stay with our sleeping friend in case he wakes."

"Oh, I doubt that will be any time soon," Jack said, looking down at the cattle prod. He held it out to Mandy. "But just in case, it's all yours."

Chapter 6

Everything was dark and still. The boy was dead. There could be no question. From the silence came terror.

I died, he said to himself, horrified at the thought. Then felt his shoulders shake. The cold feeling of death pressed all about him. He tried to remember his name and how he died, but could remember nothing. All he could recall was a terrible flash and a horrible pain.

Pain … the pain lingered even after his life had gone. Mostly his head hurt. And he tasted metal in his mouth. Funny, but death should not be like this. He wasn't sure how he knew this, but he remembered death being about meeting angels and going to a better place … unless he'd been especially wicked. Then he would go down to terrible fire. Cold struck again and he longed to meet a fire. Then he became aware of an awful burning pain on his right shoulder. Perhaps he'd been among the wicked after all.

His eyes blinked open. Each eyelid felt like a slab of metal. Awake now, he found himself lying inside a roomy coffin. It smelled like death. A few inches from his face was a wall of cloth.

Puzzled, he tried lifting himself, but couldn't move. His muscles were like gelatin and his mind like mush. A loud buzzing noise filled his head.

Dimly, he became aware of voices. He wondered if they were angels. Then he heard a word no angel would ever say.

Groaning, he again tried rising. He lay mostly on his stomach and his face stuck to the coffin's floor. An arm dangled below him, while his burning arm lay smashed against his side. With great effort, he stretched out his feet. Then he pressed his head into the coffin's floor and pushed back onto his knees, causing him to roll on his side. This squeezed his burning arm into the floor and all at once he sat up, gasping in pain.

He wasn't dead and wasn't in a coffin. That would have been better. He found himself sitting in the back of an old musty car smelling of stale French fries and body odor. The windows were closed tight and the foul air pressed against him like a suffocating blanket.

Blinking, he tried to remember how he got there. Nothing made sense. Looking down, he saw he wore scratchy gray sweatpants at least two sizes too large and a plain black shirt with sleeves that hung over his hands.

What had happened to him?

Sweat formed on his brow as the wracking pain continued to pulse through his head and up and down his spine. Everything felt fuzzy …

How did he end up here? And where was here? More importantly, *who was he?*

He didn't have an answer. It felt as if his mind had turned into an empty cave guarded with electricity. Thinking only brought more hurt. Instead, he took in his surroundings. Food wrappers littered the car floor. A dirty brown towel had fallen from him when he'd rolled over. Otherwise the car was empty.

Staring into the rearview mirror, he wrinkled his brow. A young frightened boy stared back with short spikey hair sticking up from around a narrow face. For a moment his entire body trembled. Everything seemed terribly wrong.

Trying to swallow was like trying to eat sandpaper. He coughed hoarsely and looked out the front windshield.

Three grown-ups stood in front of the car and were arguing. Two women and one man. Their raised voices had woken him. Though muffled, they were still loud enough to be made out from inside the car.

He narrowed his eyes but could not place any of them. Then he shuddered when one of the women held up an odd-looking stick. For some reason, the sight of the stick made him want to faint. Breathing deeply, he managed to remain conscious. He leaned forward to try to understand what they were talking about. Slowly he did, and his body started to shake, not just from the cold, but from fear. They were talking about killing him.

The man claimed it would be best to do it now and hide the body.

"I ain't afraid of getting my hands dirty," he sneered.

One of the women was crying silently and shaking her head. The other argued that they should wait until the proper time. She kept saying everything would've been for nothing if they messed up now.

The boy didn't need to hear anything else. He just knew he had to get out of there. Fast.

Thankfully, the grown-ups were too intent on arguing to look back at the car. It was parked on the side of a narrow road partly in a small ditch so it leaned to the right. In this direction, he saw a line of trees rising above tall grass. On the other side of the road was a steep hill naked of trees. He looked back to the tree line. The trees were bare, so he knew it had to be winter. But winter *where?* Where was he and who were the grown-ups and why did they want to kill him? A breeze hit against the side of the car. In the distance, the tree branches seemed to beckon him to come. *Forget about the questions*, they seemed to say. *Just get away!*

"Do we have to hurt him?" wailed a panicked woman's voice.

"No, just kill him," barked the man's voice. He sounded serious. Dead serious.

"How?" asked another woman's voice, this one deeper. She sounded more curious than horrified.

The boy needed no more urging as he ducked down. Scooting back, he hit the door closest to the trees. With his heart pounding, he twisted to his stomach and found the latch. Carefully and quietly, he eased the door open and crawled free of the car. Using his back foot, he gently closed the door softly behind him. He briefly paused to listen, holding his breath and biting his lower lip in fear. When he heard no cries of detection, his breath returned. For a moment, he allowed his lungs to fill with fresh air. Then it was time to move.

Keeping on his belly, he began crawling into the tall grass, ignoring the cold and the fear pressing around him. The sun descended behind the hills, taking away most of the light. Despite the chill, sweat formed on his forehead.

Not knowing where he was heading, the boy continued toward the trees. His heart hammered in his chest. Yes. He was alive. And he wanted to stay that way.

"It doesn't matter how!" roared the man behind him. Outside the car, the voices were louder and harsher. "He's going to get it in the end. It's better to do it now and bury the body. Otherwise we can be caught at any time with him."

"Not so loud!" wailed a woman's voice. "Somebody can hear us!"

"Somebody like the boy," the deeper woman's voice said. Then she said a bad word. "The light is on in the car. Quick, check on him."

The boy didn't wait or look back. Staggering to his feet, he started running.

"Look! He's getting away!" screeched the first woman's voice.

"I told you!" yelled the man. "Hey! Get back here!"

The boy only ran faster. Slowly but surely, his body was waking up. Propelled by fear, it chugged to the trees and into the shadowy woods. Crashing through a low branch, the boy fell and rolled into a pile of dry leaves. Gasping, he landed on his bad shoulder, sending searing pain shooting down his arm.

For a moment he nearly blacked out. Crying out, he forced himself to his knees while resting his forehead on the ground. Seconds passed and when the pain had dulled to a roar, he scrambled to his feet with his good arm. He clutched his burning shoulder as he resumed crashing through the brush ahead.

Shouts and sounds of pursuit were not far behind. Thankfully, the deeper he went into the woods the thinner the brush. Still, with the fading light, he smacked into several branches and found himself in the midst of thorns more than once. His clothes tore, but he continued onward.

"He's this way!" roared the man. "I see him!"

The boy panted in fear as he continued his desperate retreat. The dry fallen leaves did very little to muffle his footsteps. Thankfully his pursuers were just as loud.

"We're going to get you, so give up now!" hollered the man.

"We won't hurt you!" called one of the women. "You're just going to get lost!"

The boy decided to take his chances on getting lost. He crashed on to a place he knew not.

Brittany stomped her way home, taking the shortcut by following the train tracks. She knew she wasn't ever supposed to use the tracks to travel home, but she didn't care. At least this way nobody would bother her.

School had been horrible again. The girls from basketball had spread the story of how "Stink Fish" thought she could be an athlete, but played ball like a blind bat trying to walk a dog. "She was all over the place trying to dribble," one of the girls said during homeroom. "She spent more time chasing the ball than anything else. I thought coach was going to have a heart attack!"

Brittany had walked in just in time to hear that. When the girls saw her, they'd quickly covered their mouths and muffled their laughter. The rest of the day, Brittany caught kids pointing her out and miming trying to dribble an imaginary ball while blind.

During lunch, Mason had found her sitting dejectedly at one of the back tables all by herself. Not even the other rejects had wanted to be near her on this day.

"Don't worry," he'd mumbled to her. "It's the last day before break. They'll all forget about it by January." Then he'd left her to sit with his soccer buddies.

After school mercifully ended, she'd walked to the library to check out books to get her through the two weeks of no school or friends. It took twenty minutes to walk there from her house, but it was worth it for a few good books. The usual librarian had not been there. Instead, a pinched-faced lady with short blond hair had waited behind the desk. She'd adamantly refused to let Brittany check out any more books. "You already have three books out. Return those and you can get more," she'd told her in a shrill, grating voice.

Brittany had tried to explain that her mom and Mason shared her card and those books were for them, but the librarian clearly hadn't believed her.

Kids, the librarian had told her, needed to learn responsibility. Borrowing books was a privilege, not a right.

Brittany knew the real reason she couldn't take the books. She was all alone and dressed in a smelly gray hoodie and unwashed jeans with a hole in one knee. With the wrong skin color.

At the time, she'd resisted the urge to slam down her wanted books, or to take them and run, but instead had politely thanked the woman and walked briskly from the library.

Hot tears had run down her cheeks when she'd met the cold air of the Friday afternoon. Wanting to walk briskly, she'd left her coat at home. So she took the shortcut.

If only I could find a shortcut to a better life, she now thought miserably.

The tracks were behind the library just past a thin copse of trees. They ran a little ways before reaching the old warehouse once used for stocking lumber to ship out by train. The Burnhurst Lumber Mill had closed ten years ago and the town of Burnhurst had never recovered. Now the warehouse sat abandoned except for a few leftover piles of forgotten wood too rotten to salvage.

Only elite people like Melissa's parents, who were lawyers, didn't seem affected by the economic hardship. For others, it proved to be a disaster. The homeless population spiked as houses were lost and families moved on, sometimes without their fathers. Many stores had closed.

In the downtown area alone, three restaurants, two shopping centers, and a music store had gone out of business in the past two years. Cooligan's Department Store, where her mom worked, looked to be the next on the list of closures, unless a holiday miracle picked up sales. Not too likely since nobody in town could afford an elaborate Christmas.

Brittany kicked a rock on the tracks, sending it skittering into the trees on her left.

Holiday miracles are nothing but fiction, she thought darkly. They only came true in stories ... or for people like Melissa. Earlier that day, Brittany had watched her leave school with her mom. They, Melissa had let the whole school know, were leaving for New York City to catch a glimpse of the wonder boy Shio Slaydon before going Christmas shopping.

Brittany sighed. Christmas for her was like another day. At least her mom would have it off. But the only thing to celebrate this year was being together. There would be no tree or presents. Just like last year and the year before that.

She'd just reached the warehouse. Once she passed it, she would cross a road and then go another half mile before coming to the back of her block. She shuddered when the large shadowy building came into view. It reminded her of a graveyard, only it was a place where dreams and futures were dead instead of people.

Piles of scrapped wood sat covered with cloth tarps on the warehouse's platform like tombstones. A few of the tarps blew in the wind and resembled ghosts.

Brittany shook herself free of the dark thoughts. The scrap wood, she knew, was used by the homeless community of Burnhurst. They were burned for warmth and for cooking.

Being alone at twilight didn't bother Brittany. She knew there were homeless men and women around this area. Unlike most girls her age, she felt comforted by this fact. This was because she met and worked with many of the homeless through her church. One of the men was a giant named Derek Murdock, better known as Big Murdock. He was the one who told her about the warehouse and the wood. He had a place nearby, she knew.

She wondered if she should stop and try to find him. Big Murdock definitely looked like a homeless hobo, but he didn't act like one.

When she first saw him at the shelter her church worked at each week, she'd been too afraid to speak. With a wild beard and mustache streaked with gray covering much of his face, wearing layers of musty, smelly coats and sweaters, he looked like an Arctic explorer lost in bitterness and right out of a horror film. His hair, thick with grease, grew like his beard and, unless tied in a ponytail, would stick out in all directions like he'd been electrocuted. When he spoke, his voice rumbled like a volcano about to blow. He never washed his clothes and always carried a foul odor.

She learned from the ladies in the shelter that he'd come from out of town a few years before but had decided to stay in Burnhurst. Nobody knew his past, and rumors about military service and a former felon circulated. Brittany made sure to stay away from him.

Helping with the homeless opened her eyes. Suddenly, they were no longer faceless beings but real people with real personalities. Many had a great sense of humor. She often saw them on the streets and would wave and stop to talk to the ones she knew, except for Big Murdock.

Then, one day, a group of teenagers followed her from the library and started calling her names. One asked for her to come over. She tried running, but they easily ran her down. Four of them formed a rough circle around her.

Then a large shadow fell over them. "Leave her alone," growled a deep, angry voice.

The boys turned to see Big Murdock with clenched fists and bared teeth. Without a word, they fled.

Big Murdock watched them go and then turned to leave.

"Wait!" Brittany called out. "I, I want to thank you. And say I'm sorry for … not being nice to you before. You know, at the shelter … I, uh, work there."

Big Murdock stopped and turned. He grinned widely, showing off chipped, yellow teeth. "No thanks needed, missy. I wouldn't be nice to me either. Didn't your mother tell you to stay away from strangers?"

That began their friendship. After some months of talking at the shelter, Big Murdock reluctantly told Brittany about how he lived among the ruins of the lumber mill. He rarely slept at the warehouse, because the owners still occasionally sent guards out to chase out any squatters. But he did regularly use the scrap wood. He was the one who started putting tarps over the scraps so he and others like him had dry wood for fires when needed.

Brittany learned that Big Murdock was like a leader for many of the homeless. And soon after, word had gotten passed around to keep an eye out for her. Now, almost all the homeless people she met would greet her with a smile and kind words. These she never failed to return.

Still, Big Murdock constantly warned her to avoid the tracks and warehouse. Poverty hurt people on many levels and some were dangerous. Also, trains still ran on the track—they just no longer stopped at Burnhurst.

Thinking of Big Murdock, Brittany gazed over the shell of the past and saw no life. Everything appeared cold, gray, and still.

Suddenly, she heard a noise behind her.

Whirling, she stared into the trees above the tracks. Acres of woods lined this side of the tracks and stretched out over a mile to the western boundary of Burnhurst. They'd been planted for timber years before but had since been saved due to the mill's closing. Now the homeless and teenagers looking for places to hide were the only people who used the woods. Kids were told to stay out. There were coyotes and rumors of wolves that hunted a vast deer population.

Brittany shivered and wondered what she would rather see coming out of the trees. A person or a wolf. Both would probably freak her out.

"Who's there?" she asked boldly. If it was a homeless friend, it wouldn't be too bad. But she didn't think that was the case. Whoever or whatever was out there was trying to be too quiet. She sensed eyes on her. Fear gripped her stomach and she stepped back from the tracks toward the warehouse. Another rustle of leaves and she placed the sound behind a clump of bushes just below a large oak tree.

"I know you're there," she said, gulping. "You can come out … now."

A shadow stepped out.

It wasn't a man or a wolf. It was just a boy.

Brittany bent over with relief when she saw the slight figure of a scared kid standing in front of her.

"Good grief, you scared me!" she said. "What are you doing, playing war?"

He looked slightly younger than her and well cared for. A sharp haircut and smooth skin, tanned to a light brown, highlighted an extremely good-looking face that she found somewhat familiar.

Immediately, she dismissed him as a kid who wouldn't give her the time of day in ordinary circumstances. She was about to keep on going and leave him when he made a sound. It sounded almost a whimper. Pleading.

She took deep breaths and stared at the boy harder. Cared for, maybe. But not recently. Even in the fading light she could tell the boy had run into trouble.

He held up filthy sweatpants with a thin hand and had an equally grimy shirt draped over his small frame. Dirt covered his face and she could see scratches all over his hands. Spikes of dark hair stuck up from his high forehead, but otherwise it was matted with dirt and sweat.

What drew her attention most was his eyes. Wild with fear and confusion, they stared at her as if begging.

"What's wrong?" she asked him. "Can't you talk?" she said sharply. "Are you lost?"

The last thing she needed was some stupid light-skinned boy lost at nightfall. He looked so pathetic standing there.

She sighed. "Come on. What's your name?"

Then he spoke. "I … I don't know." It sounded almost like a whimper.

A branch broke in the trees behind him and he reacted as if shot. Glancing back, he flew down to the tracks where Brittany stood.

"Th-they ... they're after me," he hissed. "They're trying to kill me!"

Brittany choked back her fear. The boy seemed out of his mind. "What? Who's after you?"

"I ... I don't know." The boy grabbed her sleeve and looked up with pleading eyes. "I don't know how ... but I woke up in a car. They were talking about killing me, so I ran. Please help me. They're chasing me!"

Then they both heard it. A deep voice calling from the woods. "This way, I think I found his trail!"

It sounded very close.

Brittany's heart hammered against her chest and threatened to climb up her throat. Quickly, she made a decision. "Come with me," she said, grabbing the boy's arm.

The boy cried out in pain and nearly sank to his knees.

"Hurts there," he gasped.

"Sorry," Brittany said, alarmed. "Here, just follow me." She hopped from the tracks and raced to the edge of the warehouse's platform. It reached up to her nose.

"Here, climb up," she told the boy. Bending low, she grabbed the boy's ankles and hoisted him upwards to the platform. She was alarmed to see the boy had no shoes, but wore only filthy socks on his feet.

Then, she hoisted herself up the platform with both hands and scrambled up after him, tearing skin on her palms in the process.

Behind her, she heard voices closing in.

"There's some kind of building up ahead," said a woman gruffly. "I bet he's hiding there."

"Search everywhere," returned the man's voice. "We're not leaving without him."

"No kidding," snapped the woman's gruff voice.

The children were caught in the middle of the platform. Brittany didn't want to even risk trying one of the doors. Opening would cause noise. Her eyes darted to a wood pile covered in a tarp.

"Down here!" she hissed. She shoved the boy down and pulled the tarp from the wood and over the boy. Then she crawled under, laying herself across the boy's back, praying they looked like a pile of old, rotten wood.

Like this, they huddled together in the dark, breathing in musty fumes of rotting wood.

Brittany didn't dare breathe unless necessary. When she did, the air proved stale and full of sawdust. Under her, she felt the boy trembling like a leaf. She pressed her weight down firmly.

"Just relax," she whispered. "If you don't move, they won't notice us." This was more like a prayer than the truth.

Silence followed and then the voices were suddenly right next to them. The boy went still.

"I'll search on top. You two go around, look for him in the back." The man spoke roughly. "When I find him, he's dead."

The woman's deep voice grunted more in agreement than protest. "Just find the brat," she snarled.

Brittany felt her blood freeze. The boy had been telling the truth. He was being hunted by killers. Suddenly her problems from earlier that day no longer seemed so big. She just hoped to live long enough to see the next day.

The sound of deep grunting near her feet let her know the man was climbing up the platform. Her arms squeezed the boy's shoulders. The voice of death would soon be upon them.

Chapter
7

The wood squeaked next to her and she could feel the heavy tread of a large man standing on the platform only a few feet from her head. She nearly screamed when a foot nudged the tarp. Then it moved on. A loud thud came from near her head and she heard the sound of wood pieces skittering off the platform. The man had kicked the uncovered wood pile in frustration. Next, she heard the sound of the door being tried.

"Anything?" called the deep woman's voice.

"Nothing," spat the man. Only two voices had been heard, but the man had mentioned two others. "All that's up here is rotting wood covered in these rotten tarps."

Brittany worked hard to control her breathing. The squeak of wood approached and she knew he was standing just above them looking down.

The boy groaned softly from beneath her.

Brittany wondered if he'd fainted. That would probably be for the best. Thankfully the man didn't seem to hear.

"I think I found something!" called a shrill voice of another woman. The third voice.

Immediately, he heard a heavy fall as the man jumped down. Footsteps retreated around the warehouse.

Gasping for a breath and shaking wildly, Brittany rose to her hands and knees. "Are you okay," she whispered hoarsely.

The boy shifted slightly as if just waking. "Brilliantly terrible," he moaned.

"Well, it'll be a lot worse if they come back and find you here." She shook the boy, but he didn't budge.

"That's a man's footprint, you idiot!" she heard the man bellow from around the corner. "And it looks too old. Move around the front. I doubt he went too far this way. I know he's close by. I can feel it!"

Brittany's entire body shook. But then she made a decision. "I hope this works for both our sakes," she hissed at the boy. Then she crawled out from the tarp, making sure it covered the boy.

Quickly, she slid down from the platform and started walking as naturally as she could along the tracks. As naturally as she could with legs that suddenly felt as if they were filled with jelly instead of bones.

She froze when she heard heavy footsteps coming from the back of the platform. They must have climbed up the back way and were heading right to where the boy lay.

She glanced at the tarp and was alarmed to see the boy poke his head out and stare out. He must have thought she'd abandoned him. His eyes were wide with fright.

Hastily, she put her finger to her lips and motioned him to get under cover. Then she went to a knee and pretended to tie her shoe.

She was just in time as the man came around the corner of the warehouse on her left. From the right of the warehouse came two women also on the platform. Brittany risked a peek up and instantly went back to her shoes. None of them looked very full of the holiday spirit.

"Any sign of the boy?" asked the deep-voiced woman. She was a large woman with a wide, unpleasant face dotted with brown specks that made her features appear even darker in the fading light. Cruel, beady eyes pressed tightly against a large nose.

The smaller woman by her side seemed frail in comparison.

"No, I—" The man spotted Brittany. "Hey, you! What are you doing here?" he shouted.

Brittany jerked up her head and did her best to look innocently surprised. "Are-are you talking to me?" she asked, her voice shaking.

"Yeah, who else?" barked the man. He was exactly how Brittany imagined him to be. Big, burly, and mean looking. He wore a heavy plaid shirt stretched across a wide chest. Sweat dripped from his face. "We're looking for a kid. A boy about your age, maybe slightly smaller. Skinny with brown hair. You see anybody like that?"

Brittany shook her head vigorously. "I was just walking home," she said hurriedly. "I've seen nobody except for you." She did her best to sound clueless. Then she swallowed. "What are you looking for him for?"

"He's a runaway," the larger of the women said. "He's a bit confused and paranoid." She laughed lightly. "I'm afraid he has some mental health issues and thinks we're after him."

"You should call the police," Brittany said, biting her lip. The man stood just next to the tarp.

"Oh, we did that," the larger woman said smoothly. Her face was lost in the shadows as night fast approached. Brittany could feel her hard gaze staring at her. "They're looking for him too. But if they find him, they'll probably lock him up and we don't want that. We'd rather take him home quietly and give him time to recover."

"Yeah," chimed in the second girl. Smaller and much more timid, she hung back in the shadows and sounded slightly scared. "All he needs is his medicine."

The man snorted. "You got that right."

Then Brittany watched in horror as the man squatted his big backside right on top of the boy's hiding place. He sat back with a sigh and then frowned.

"I wouldn't sit there," Brittany said desperately. "That's all rotten wood and you can fall right through. And there are black widow spiders all over those tarps. Also snakes live there. My brother played in one and nearly died."

The man quickly shot back to his feet and wiped the back of his pants. "That's just great," he growled. But he sounded a little shaken. He started at Brittany. "You sure you haven't seen him? He came this way not more than a minute ago."

Brittany trembled as she shook her head. She didn't like how the man and large woman started moving toward her. Also the other woman was eyeing the tarp.

A loud bellow from behind the warehouse saved her. "Who's that there?" cried a loud, thundering voice. "Whoever you are, you're on my territory and better scram!"

The women and man stopped suddenly as if caught in a beam of light. They stared wildly at each other. The smaller woman moved first and the others quickly followed. All three scrambled from the platform and moved to the tracks.

Brittany quickly dashed toward the voice. She had never been happier to see Big Murdock than at that moment. The large man lurched from around the warehouse like a drunken lunatic. His wild beard and hair made it look as if his face were on fire.

"Scram, I said!" he bellowed even louder.

The man made to say something, but stopped when Murdock staggered in his direction.

Though not small by any means, the man looked puny compared to Big Murdock. The three quietly but quickly fled up into the trees.

Murdock lurched after them until he was certain they were nowhere near. Then he turned on Brittany, straightening up. "What in blazes was that all about?" he demanded sternly. "What are you doing here this late at night? And all alone?"

"Forget that, Murdock," Brittany said desperately, rushing for the platform. "Help me up!"

"Why? Wh—" Murdock stopped when he saw the wood pile move and turn into the frightened form of a boy crawling from the tarp.

"Those three were after him," Brittany explained. "I think they wanted to kill him."

"Ha!" Murdock laughed. "He's probably a runaway with an imagination to match."

An automatic light from the warehouse switched on, bathing the three in a pale yellow light.

The boy flinched from the light and then stared at Murdock. He slowly sat down and hung his legs over the side. "Who are you?" he asked suspiciously. For a moment, he looked relaxed and not like a scared, lost little boy.

"Doesn't matter," snapped the homeless man. "The question is, who are you?"

The boy looked pained. "I don't know," he answered, suddenly sounding pitiful again. "I can't … I can't remember."

"Listen, Murdock," Brittany said, crouching next to the boy. "We have to help him. Those guys can come back any moment."

Big Murdock frowned for a moment. Then he shrugged. "Very well," he muttered. "You two come with me until it's safe and then you can take him to your home, Brittany. I want nothing to do with him."

"That's … that's a plan," Brittany said. "Thank you, Murdock!" She grinned at the boy. "Did you hear that?"

The boy and the homeless man ignored her and stared distastefully at each other for a long moment.

"You mean *this* guy is helping *us*?" the boy asked, his handsome features twisting in a grimace.

"What's wrong with that?" Brittany demanded.

"He smells like a sewer," the boy said to her.

Brittany bit her lip and kept from shouting.

Big Murdock snorted. "So do you, boy. What happened, you wet yourself?"

The boy gulped and looked ashamed, drawing his knees to his chin. "He … he sat on my bum," he said sourly. "I thought I would be crushed."

Big Murdock barked out a laugh. "Don't worry, I've done the same many a time. Only I was just a baby, or falling down drunk. Come if you want, but I'm not staying here any longer smelling your stink."

The boy frowned, his black eyes flashing, but he said nothing.

"If you don't come," Brittany told him, "those three will be back before you know it."

The boy got up miserably and followed Brittany and Murdock into the shadows.

Murdock led them from the warehouse to an old abandoned brick building at the edge of the mill property. Climbing a rickety staircase, he produced a key and proceeded to unlock the door at the top of the stairs.

"This is my humble home," he mumbled as he made way for the kids.

"Smells like an outhouse," mumbled the boy.

"You're just smelling yourself," Big Murdock growled back.

"Where're the lights?" the boy asked, stepping hesitantly in the darkened room.

"In this home there is no electricity. Now be patient!" snapped the big man.

Brittany sighed. "Look," she said to the boy. "I know you're lost and confused, but he is helping you. So you can be a little more polite."

Big Murdock grunted in agreement as he fumbled in the dark. The boy fell silent.

A beam of light shot through the dark and Murdock grinned as he held a flashlight to his chin. "Just a moment more …"

Soon three burning candles and a single flashlight illuminated the room. The plastered walls were bare and suffered from erosion in some areas. Otherwise, the floor had been swept clean. Two sleeping bags were laid out in the far corner, next to a pile of clothes and camping gear. Two large coolers sat at the foot of the sleeping bags. Between the coolers were neat stacks of boxes and cans of food.

Big Murdock offered granola bars but Brittany politely declined. The boy only stared in disbelief before taking a seat by the door.

On the way, Brittany couldn't stop staring at the boy's feet. His socked feet were covered in mud … and blood. Thorns had done a number on his feet, but he didn't complain. He just held his injured shoulder and stared blankly, struggling to understand.

Brittany couldn't help but feel sorry for him. Even if he did act like a spoiled, rude brat. After a while, the boy slid into a restless slumber. His head sank to his chest and then slowly rolled to lean on Brittany's shoulder. He folded up his knees and lay against her.

"You should shake him off," Big Murdock grunted from where he sat by his sleeping bags across from them. He'd offered the bags for more comfortable seating, but the boy had silently refused. "He might be contagious. Kids like that are spoiled brats who grow up to be punks."

That was exactly what she thought and would've have said so less than an hour before. Now, though, she made a face. "How can you say that? You don't even know him."

Big Murdock snorted. "Are you sure about that? People like him are all the same. They don't give people like us a care in the world unless they need us."

Brittany pretended to ignore him. Instead she looked curiously at all of Big Murdock's stuff.

"So this is where you live," she said to change the subject.

"Mostly. I have lots of places, really. You know people. To them the homeless are like stray dogs. They're an unwanted nuisance. If I'm ever run out of one place, I just go to another." He sighed. "Sometimes I wish things could have turned out differently …"

Brittany shifted to let the boy lean against her more comfortably. He wiggled his shoulders, but didn't stir. Instead of being repulsed, she actually felt comforted by his presence. He was like a lost puppy.

Big Murdock caught her looking at the boy. He grunted. "You know, once I was like that boy. So full of myself and had the looks to match. I played football back then. Was quarterback, and got to be pretty good."

Brittany swallowed. Big Murdock had never opened up about his private life before. She lifted her eyes to look at him, but didn't say a word. She was afraid if she did he would clam back up.

The large man licked his lips and stared at the candle's flame, but seemed to be looking someplace else far away.

"Yeah, I was a good player back then. You know, by my senior year I was being scouted by lots of big schools ..." He trailed off, dropping his bearded face to his chest.

"What happened?" Brittany asked quietly, afraid the moment had been lost. "How did you ..."

"End up here?" Big Murdock snorted, looking at her. "Like I said, I was like this kid. Full of myself, but no clue of who I really was. Well, I started drinking after games. Thought it was cool and all. Had a lot of friends then. We all thought we were cool. Weekend parties became the only thing that mattered. I ended up just barely finishing high school and stuck with only a junior college that would take me. My parents had split up and were no help. So what did I do?" He laughed bitterly.

"Claimed the world treated me wrong and I deserved better. I started stealing and drinking. See, I needed the money ... and the alcohol. One thing led to another and soon I found myself kicked out of college and threatened with jail time. So I gathered my stuff and started traveling. I've worked many a job since then. Until one day I found myself stuck in a line to a homeless shelter. Never seemed to get out of it since." He shook his head. "All that time and you know what? I haven't changed much. I'm not as full of myself as before, but I still have no idea who I am or what I'm supposed to be doing."

"Wh-what about your parents?" Brittany asked softly. "Don't you miss them?"

Big Murdock coughed. "Don't know why I'm saying this," he muttered. "Just seeing that young punk talk about me like that ... look at me like that ..." He stared at Brittany. In the flickering shadows, he looked positively scary—like a monster, only sad.

"My parents never cared about me once I started getting into trouble," he said flatly. "They were too busy blaming each other for causing all my problems. When I left they were both better off." He stared at Brittany. "You have a good mom, Brittany. I know things aren't easy for you, but you have a mom that loves you."

Brittany swallowed. "You're a good man, too," she said. "You helped us."

Big Murdock snorted. "Really? Did I? Who knows. Maybe those people were telling the truth and the kid is a runaway. For all you know he's a dangerous lunatic. Like you once thought I was." He smiled sardonically. "Only difference he's a cute little kid and I'm an ugly old man."

"That's not true," Brittany said, biting her lip. "I mean, it's different with kids. I, well …" she stopped, too tired to go on. She knew what it was like to be judged and treated unfairly. Maybe Big Murdock was right. She did the same—judged based on looks and nothing else.

Seeing her face hurt, Big Murdock quickly rose to his feet.

"I'm sorry, Brittany," he said hastily. "I have no call to babble on like that. You're one of the few people I trust. You know, I never told any of what you heard tonight to anyone. Not for more than twenty years. You have a good heart. I just don't want to see it broken … especially by the likes of that kid."

Brittany shifted in her seat and the boy jerked awake.

"Wh-what time is it?" he blurted, staring around wildly.

"Time to go," grunted Big Murdock. "I'll walk you two to your house, Brittany. You sure your mother would take in the kid? We can always go to the police."

Brittany started to nod her head, but then shook it vigorously. She never told Big Murdock that her mom was rarely home at night. Usually a neighbor looked in on them, but even that was rare.

"No police," she said firmly. "Not yet. I don't know what those people want with him, but if they're right and the police are looking for him too …"

Big Murdock shrugged. "I don't always trust the uniform either. Most are good, but a few bad ones can really make your life miserable. Come on."

The boy stood up shakily, looking exhausted and confused.

Brittany looked at him worriedly. "Once we get home I'll look at your arm and feet," she told him. "But until then, I think Murdock should carry you."

"No!" both boy and man shouted at once.

"I don't want that guy touching me," the boy said, crossing his arms defiantly.

"And I don't want that stinky kid wetting my back," Big Murdock responded, crossing his own arms.

"Fine," Brittany snapped. "Then I guess we'll have to spend the night here!"

Sulkily, the boy allowed Big Murdock to carry him on his back. The large man spent the whole time complaining under his breath.

After making sure none of the three strangers were around, Brittany led the way from Big Murdock's home to her house. There were few streetlights in this area of town and they passed through the night mostly in dark shadows. Avoiding the train tracks, she took the road once used by lumber trucks but now mostly abandoned, before cutting onto a trail through a cluster of trees. The trail led to the street near her bus stop.

Minutes later they arrived at her front yard. All the lights were dark and Brittany was relieved Mason had yet to return home. He was likely at Ben's house playing video games or watching old soccer games.

Big Murdock slid the boy from his back and gave a curt goodbye. The boy never said thanks, so Brittany said it for him.

Big Murdock just raised a hand. "Good luck," he mumbled before melting in the darkness.

Brittany shuddered as she watched the big man go.

"Is this where you live?" the boys asked doubtfully, sounding just as critical as when he'd seen Big Murdock's place. "It's really small."

"It isn't much, but it's better than standing in the cold," Brittany told him tiredly as she turned to her humble home. "Come on."

The temperature had dropped with the sun and the boy needed no more urging. He still had to hold up his pants as he trotted after Brittany.

Brittany took him in the front door and flipped on the lights. They were greeted with a blast of warm air. Ignoring the bare meager surroundings, the boys sighed with pleasure.

"Oh, no, you don't," Brittany told him when he started for the couch in the family room. "We're going up to the bathroom and you're taking a shower before you touch a lick of my furniture. If my mom comes home and smells what you smell like, we're sunk. And believe me, you look like a mess too."

Allowing no argument, Brittany led the way up the stairs and straight to the tiny bathroom she shared with Mason. Having the boy sit on the counter, she gingerly rolled up the sleeve of his injured arm. He winced and gasped with pain at each movement until he finally told her to stop and took off the shirt without help.

Brittany's eyes widened at seeing the boy's skinny but muscular chest. Not even Mason had a hard, flat stomach like this kid, and he did more sit-ups a day than she cared to count.

"Do you play sports?" she asked without thinking.

The boy blinked and twisted his mouth. "Uh, I think so … yeah." He had a high but pleasant voice with a distinct English accent. She'd noticed it before but had been too busy and scared to think about it.

Who is this kid? she wondered for about the millionth time. Clearly he came from a good family. Even in the middle of winter she saw tan lines on his arm. Then she saw his right shoulder.

She winced. "Ouch. I bet that hurts," she muttered.

The boy looked himself and made face. "I don't know what happened there."

"Looks like a burn," Brittany told him, fingering the skin under the wound. On the outside of his right shoulder was a nasty red spot on the skin with bits of blackened spots. A small blister had risen in the center. "Does it hurt?" she asked, already knowing the answer.

"Yeah. Only when I think about it."

Brittany turned on the water to its coldest setting and gently washed the arm. "I'll leave and you take a shower. Throw out your clothes and I'll put them in the wash."

The boy stared at her. "What will I wear then?"

"I have a brother. He's a bit bigger than you, but our mom never throws away clothes. I'll find something that fits. Don't worry about her," she said hastily when seeing his look at mentioning her mom. "She's working late. I don't think she should know about you yet, so you can sleep in my brother's room tonight."

"What about your dad?"

"Oh, he's … he died," she said quietly.

The boy asked nothing else, just swallowing hard. "That's too bad," he said after a moment.

"Yeah, well, hurry up with the shower. Mason, that's my brother, should be coming home soon. After I put your clothes in the wash I'll find something to eat. Okay?"

Brittany left the room and waited for the door to crack open and dirty laundry to come flying.

Doing laundry was nothing new to her. Having washed Mason's uniform after games in the mud, she could stand the dirtiest of clothes. Still, she took care to wrap the boy's pants and underclothes in the shirt before carrying it down. The acrid smell of urine mixed with sweat and dirt was pretty unbearable.

Next, she ran up to her mom's old dresser and hunted clothes to fit the boy. Her mom never threw Mason's clothes away because she never knew if some might fit Brittany one day. For the first time in her life, Brittany thanked her mom for being this thoughtful. She grabbed a pair of pajamas that Mason wore when he'd been nine and the smallest pair of boxer shorts she could fine.

Banging on the bathroom door, she hollered that the clothes were outside the door. The water stopped for a moment and then resumed. She guessed the boy would be in there for a long while.

Thirty minutes later, the boy finally did emerge, bringing a cloud of steam with him. The pajamas hung on him a little but fit fine. He smiled sheepishly at Brittany. She'd just come up the stairs to tell him toasted pizza was ready.

Cleaned up, the boy looked vaguely familiar, but she couldn't place where she'd seen him before. He was, she had to admit, very handsome. When he smiled, as he did now, his whole face lit up.

"Er, thanks," he said. "For, er, everything."

Brittany ducked her head, suddenly feeling shy herself. "Yeah, well, uh, the pizza is getting cold. I hope you like it."

"I don't really remember, but I think I would like anything right now. I'm starving."

The boy ended up eating two entire toasted pizzas on his own and then finishing the leftovers of a third when Brittany proclaimed herself full. He also drank over five glasses of milk. As he finished the last bite, Brittany saw the boy's eyes start to slide close.

Quickly, she hustled him back up to the bathroom and had him remove his shirt again so she could bandage his arm. Her mother had wanted to be a nurse but never could afford nursing school. This hadn't stopped her from buying books on first aid and basic nursing. She even used to practice on her kids. Brittany had enjoyed these times and had later read more than one of the books. She was secretly happy to now practice on a live patient. Mason had never let her near him.

After she wrapped his arm in a clean bandage, the boy pulled his shirt back on and she checked his feet, relieved to see there were no deep scratches. She smeared ointment all over them anyway. Finally, she found an unused toothbrush from a dentist visit and had him brush his teeth.

"Come on," he groaned when presented the toothpaste. "You're like my mum."

"So you remember your mom?" Brittany asked, her eyebrows rising.

The boy pursed his lips and shook his head dejectedly. "Not really ... I know I have one though ..." He hopped down from the sink and stared in the mirror. His bottom lip started to tremble. "I just can't remember anything."

"Don't worry," Brittany said hurriedly, patting his back. "I'm sure you just need a good night's rest."

She sent him to Mason's bed and stood outside the door until she heard his soft breathing even out. He went out in minutes.

Exhausted herself, she trudged back down the stairs and settled on the sofa. She found the controller to their small TV and sighed.

Hooked up to an antenna, their set captured a total of six channels. None would have anything good on. Before she could even find out, her eyes slid shut and the controller slipped from her hand.

She never saw the news report about the Slaydon press conference at the airport coming to a sudden, abrupt end. Michal Slaydon, after answering two questions had gotten a text on his phone that sent him shooting to his feet and almost fleeing the room. Many speculated that there were more problems between him and his wife. The Annual Slaydon Charity Ball, the newscaster said seriously, looked to be in danger of being cancelled.

Chapter
8

Mason came home to find his sister sleeping in a quiet house. He sniffed the air and grinned. "You made pizza?" he said, pumping a fist. "Right on!"

Going straight to the fridge, he was puzzled to find no leftovers. His sister ate like a chicken—always pecking at her food as if it tasted like dried corn. There was no way she ate an entire toasted pizza. Checking the trashcan, he gave a double take. Not one box, but three boxes of pizza were in the trash. Three.

"No way," he said, staring out where his sister slept. "Are you getting depressed, sis?" he asked in wonder.

He settled on making two ham sandwiches using the last of the meat, which meant he had none left for the weekend. He always had a ham sandwich on game day. Apparently not this weekend—the United game really had the makings of a disaster.

Now in a bad mood, he finished off his supper and stomped up the stairs. His sister turned a little but never woke up. As he stopped at the bathroom, his eyes widened.

"What's going on?" he muttered.

Steam covered the mirror, but when he'd passed his sister she still wore her school clothes. The first aid kit sat open on the counter. Rolls of bandages were laid out next to disinfecting ointment. Then he stared at the floor. Puddles of water clustered around very dirty footprints that led into the tub. The showerhead dripped above the tub. Mason watched drops of water plop on a dirt-streaked drain. A dripping washcloth covered in filth hung on the tub's edge.

Mason scratched his head in puzzlement. Brittany hated dirt and always cleaned up after herself. *What is going on?* he wondered again.

Still shaking his head, he made his way to his room. Funny, he hadn't closed the door when he'd left that morning. Then he switched on the lights and started for his bed. He just wanted to lie down and close his eyes for a moment.

He drew up short. His bed. There was a body in his bed. Biting off a strangled yell, he rapidly retreated from his room, slamming off the lights. Then he raced down the stairs to his sister.

"Brittany," he hissed. "Wake up!"

"Oh ..." she groaned, sitting up and stretching her arms over her head. "You're finally home, Mase."

"Look, sis, we have a problem. There's somebody in the house! He's in my bed!" Mason's eyes looked as big as soccer balls and he danced from foot to foot like his socks were on fire. He waited for Brittany to react.

She smacked her lips and yawned. "I know ... I hope you didn't wake him."

"Wh-what?" Mason stammered. He struggled to control his voice. "Wake who?"

"Oh, some boy ... he doesn't know who he is yet." She yawned again.

"What!" Mason shouted.

Brittany jerked and her eyes snapped wide open. "Hush, Mason!" she hissed. "You'll wake him for sure!"

"Wake who? And what is he doing in my bed?"

Brittany got up from the couch and motioned him to be quiet. She quickly told him how she'd found the boy being chased and how the kid didn't remember anything.

Mason took it all in dubiously. "You must know something. You can't let some strange kid in our house. Tell me what you do know about him," he demanded.

"Well, he wore clothes that didn't fit him, had a bad burn on his arm, but otherwise he looks well cared for. I mean, well, he has, um, a nice haircut. Oh, and he speaks in a funny accent. Like he's from a movie, you know, an English movie."

Mason scratched his short curly hair. "Boys like that don't come from nowhere," he said at last. At least he sounded more curious than hostile. "What else about his clothes? Did they have any markings or anything in the pockets? In TV shows, there's always something in the pockets."

Brittany shrugged. "Go see for yourself. I put them in the wash. They should be done now."

Mason stared at her and shook his head. "For somebody with no friends, you sure do act nice to complete strangers." He spoke without malice but almost with pride.

Brittany rolled her eyes, "He needed help. I wasn't going to leave him!"

"Well, let's check out his clothes and see if we can find some clue about him. You say he can't remember anything?"

"He doesn't even remember his name," Brittany said, shaking her head. Mason kept going for the washing machine. "His clothes are a waste of time," she called after him. "I told you, they have no markings. Besides, they were much too big for him."

She sat back on the couch until she heard Mason's triumphant yell.

"I think I found a clue!" he hollered.

"Let the whole world know about it," Brittany said with a huff, hastily getting to her feet.

She met Mason coming out of the laundry room just beyond the kitchen. He held up a wet pair of boxer shorts like a trophy. Dark red with a royal blue waistband, they had symbols of lions on either side.

"Why," she asked, her eyes wide with disbelief, "are you holding up underwear?"

"These aren't any old boxers, sis. Look!" Mason thrust the waistband at her. "These are Slaydon shorts. They cost more money than all my clothes put together."

Brittany gave a start and grabbed Mason's arm. "Slaydon!" she yelped.

"Yeah. Remember Melissa talking about Michal Slaydon coming here? Well, he and his wife have their own clothes they sell. And I promise you that only somebody rich could afford them. That kid is someone from money. I don't know where those other dumpy clothes came from—"

Brittany struggled to speak as suddenly she understood something terrible. "Qu-quiet!" she burst out. "I think I know who the boy is!"

"Huh? Who?"

"I knew I recognized him, but I just didn't know from where! But it's impossible!"

"Sis, what are you going on about?"

"I told you, I think I know who the boy is!"

"You didn't tell me. You just said you think you know who he might be. Now tell me!" he pleaded.

Brittany took a deep breath. "Shio Slaydon."

Mason barked out a laugh, but stopped when he didn't see Brittany join in. "Wait, are you serious?"

"Come with me," she said and started for the stairs. Mason had to rush to keep up.

Brother and sister crept to Mason's room and over to the bed.

"I can't see," whispered Mason. "It's too dark."

"Hush, go turn on the light. Just for a second. I just want to see if you agree with me."

Mason did as he was told. Then he gasped when he saw the sleeping boy. Lying on his side, his hair tousled, the boy's profile was plainly visible.

"I saw his picture this morning," Brittany whispered. "Don't ask me how, but it's him."

There could be no question. Mason had Shio Slaydon, son of world-famous soccer player Michal Slaydon, sleeping in his bed.

Just above the boy's head was the poster of Manchester City soccer players.

"No way," he breathed. "Nobody will believe this."

"Because you won't tell anybody," Brittany growled. "Let's go before he wakes up. We have to talk."

They quietly left the room and returned down the stairs. Sitting on the couch, they spoke in low tones. After much debating, they decided they wouldn't tell the boy the truth about his identity. Not knowing what or who caused the boy to be in this situation, they didn't want to shock him. Instead, they hoped his memory would return on its own and he could tell them the next move.

So far there had been no news about a missing celebrity's son. How come? They had snapped on the evening news and searched for updates but saw nothing.

Finally, on the eleven o'clock news they saw the report on the strange Slaydon press conference ending earlier. That was when Mason suggested that perhaps one of his parents could want Shio dead.

"Out of some twisted revenge?" he wondered. "They are having marriage problems," he said defensively when Brittany gave him a look of utter disgust. "If we turn him back to his parents, we could be putting him in mortal danger!"

That gave Brittany reason to stop and think. "You could be right," she allowed. "There are crazy people all over doing horrible things. And I can't think of a better explanation … this whole thing is so bizarre."

So it was decided. Neither would tell Shio his identity, but they would let the boy find out on his own. Then he could explain what happened to lead him to Burnhurst.

Until that time came, they had to keep his presence and identity a secret. Brittany was sure the three people looking for him hadn't given up their search.

When they were finished talking, it was nearing midnight. Their mom would be coming home soon.

"Where're you sleeping?" Brittany asked, getting to her feet.

"The couch, I guess," Mason said, shrugging. "Mom wouldn't mind. It wouldn't be the first time I fell asleep watching television."

Brittany snorted and went off to her bed. It had been a long day … and a longer night.

Mrs. Tiff arrived home shortly after to find the house dark except for the light of the television. Mason lay curled up in some of Brittany's blankets, fast asleep.

"What am I going to do for you," she mumbled, smoothing down a crease in the blanket. "My poor babies … what am I going to do for you?"

She clicked off the set and stumbled upstairs.

Mason cracked open an eye and frowned. He'd smelled alcohol on his mom's breath. He had a hard time falling back to sleep.

Brittany woke up just as the sun started peeking over the trees outside her window. She glanced at her alarm clock and saw she'd awakened before her normal school time. Vaguely she remembered that she had a reason why … Shio!

She sat up with a start. He needed her help. Rolling out of bed, she raced out of her room.

After a quick trip to the bathroom, she crept to Mason's room and peeked in. The boy lay fast asleep with his mouth parted and feet curled tightly. Still on his side, he had one arm dangling off the bed while the other bent over his head, clutching the pillow. He looked even smaller under the mountain of quilts she'd piled on him the night before.

How anyone could go out of their way to hurt another human, especially a kid, was unfathomable. Just thinking about it made her feel sick.

She shivered in the morning chill. Her mother always turned the heat off when returning home at night to save money. Thinking of her mom, Brittany knew she had to have breakfast made and finished before her mom woke up.

She quietly retreated to let the boy rest in peace. Later, he would have to hide until her mom went to work. Going down to the kitchen, she started preparing a big breakfast.

Mason opened his eyes on the couch to the din of pots and pans rattling in the kitchen. "That you, sis?" he asked tiredly. "What are you trying to do, tear down the kitchen?"

"No, I'm trying to make pancakes! I can't find any of the ingredients!"

Mason immediately perked up. Pancakes were a real treat in the Tiff house. "Let me help then," he said, rolling off the couch. Immediately he hugged his arms close. "Man, it's freezing!"

"I just turned on the heat, but it'll take a while to warm up. Oh, hurry and help! I want to finish before Shio wakes up!"

Mason padded in the kitchen wearing a smirk. "Is that right?" he said, wiggling his eyebrows. "Don't tell me you're getting a crush on—"

A dishcloth nailed him in the face.

"Don't be stupid. Think about it. What if he wakes up at the same time as Mom? Do you think Mom will be happy to find some strange celebrity kid sleeping in her house? She'll blow up!"

Mason swallowed and grew sober. "Uh, yeah … you're right. Mom is having a hard enough time. So what do we do?"

Brittany threw up her hands. "I don't know! I'll make some kind of pancakes with whatever we have, but after that it's up to you."

Mason frowned. "What do you mean by that?"

"It's Saturday. We have our holiday party for the homeless today. I'm being picked up in a few hours. That means you have to get Shio—that boy—out of the house and away from Mom. She doesn't work until tonight."

"But I was planning on hanging out with Ben! We were going to the soccer field!"

"Mason," Brittany said, clenching her teeth. "We have a boy to protect. Take Shio instead to play soccer, but stay away from any public places out in the open. Practice soccer in the old lot at the end of the street."

"What about Ben?" Mason asked sullenly. "I promised I'd see him today."

"Tell him you'll see him tomorrow! Oh, and make sure Sh—the boy wears a hat and something bulky, just in case. We don't want anybody recognizing him."

"Right," muttered Mason. "My first weekend of break and I have to babysit some rich kid while avoiding all other people. That's just great."

"It's only for today. By tomorrow we'll figure something out. Please, Mase? I'll let you have one pancake."

"One?" her brother asked, alarmed.

Brittany nodded firmly. "The rest are for ... the kid. There aren't enough ingredients for a lot. You should see how much he eats."

Mason took a deep breath and then sighed. "Let me go tell Ben that I can't make it today," he said finally. "But when I get back I want *two* pancakes."

The boy lay trembling. Cruel green eyes peered down over him and gave a sneering laugh. "You'll never play soccer again, boy!" Hands suddenly yanked on his shirt, trying to rip it off. Another woman kicked a soccer ball through his legs. "Goal!" she screamed, pumping her fist. Then the green eyes were leering down. "You're mine, boy!" The boy cried out desperately. "Dad!" he cried. "Dad! Where are you?" The green eyes laughed mockingly. "You have no dad, boy!" Blue lightning flashed from the eyes, striking the boy's shoulder.

He cried out as his eyes snapped open. Instinctively, he rolled away from the light but found himself tangled in sheets. It had all just been a bad dream.

Flipping to his stomach, he stared around at the strange room. Early morning sunlight broke through windows on either side of the bed.

A dresser supported a full bookshelf on one wall and a he saw an open closet on the other side. His eyes lifted and he shivered. Above him, he saw a huge poster with soccer players. Something about it was awfully familiar ...

Twisting to his back to get a better look, he rolled right off the bed. He landed with a soft thump in a pile of sheets. Slowly, he remembered—waking up in the car and the terrible chase ... it hadn't been all a bad dream. It had all happened.

Moving to a sitting position, he winced at the pain in his shoulder. He hugged his knees tight and fought back tears. Everything started coming back ... Brittany, she had saved him. He wore pajamas a little too loose and was in Brittany's brother's room.

He wondered where he had slept. His eyes went back to the poster and widened. It was a poster of the Manchester City team and he recognized three players because they had come to his birthday party before ... right? That didn't make sense ... His head hurt and he just wanted to curl up and close his eyes ...

Then he smelled pancakes cooking.

Soon after, Shio wandered down the stairs, rubbing his eyes. He stopped short of the kitchen and stared in with a frown.

A strange boy about a year or two older than him sat on a stool at the corner licking his lips. Dark-skinned like Brittany, he had a round face with smooth cheekbones and short dark hair cut close to his scalp. At the moment, he looked miserable. A small pile of pancakes sat on a plate before him. Shio gulped. This had to be the brother. He didn't look too happy.

Brittany stood at the stove wearing an apron over camouflage pajamas too large for her frame. Flour covered her forehead and right cheek. She held a raised spatula in her right fist and shook it at the unhappy boy. "If you touch one more, Mase, I'll put this spoon between your ears."

"Come on, sis," whined the boy, "it's rare that I ever compliment your cooking! For running out of milk and butter, these are good. Can't I get more?"

"They're for—" she stopped and turned to see Shio standing there watching.

Shio smiled thinly and raised a hand. "Hiya," he said shyly.

"Oh, good morning, er, boy," Brittany said. She hastily put down the spatula and wiped her hands on her apron. After exchanging a quick look with her brother, she turned to Shio and smiled widely. "I called you boy because I don't know what else to call you …" She trailed off as if waiting.

Shio shrugged and shuffled in the kitchen. "That's fine," he said, stifling a yawn. He looked around and scratched his unruly hair. "Do you have a horn here? Um, I mean a phone?"

Brittany's brother cleared his throat and then spoke. "I'm Mason, Brittany's older brother. Sorry, but our phone was, uh, disconnected last month. Our mom has a cell phone, but she keeps it in her purse for emergencies. Why do you ask?"

Shrugging, the boy grabbed a stool next to Mason and sat down. "Just curious." He eyed the pancakes.

"Oh, those are all yours," Brittany said, rushing to grab the plate and push them in front of Shio. "Mason has already eaten, *haven't* you, Mase?"

"Yeah, I had a whole bite," Mason growled.

Shio grinned and ran a hand through his hair. "I'm not that hungry. I can split them with you." He looked at Brittany. "Three ways?"

Mason groaned. "Great. I might get three bites now."

After a quick breakfast, while Brittany cleaned up, Mason asked grudgingly if Shio wanted to kick a soccer ball around outside.

Immediately the boy perked up. During breakfast he hadn't said a word. After receiving his share of pancakes, he'd barely touched them and, after only a few bites, he'd pushed his plate to Mason. When Brittany was not looking, Mason had smoothly transferred Shio's share onto his plate and had started eating quickly.

Shio had spent the rest of the time looking down at the counter, lost in thought. Only after Brittany had spoken to him did he lift his head and offer one of his bright smiles.

But at the mention of soccer, his eyes and mouth stretched wider.

"That would be brilliant. Do you play?" he asked, barely containing his excitement.

"Well, a little," Mason said modestly. He glanced at Brittany, who'd stopped scrubbing the pan. "Do you play soccer, um, boy?"

Shio's face clouded. "I, I think so, yeah," he said. "At least I'd like to."

"Before you go out," Brittany told him, looking slightly disappointed, "you'd better wear something so nobody will recognize you easily. I mean, so those people from last night won't recognize you."

Shio nodded. "What do you have?" he asked.

Soon after, Mason left with a boy dressed in a black winter's hat pulled low over his ears, a jacket much too large covering everything from his neck to his knees, and a tight pair of sweatpants leftover from Mason's younger playing days. Large gray gloves covered his hands. On his feet was a pair of faded pink and gray sneakers. Brittany's shoes were all that fit him.

"I look like rubbish," Shio complained as he followed Mason down the steps to the front yard.

Mason didn't disagree. He carried a soccer ball under his arm and a sour expression on his face. "At least," he muttered, "I'll do everything possible not to get seen by anyone. That's for sure."

The sun had yet to go up very far and the cold air caused their breath to be visible. The early Saturday morning and cold air combined to keep the streets almost entirely clear.

Mason started jogging, not waiting for Shio to catch up. He was surprised when the younger boy easily pulled even with him. Together, the boys jogged past Ben's house and down the street to the end.

Passing Ben's house caused Mason to wince. His best friend had not been happy when he woke up to Mason throwing pebbles at his window.

When opening the window, he'd stared in disbelief down at Mason. "You better be doing this for a good reason," he'd grumbled. Then his entire face had brightened. "Does this mean you decided to call off tomorrow's game? You know, if you don't go, nobody will go, except for maybe Shelly. Then who cares?"

Mason winced at the memory. When he'd told Ben that absolutely they would play the game tomorrow but that he just couldn't practice with him today, Ben's face had dropped both stories to the cold, hard ground. "You woke me up for that?" he'd groused. Then the window had slammed shut.

Today he may have lost a best friend. Tomorrow he would lose a big soccer match. He glanced at Shio and silently hoped it was all worth it.

At the homeless holiday party, Brittany was happy to find Big Murdock among the men in line for the holiday eggnog—completely free of alcohol, of course.

Seeing her, the big man shuffled to the side and sat with her in the corner of the room next to an artificial tree decorated with paper and lights.

They were in the fellowship hall behind the church. About fifty men and women from the street had shown up to be served by the handful of volunteers. Luckily, there were enough so Brittany wasn't needed at the moment.

"Is the boy still there?" Big Murdock growled in greeting. "If he bothers you in any way I'll take his skinny behind and drop it right on the tracks where we found him."

Brittany sighed. "Look, Murdock, it's nothing like that. He's fine. I just want to thank you again for all your help."

Big Murdock grunted. "Well, for your information, those three goons are still around. They poked around the warehouse last night but then left. I stopped by there on my way home." He made a face. "But they're staying at a motel just on the edge of town."

Brittany stared at him in alarm. "They're still here? How do you know all this?" she asked. "Did you follow them?"

Murdock barked out a laugh. "Huh-uh, no way. Fred, the guy in the end of the line with his girl Myrtle stayed in the same motel last night. I asked around the group and they're the only ones who saw anybody who matched the description. The good news, they're not in this area at the moment."

Fred and Myrtle were two scruffy individuals who looked to be anywhere from forty to eighty. Their faces looked like road maps of all the paths they'd traveled together. Fred had a thick graying beard that matched Myrtle's shoulder-length hair. Otherwise, they were hard to tell apart—both were big-bodied, silent, and extremely unfriendly. Brittany always wondered if they were married, siblings, or just good friends. They mostly only talked to themselves. Only Big Murdock could have gotten any information from them.

Without thinking, Brittany reached up and gave the man a giant hug. "Thanks, Murdock," she said.

"Anything you need, you just tell me, young lady. Not many give people here the time of day. You do. Now let go before you get yelled at. You know there's no contact with people like me."

Brittany let go. "Right. Since you mentioned it, there is something else. Do you know anything about injuries?"

Big Murdock shot her a look and she quickly explained about the burn on Shio's arm. Before Shio had gone out with Mason, she'd changed bandages and made sure it was clean. It hadn't looked much better than the night before.

Big Murdock frowned as he listened. "Sounds like an electrical burn," he said after a moment. "That could explain the memory loss. A powerful jolt of electricity could cause your brain to go haywire. But don't worry, he should settle." He ran his hand through his beard. "But you're right. Those people definitely sound like bad news. You sure you don't want police involved?"

Brittany shook her head. "Not yet. Not until we know what he's up against. Trust me, Murdock. We have our reasons."

The big man nodded and held up his hands. "Okay, I'll keep an eye out for them. But first I need to grab me a cup of eggnog. Just make sure you keep the boy out of sight for a while."

"Don't worry," Brittany promised him. "We have that totally all under control."

Big Murdock only grunted.

Chapter
9

All bad feelings quickly evaporated. Mason couldn't believe his luck. He was playing soccer with a prodigy, with a bona fide soccer star. All doubts about the boy's identity vanished just after the first touch of the soccer ball.

On first touch, the boy flipped it straight up in the air, catching it on his head, then bending low, cradled it on his back. Next he stood up, causing the ball to roll down his back before stopping it behind his right knee against his backside.

Pausing a moment, he hopped up, flicking the ball back up and over his head, only to catch it on his right foot. The ball never hit the ground.

Seeing Mason's jaw hanging open, Shio looked sheepish and calmly flicked the ball to Mason.

The two fell into a game of pass that turned into a one-on-one battle. Mason proved overmatched from the start. Shio kept the ball at his feet like it was attached by an invisible string. His movements were a blur and Mason fell twice when trying to stay in front of the boy.

When Mason had the ball, he could never get past the lightning-quick boy. Every time he tried, a quick foot knocked the ball loose, or Mason would tangle his own feet and lose the ball on his own.

Soon they resumed the game of pass. Shio kept complete mastery over the ball and all his passes were right on target.

Finally, Mason sat down on the grass. "Man," he wheezed, "you play like a pro." He gulped and looked at the boy carefully. "Uh, your father must have been pretty good."

Shio, who'd long shucked his jacket and gloves but kept his hat on, sat on the ball, facing Mason. He wore a heavy hoodie and looked ready to disappear inside it. For a brief moment, he looked utterly lost and scared. Then he dropped his gaze and gave the briefest of shrugs.

"I don't remember," he said softly. He stared curiously at Mason. "Do you play on a team here? You have talent too."

Coming from Shio, Mason took it as a compliment. Still, he waved his hand. "Not compared to you. But, yeah, I play on a small team here."

Slightly embarrassed, he proceeded to tell Shio about the Sharks and the impending showdown with the powerful Burnhurst United team.

"We're going to be crushed," he finished, grimacing.

Shio pursed his lips and rested his arms on his knees. "Your team can't all be rubbish," he finally said. "You're good. Trust me. You just need to learn some moves and get quicker off the ball."

Mason grunted and shook his head. "Yeah, right," he muttered.

Shio frowned and shot to his feet. "Here, I'll show you."

The boys spent the next hour going over individual soccer moves. First, Shio would demonstrate in slow motion and then show how it had to speed up to work properly.

Mason then tried it in slow motion before working on getting each move faster and faster.

After getting the hang of about three of the moves, he stepped back and cried out in pure joy. Then he stared at Shio with complete sincere thanks.

"I've been trying to teach myself for years, man, but you showed me more than I've learned in less than a day! Man, I wish you could play with us tomorrow."

Shio grinned and tilted his head up at the sky. "Me too," he said wistfully. "Would be brilliant."

Mason's face lit up and, all at once, he broke into a grin so wide it threatened to split his face. "Oh my goodness, man. I think I know a way. I know a way you can play!"

For the entire time they'd been together, Mason avoided having to call Shio any name. He didn't want to slip and call him Shio out loud. But now he had a plan to keep that from ever happening … A plan to give Shio a new name and to get him on the field the next day playing for the Sharks.

When he told Shio his plan, explaining it in detail, the boy could only say one word. "Brilliant."

Halftime

Chapter
10

"**A**bsolutely not!" Brittany said to Mason when hearing Mason's brilliant plan. "That's the stupidest thing I have ever heard! Are you crazy? Are you insane?"

The two siblings sat on Mason's bed glaring at each other.

"But you don't understand," Mason said. "You should have seen him out there. Soccer is his life. He wants to do this! Come on, sis, you have to be on this. He'll die if I tell him he can't play."

"That's the problem. He could die if he does play! Mason, there are people looking for him to kill him!"

The boy being discussed currently was in the shower. He had returned with Mason shortly after Brittany came home from the homeless party.

They'd found Mrs. Tiff sleeping on the couch and the children had tiptoed past her and up the stairs. It was a few hours before sunset and Brittany had been shocked to hear how the boys spent the entire day kicking the ball around in the cold.

Seeing Shio's exhausted, though elated, face, she'd immediately sent him to the shower. Then, she'd grabbed her brother and dragged him to his room. Before she'd had the chance to launch into a lecture about keeping an injured kid out in the cold playing soccer, her brother went in on her with his crazy plan. Thus the argument started.

"Nobody is going to look for him at a local soccer tournament," Mason said. "That's the last place they'd expect him to be!"

"Keep your voice down," Brittany told him. "He might hear!"

Mason made a face but then stopped. "I don't hear the water running."

"He probably collapsed with exhaustion."

"I doubt that. That kid can run like a horse. Quiet, and listen."

The siblings both sat still. From the hall, they heard the bathroom door close. Moments later the shower started.

"Odd," Brittany said. "He must have forgotten something,"

"Or he was making sure you would let him play. Look, Brittany, I know you think I'm being selfish."

"Yeah, all for your stupid soccer game."

"It's more than that!" blurted Mason. "Don't you get it? Soccer is the link to his memories. If he plays tomorrow it might trigger who he really is!" He stood up and jabbed a finger at the poster of Manchester City over his bed. "He already asked me if Man City was my favorite team."

"So?" asked his sister.

"You don't get it, do you? Soccer is making him remember."

Before Brittany could reply, their mom hollered from down the stairs. "Brittany, Manson! What are you two doing? I hope it's not fighting!"

Brittany answered first. "Just talking, Mom!"

"Then why is the water running?" called back their mom.

Mason gulped. "That's me!" he yelled. "I'm letting the water warm up!"

"It's been warming up for at least five minutes! You get in there before I warm up your backside, Mason! Don't you think you're too old! We can't waste water, you know that!"

Brittany and Mason exchanged glances. Then Mason got up.

"Yes, Mom!" he yelled. Opening his door loudly, he trudged to the bathroom. Stopping outside, he took a breath, then quickly opened the door and slammed it.

A startled high-pitched yelp came from the other side.

"Guess it didn't warm up enough," Mrs. Tiff called up. "Boy, Mason sounded a little high there."

"Maybe he slipped," Brittany said, watching from Mason's door.

Mason stood frozen in front of the bathroom. "You have to let him play after this," he hissed.

In the end, Brittany relented. She would help the boys with their crazy brilliant plan. Seeing Shio's hopeful look and hearing Mason's relentless arguments proved too much.

Just before dark, with her mom gone for work, she left the house with the boys to find Big Murdock. The success of the plan all relied on him.

Secretly she hoped he would call them all idiots and flat-out refuse. Actually, she knew he would. Sticking out his neck for Shio to play a dumb game was the last thing the big man would ever do.

When they reached the building of Big Murdock's last known address, the room he'd showed her the night before with Shio, she motioned Mason to stay put. Then, grabbing Shio's uninjured arm, she led him up the stairs.

"Why are we back here?" Shio asked her nervously. "I thought you were helping us for tomorrow."

"I am," Brittany hissed. "You need a father, right? Well, Murdock is the only adult who can stand in for the job."

Shio jerked to a stop at the door. "You mean you want that big smelly guy to be my father?" he asked in disbelief.

"Who else?"

Shio had no answer. Mason's plan was to have Shio pose as Marco Reese, the boy who'd signed up for the Sharks but had never appeared. To pull it off, he needed a father to vouch for his identity. That and a lot of luck.

Brittany knocked on the door. "Murdock, it's me," she said loudly. "Are you there?"

The door remained shut and Brittany sighed with relief. "Nobody's home, I guess we'll have to nix the—"

The door opened a crack. Then it was thrown open with a crash.

"Are you kids crazy?" hissed Big Murdock. "Get in here!" Once they were all inside, Murdock shut the door firmly and locked it. "I thought you two were the authorities coming to throw me out! You woke me from a nap and I was so scared I started packing without thinking!"

The big man breathed heavily. The only light came from a candle burning on one of the coolers. The sleeping bags were tossed in heap and his neat stacks of food were a mess. One of the coolers was open and stuffed with food and pots and pans.

Shio coughed lightly. "I hope you didn't wet yourself," he said innocently.

Big Murdock glared at him. "Good to see you're feeling better, boy," he growled. "Keep it that way."

Brittany wrung her hands. She'd never seen Big Murdock so angry before.

"We're sorry," she said. "Really, we are."

Murdock snorted as he lit more candles, soon bathing the room in a glowing light. "At least you're sorry," muttered. "The boy needs a good hiding before he'll ever be sorry." Then sighing, he took a seat by his tumbled sleeping bags. "Now please tell me why you invaded my space like a horde of Vikings. It had better be good."

Shio shuffled next to Brittany and licked his lips. "It's all her idea," he mumbled.

"What's her idea?" barked Big Murdock. He looked at Brittany. "Tell me."

Taking a deep breath, Brittany told Big Murdock the plan, making it sound as ridiculous as she could. When she finished she stepped to the door and waited to be tossed out.

Surprisingly, the large man seemed taken aback by the request. "You, you want me to be the boy's father?" he asked. He swallowed hard.

Shio had cringed when Brittany stopped talking, but now he looked up hopefully. "It would only be for a short while," he said. "Just as long as the game lasts."

"Murdock," Brittany began, "I know you said you would help me, but this is way too—"

Big Murdock raised a hand to stop her. "No, no," he said. "I … I actually have a son, you know." He sighed. "I haven't seen him since he was a toddler, barely two. That was twenty years ago. Not once did I ever see him play a game. I never took him anywhere."

Brittany swallowed. "I'm so sorry. I had no idea. We shouldn't have come—"

"Brittany, it's okay," Murdock said gently. "Don't you get it? I've been a father almost half my life but have never once acted like one. Ever." He eyed Shio and grimaced. "Even if it is for a spoiled brat, I … I think I owe it to myself, and to my son, to do it."

Shio raised his eyebrows. "Thanks … I think."

Brittany just stared speechlessly at the man she thought she knew.

"Quiet, boy," Big Murdock snapped. "If I'm to be your father then you'd better start showing me some respect."

Shio made to say something back, but smiled. "Sure … Dad."

"Go on before I really act like a father and take you over a knee. Get out, both of you."

Brittany stopped at the door. "But Murdock," she said desperately. "How will you look the part? I mean, if you show up like …"

"A homeless bum?" Big Murdock asked. He laughed at her mortified expression. "Don't you worry about that. I have some friends who will lend me a shower and some clean clothes." The large man sounded jovial, even excited.

"And a razor," Shio added under his breath.

"And a belt," Big Murdock said sharply. He looked at Brittany. "What proof must I bring to show I'm the father? I mean, I'm guessing they'll ask for something."

This would be the tricky part and would probably end in failure. Brittany reached in her coat pocket and pulled out a folded paper. "This is an extra signup form for the team my brother had. You have to fill it out with all the, uh, information." She felt her face grow warm. "You'll have to make up an address. You're to be

Mr. Reese and he's going to be Marco Reese." Surely, she thought, Big Murdock will now laugh and say it was all a joke.

Instead, the big man grunted. He took the form and squinted at it. "Oh yeah? And how old is the boy?"

Shio looked helplessly at Brittany.

"Um, eleven?" she said. "The league already has the original form, but we're hoping they won't bother to check them."

Big Murdock raised both his eyebrows. "Is that right? Well, we'll see what we can do … I guess I'll make up the rest and hope it passes. You two better get on home before it gets too cold."

Brittany already felt too cold. She couldn't believe Big Murdock agreed to all this. She trudged down the steps with Shio bouncing behind her.

Mason greeted them at the bottom of the stairs. He stamped his feet and blew into his frozen hands. "W-well?" he asked. "Are w-we in?"

Shio grinned and nodded, causing Mason to whoop and embrace the boy in a bear hug.

Brittany shook her head. "It'll never work," she said. Nobody listened.

Once back at the house, she went straight to the shower and spent a long time wondering how everything happened so fast. Just a few days ago, she'd been the laughing stock of basketball tryouts. No friends and a popularity score near zero. Now a heartthrob celebrity slept over at her house and trusted her with his safety that he wanted to risk over a meaningless soccer game. How did these things happen?

If only Melissa could be in her shoes …

Pounding at the door let her know she'd been lost in thought too long.

"Hurry up," Mason called. "We need you to make dinner and I need a shower!"

"You already had one," she yelled back. "Remember?"

Poor Mason was left with no hot water … it did little to dampen his spirits.

Late that night, Shio slipped from his bed and crept downstairs. Moonlight filtered softly through the windows and guided his soft steps.

Mason lay asleep on the couch, snoring softly. He never stirred when Shio knelt behind him.

The young boy carefully pulled out a cell phone from under the couch. He'd slipped it from Mrs. Tiff's purse earlier that afternoon before taking a shower, hiding it beneath the couch.

Now, crouched behind the couch, he flicked it open and smiled with delight at seeing it did not require a password. Minutes later, he flicked it shut and placed it on the stand next to the couch. He was about to return up the stairs when he heard a noise outside.

Fear struck him like a knife and he froze in terror. He was sure the man and two women had found him. He'd worn the winter hat and large coat when they saw Murdock, but perhaps he'd still been spotted and they'd followed him to Brittany's house.

His knees shook below him and he nearly wet his pajamas. Swallowing, he picked up the cell phone and eased to the front window, very slowly.

Peering out, he saw nothing at first. It was a clear sky with a full moon watching from overhead.

Licking his dry lips, Shio searched the yard again. Then he saw the shape lurching on the street in front of the house. In the moonlight he made out the figure of Mrs. Tiff.

Shaking with relief, he returned the cell phone to the stand, instantly feeling guilty. The poor woman probably thought she'd lost her phone. She could even be looking for it that very moment. He returned to the window and watched Brittany and Mason's mother lurch and fall to her knees. She sobbed so loudly Shio could hear her.

Without thinking, Shio opened the door and slipped out in his bare feet. Running lightly over the frozen grass, he reached Mrs. Tiff as she regained her footing.

The Tiffs had no working car—Brittany had told him it was currently in the shop—and Mrs. Tiff had to walk a half mile to the bus stop when going to and from her work. She had to be exhausted. But as Shio neared her, he also knew she'd been drinking.

"I'm being fired," the woman mumbled. "They threatened to fire me today," she said, slurring her words. "Isn't that rich? A poor woman like me, being tossed from her job like a piece of garbage. I'll never sell another stitch of clothing from that place." She staggered forward and nearly pitched to the ground. "And now … and now I can't even find my home …" The woman started sobbing. "Why? Why, Lord, do you do this to me? Ain't it enough you got my husband?"

Shio gulped and stepped out from the shadows in front of the woman. He'd seen drunken people before. Some were mean, but others were just plain sad.

Mrs. Tiff had no meanness. She just had the weight of three worlds on her shoulders—her world and the worlds of her children. They were crushing her.

"Mrs. Tiff, your home is over here," he said softly.

"My, my," the woman said, blinking at him. "An angel. What a sight you are. Bless you, child. But you're too late."

Shio glanced worriedly back at the house. He wondered if he should run and find help. But then the woman grabbed his shoulder.

"I know who you really are," she hissed, ducking her head down to Shio's face.

He flinched from the sour breath.

"You're an imposter. There are no angels. Nobody cares about nobody no more."

"That's not true," Shio said nervously. "Brittany cares, yeah? She helped me when nobody else did. She saved my life."

Mrs. Tiff lurched back to her full height and wavered. "You're a funny little angel," she said. "But speak the truth. I do have a precious daughter." She belched. "Very well, lead on. Take me to my paradise."

Shio, frightened but determined, supported Mrs. Tiff to the front door and helped her in.

"Got to turn off the heat," muttered the woman. She staggered from Shio and over to the thermostat. After shutting down the heat, she turned on Shio. "Now you better get off to bed. It's late, even for angels."

Not knowing what else to do, Shio nodded and raced up the stairs.

Muttering about drinking too much and needing church, Mrs. Tiff followed a little while after. Quiet then came over the Tiff household. It lasted until the sun stretched over the trees.

Brittany opened her eyes and sighed. It was Sunday. The day for church and then the soccer game … the soccer game!

She jolted to a sitting position. She couldn't believe she'd agreed to let Mason and Shio go along with their crazy plan. And even Big Murdock had become part of it!

Groaning, she flopped back to bed and had the urge to roll over and sleep until Christmas. Instead she dragged her tired, worried body out of bed and got dressed for church. One of the ladies would be picking her up. Usually Mason went with her, but this morning he had to stay behind and watch Shio.

Their mom always slept late on Sundays and attended a late afternoon service. Sunday was the only day of the week she had off.

After church, the plan was for Brittany to return home and then go with the boys to meet Big Murdock at the top of their street. Together they would walk to the Burnhurst Sports-Plex, just over five blocks toward the center of town.

Full of nervous energy, Brittany couldn't sit still. Unable to eat, she found herself pacing in front of her driveway waiting for her church ride.

"What are you doing?" asked a snide voice from the street.

Brittany looked up to see Melissa standing on the other side of the road walking a puppy.

"Oh, just waiting for a ride."

"You were talking to yourself."

Brittany's face burned. She looked at the small dog, a beagle, at Melissa's feet. It looked barely awake as it wagged a short tail in her direction.

"Is that a new dog?" she asked, hoping to change the subject.

"Of course it is," Melissa snapped. "I got it yesterday to make up for missing the Slaydons." She turned her face into a pout. "All that way and Shio Slaydon wasn't even there. My mom and I were so angry we got the puppy and named him Shio." She glared at Brittany, daring her to make a comment.

Brittany swallowed and only shrugged her shoulders with a grin. "I think that's, uh, great," she said. "You know, I don't think Shio is so bad after all."

"You mean my dog?" Melissa said suspiciously. "You did say it was a good dog's name."

"I was wrong, Melissa, okay? I'm sorry for all the things I said. I mean it. I'm sure Shio is really nice. Oh, there's my ride. I have to go."

Melissa frowned as the car pulled up and Brittany climbed inside.

"Must be Sunday," she muttered. "Everyone is nicer on Sunday."

Chapter
11

Later that day, just past noon, everything seemed to be going according to plan. Brittany had prayed all morning for something to go wrong—for rain to start falling, or for Shio to remember who he was and ask to go home. But the sun remained out and she returned from church to find Mason and Shio waiting impatiently at the door.

They'd just finished a brunch of oatmeal and fried sliced tomatoes and were ready to unleash. The meal had been Shio's creation after Mason complained of nothing left to eat. Only a tomato and leftover oatmeal had been found in the fridge. Shio just took charge and sliced the tomato with a knife and fried it up while Mason heated the oatmeal. Then Shio emptied the sugar container on the tomatoes and oatmeal. Surprisingly, it hadn't been bad. When finished, both felt ready to take on the world. They'd changed right after and waited for Brittany.

Mason had a jacket over his Sharks uniform, while Shio wore borrowed shorts, pads and socks, and soccer cleats. Under his jacket was a black sweater.

The cleats came from Ben. Mason's best friend lent him his extra pair when Mason had asked earlier that morning. "For a good cause," Mason had said at the time. "To make showing up for today's game worth it."

"I'll be there," Ben had grumbled, handing over the shoes. "You're my best friend, after all. We'll go down with the ship together."

Brittany walked with the boys to where they'd arranged to meet Big Murdock and gave a sigh of relief.

Nobody was in sight.

"Oh well," she said brightly. "I don't think Murdock can make it after all." Then she gulped. "Oh, guys, is that a police car coming our way?"

The boys stopped searching for the large man and instead watched as a white county cruiser with blue lights on top coasted right up to them. At first it looked ready to pass them by, but the breaks slammed and the blue lights flashed.

Caught by surprise, the children stood frozen in fear as the passenger window lowered. An angry face glared out at them. Dark brown hair with a hint of gray was slicked back from a weather-beaten face lined with wrinkles. A thick goatee covered the large man's upper lip and chin. Seeing the children, he sneered.

"Well?" he barked. "What do you think? You all coming or not?"

"Mur-Murdock?" Brittany asked timidly, in total disbelief. "Is … is that you?"

"It ain't my granny." Murdock grinned at Shio, revealing his familiar yellow teeth. "What's the matter, son? Wet your shorts?"

Shio shoved his hands in his coat pockets and gave back a cool look. "It's about time they arrested my dad," he said.

Next to Murdock, the driver laughed. "I'm Deputy Donald. Nobody is being arrested. Derek here has explained everything to me. Climb in the back and we'll pull one over on old Burnhurst United."

Brittany gulped as she opened the door to the cruiser. "Ev-everything?" she squeaked.

"Yes, everything," Big Murdock snapped. "Deputy Donald is an old friend of mine. We go way back. I told him Marco is visiting from Brazil and has dreamed of playing on North American soil his whole life. This is his big chance."

"Look, I know this isn't ethical," Deputy Donald said, grinning, "but if it makes a kid's dream come true, then I'm all for it. I played rec soccer before and know what it's like to be crushed by that United squad. You all won't win anyway, but at least it'll be fun, right?"

"Yeah," Brittany said. "A blast." She could only wonder what Big Murdock had said about Shio to get the deputy to agree to help.

Deputy Donald dropped off his passengers just past the soccer field so they could slip in without too much notice. "I'll wait here in case you have any trouble," he said, giving a wink.

The kids thanked him as they left, and Big Murdock grunted his appreciation.

The deputy merely grinned. "Anything for old friends and new friends," he said.

It turned out that they didn't need the deputy's help.

Coach Smith looked up in surprise when Mason ran up to him yelling that Marco Reese had come. Most of the Sharks had already arrived and thought he was joking.

"You're my best friend," Ben told him. "You want to know why? You tell funny stories."

"Yeah, it's not too late to forfeit," added Craig Anderson. "Not even Marco could save us today. Whoever he is."

The United team had already taken the field and was busy with organized drills the Sharks could only dream of performing. Half the team played a game of keep away, while the other half worked on passing and shooting drills. They looked like a smooth, well-oiled machine about to be unleashed.

Even Shelly watched nervously. "We're so doomed," she muttered.

But then Big Murdock strolled from the parking lot with a large arm placed firmly around Shio's shoulders. Shio grinned shyly, but kept his head up. The big man walked slowly, but his fresh-shaven face looked slightly gray. He glanced once toward where Brittany stood off to the side. She immediately ducked her head.

"Sorry we're so late," Big Murdock boomed, shifting his attention to the coach. "My, er, son and I just, er, settled in this country." He swallowed. "I'm Mr. Reese, er, Mark Reese. I'm Marco's dad. His father." He reached in his back pocket and flashed the paperwork Brittany had given him the day before.

Stunned, Coach Smith barely looked at it. "It's, uh, great that you're here," he said. "From Brazil, right?"

Shio raised his eyebrows and looked up at his pretend father.

"That's right," Big Murdock beamed. "It took a lot longer to make it up here. And trying to deal with all this cold isn't easy. We're used to the heat. Brrr!"

Shio winced and stepped pointedly on Big Murdock's foot. True to his word, the big man had found clean clothes. He wore jeans, a bright green turtleneck sweater and brown loafers. The loafers offered little protection against soccer cleats. Big Murdock instantly gulped and bit his lip. At least he stopped talking.

Still surprised at the turn of events, the Sharks coach offered his hand, shaking first with Big Murdock and then with Shio. "Well, uh, let's have Marco meet the team. I'm Coach Smith and this is my son, Brandon."

Brandon eyed Shio critically. "Aren't you a little small to be that guy's son?"

"He's my stepson," Big Murdock said quickly, glaring.

Shio grimaced. "Hiya," he said. Then he grinned.

It was hard not to welcome the slight boy with devastating good looks.

Still, few of the Sharks thought their savior had arrived. As they took turns introducing themselves, the Sharks players offered warnings to Shio.

"I'm glad you showed up," Ben told him, summing up the overwhelming thought, "but you picked the wrong game. We're going to be creamed."

By then the rest of the team had arrived, at least those who were planning to be there. Out of fourteen roster spots, including

Marco Reese, twelve kids had shown up. That meant there would only be one sub available.

Nobody seemed to think Shio's presence would make a difference—well, aside from Shawna and Rebecca. The two girls couldn't take their eyes off the new boy.

"Some savior Marco turns out to be," Craig grumbled, as he eyed Rebecca drooling over the newcomer. "He's just a pretty boy."

Shelly shook her head and repeated herself. "We're so doomed." Then she looked at Craig. "But he is really cute."

Ben sidled up to Mason. "Is this your great plan?" he muttered. "You're my best friend. Do you want to know why? Because you're a real idiot."

Mason shrugged off the negativity. "Just wait," he said to everyone near him. "Once the game starts you'll see. We have a chance today."

"Yeah, a chance to go home now before being humiliated," Shelly said as she brushed by him.

"Okay, team, take the field!" called Coach Smith. He'd spent the last five minutes searching for Marco's jersey, finally finding it stuffed in the bottom of the ball bag. After tossing the crumpled ball of wrinkles, he clapped his hands. "Let's, er, line up and take shots. Brandon, you're in the net. Hey, let's go!"

Shawna and Rebecca stood glued to the grass watching Shio shrug off his sweater and pull on the Sharks jersey. It hung loose over his slight frame—apparently Marco was a much bigger guy when he'd first signed up for the league.

Coach Smith had to bang his fist on the clipboard to get their attention. "Come on, girls!" he barked. "Let's play soccer!"

As game time approached, a small crowd of spectators started to gather. Mostly they were parents, but a few players and coaches from other teams had also come to watch. The bigger crowds would form in the later rounds. For this game, only the parents planned to stay the entire time. Everyone knew it would likely be a double-digit lead for United by halftime.

The parents for the Sharks stood huddled near midfield on the parking lot side. They were easily identified by their glum faces.

Some of the dads were already glancing at their watches. Across the field, a stand of bleachers was quickly filling with red-clad supports of United.

Burnhurst United wore dark red jerseys and gold shorts that matched their socks. In contrast, the Sharks had light blue jerseys and shorts and socks of assorted colors. It was easy to tell which team played in the rec league.

Shio trotted on the field with his new jersey tucked in dark blue shorts and joined Mason near the centerline. He appeared mostly calm, but his dark eyes danced with excitement.

Even Brittany, who rarely watched her brother play, could tell Shio loved to be out on the field. She stood with Big Murdock just away from the other Sharks' crowd. Neither seemed to know what to do, so they did it together, which meant they mostly watched Shio and prayed nobody would recognize him.

The rest of the Sharks stood in two ragged lines and were firing wild shots toward the goal. Most missed entirely.

"We look better once the game starts," Mason said, slightly nervously, as Shio joined him. He waited to see Shio sneer in disgust and walk over to the United side. Instead, the boy grinned confidently.

"Don't worry," he said. "Everything will be sorted out soon enough."

"Yeah, well, United is pretty good," Mason said. His confidence was fading with every second. Soon the whistle would blow and the game would start. Would Shio really turn the tide?

"Look, the Sharks have a minnow!" crowed a voice behind them.

Tommy Sandhurst and Mark Claxton had finished with their drills and were walking toward them. They stopped just on the other side of the midfield. It had been Mark who'd spoken.

"You going introduce the little guy?" Tommy asked, grinning. "He looks more like a mascot than a player."

Shio stared at the two of them and then over at Mason. "Who are the clowns?" he asked.

Mason gulped and licked his lips. "They're, uh, United players," he said dumbly. He couldn't help but wish he wore the red and gold and stood between Mark and Tommy.

Mark made a fist and beat his heart. "We're United, all right. You guys are the clowns. Oh, I'm sorry, I mean girls. I forgot this was a girls' team."

"We're not all girls," Mason said, trying to smile. He didn't want trouble with the two top United players. He still had dreams of one day playing with them.

Mark stared at him. "Aren't you in the wrong sport? Your people don't play soccer."

Mason lost his grin and stepped back, feeling like somebody had punched him in the gut.

Shio immediately stepped in front of Mark and stared up at him. "You think he's in the wrong sport?" he asked hotly.

"Yeah," challenged Mark. "And so are you. Nice jersey. What did you do, sleep in it?"

"You better stay low, little dude," Tommy told Shio. "You look too nice to get dirty."

"Yeah, I bet your mommy dressed you," Mark scoffed. "Two days ago."

Shio crossed his arms. "You two are peanuts," he said.

"Oooh, good one," jeered Mark. "He called me a peanut!"

"Hey, but check out his accent," Tommy said. "You from around here? You know, my sister told me to go easy on you today. She thinks you're cute."

Shio pursed his lips. "If she looks anything like you then tell her I'm sorry. She's anything but cute."

Tommy glared and stepped forward. "Oh, yeah? That right? You're real cute, all right. Just wait until the score is five to zip and then we'll see what you'll have to say."

"I'll say I'm sorry for running up the score on you ugly duffs," Shio said sharply.

Mark snarled, looming over Shio. More than a year older and a head taller, he glared down.

"You look like a sissy and you sound like one," he growled. "We're going to rub your face in the dirt, sissy."

Mason stepped beside his teammate. "Let's just cool it," he said. "Leave him alone, Mark. He doesn't know you."

"He will soon," Mark said. "I'm the guy who's going to run him over." He glared at Mason. "Now why don't you get off the field? Take your friend Morales with you. There's no spuds to pick here today. Let the minnows swim by themselves."

Mason felt his blood rush to his head. Even Tommy knew Mark had gone too far. The United captain ducked his head and backed away a little. "Come on, Mark," he muttered. "Let's not go there."

It was too late. Shio spat at Mark's feet and stared up at him. "People like you are everywhere," he said coldly. "Mostly they troll the net and hang around dung heaps. They don't have mouths, just dung holes. Do us all a favor and shut your dung hole. It's stinking up the pitch."

Mark snarled and moved to bump into the smaller player. He never saw Shio's knee rise up. Suddenly he cried out in pain and stumbled back, doubling over.

"And stay away from me." Shio calmly turned around and walked to the sideline. Mason hurried after him.

"What did you do?" he asked, still shaken.

"Just closed his dung hole," Shio said. "People like that shouldn't play the game. They ruin it."

"Hey, Mark!" cried Coach Thompson, walking onto the field. "What are you doing on the ground? Get up!"

"He's just tying his shoe," Tommy said, looking over at Mason and Shio. "That's all." He raised his voice. "Mason, no hard feelings, but you'd better watch it!" It sounded more like a warning than a threat. Mason didn't acknowledge it. His mom always told him to ignore racism. It wasn't easy to do.

He felt Ben watching him across the field and knew his friend, whose dad came from Mexico, had heard Mark.

Mark stood up, clutching his belly. "We'll see you Sharks on the field!" he called loudly. "When we're finished you'll all be minnows and needing lots of water!"

"And you'll be needing toilet paper!" Shelly cried from where she stood in the back of the line. "To wipe your face off with!"

"That's enough!" barked the referee. "No more talk! Let's get the captains and get this game started!"

Chapter 12

Brittany ran around the back of the net and met Mason and Shio as they came off the field. The team benches were in front of the United cheering section—the Sharks were on the right of it, while United were to the left.

"You two okay?" she asked, standing up field from the Sharks bench. "I saw what happened."

Shio nodded, looking a little sheepish. "He asked for it," he mumbled.

Mason grunted. "I'm fine," he growled at his sister. "Just leave me alone."

Brittany sighed. She'd never understand sports. "Just be careful out there," she said. "The good news is, I don't think anybody recognized, uh, well, I think our plan is working." Neither of the boys seemed to be listening. They both stared back over at the United team.

"Uh, Marco, how's your arm?" she asked.

Shio rotated both shoulders. "Feels brilliant," he said without looking at her.

From the field, Coach Smith spotted them on the sideline and hollered for the boys to get back on the field and start warming up. They left Brittany without a glance back.

Brittany suddenly felt very alone. She backed up and bumped into Big Murdock.

"When's this thing going to start?" the big man asked. He tugged at his full beard that no longer existed. "I forgot what it felt like to be with so many clean people … I don't know if I can make it."

"It'll be fine," Brittany snapped, more aggressively than she intended.

Big Murdock gulped. "Yeah, right …"

Brittany glared up at him. "You know, you didn't have to do this. I kind of hoped you wouldn't have."

Big Murdock flinched. "What? Why?"

Brittany bit her bottom lip and shook her head. Uninvited tears threatened to overwhelm her eyes. All at once, all the pressure and lonely feelings pressed against her. "I don't know what I'm doing, okay? Mason and the boy wanted to play this dumb game and I didn't know how to say no. Somebody is trying to kill the kid, remember?"

"But, but I did this for you," Big Murdock sputtered. "I thought you wanted this!"

They spoke in low voices so nobody could overhear.

"What about your son? Aren't you doing this for him?"

"Yeah, sure … but, that was more of an excuse I told myself." Big Murdock wiped his mouth. "Brittany, you know I care about you. You asked for my help and I didn't want to let you down."

Brittany shook her head miserably. "Why? I mean, nobody in my school cares about me. Why you?"

Big Murdock knelt next to her. "Look," he said softly. "I've been to many homeless shelters in my life. People are there to help, but to help who? Honestly, most only come to help themselves feel better. They're feeding people in need, and that's great. But they don't really care about us. They will never talk to us or even see us again. You're different. You always come and always care."

Brittany shook her head. "I only go there because I have no friends, okay? Everybody thinks I'm a poor, dirty girl good for nothing." She gestured at the field, but kept her head bowed to hide tears. "At least Mason is good at sports and gets friends that way. Me? I'm not good at anything."

She felt Big Murdock's giant hand rest on her shoulder. "Maybe that's why you understand us," he said gently. "Besides, that's not true. You're good at the only thing that really matters."

"And what's that? Messing everything up?"

"No. It's caring about others. That's what you're good at. You may not believe this, but you made me want to stay here, Brittany. If not for you, I would've left this place long ago. And that poor kid, my so-called son, would be in a heap of trouble."

Brittany grunted and blinked away the last of her tears. "He still is," she muttered. "Somebody wants him dead."

"That's why we're here." Big Murdock stood.

Brittany turned to him and smiled. His words calmed her and put away her self-pity. "Thanks," she said. "I … I needed that."

"Just repaying what you give at the shelter," Big Murdock said gruffly. "Now, how do we protect this foolish boy?"

"Just watch out for anybody suspicious." She had already checked the crowd, but did so again. All the other adults ignored her and Big Murdock so far, but a few threw glances their way. Rumors of a new boy's sudden appearance had circulated, but nobody seemed excited to meet the father.

She was just relieved not to see the man and two women who'd been after Shio. It felt like weeks ago, but really it'd been less than two days.

And how much longer would it last? She hoped the game would bring back his memory quickly and he would provide answers to it all.

She shifted her gaze to the field. Big Murdock stood beside her, but couldn't keep still. Talking with Brittany had only calmed him momentarily. Now the nerves of acting as a father returned in full force. Together they watched as Mason took a ball and started to pass with Shio. Almost immediately, the younger boy started displaying some of his skill.

"Wow, that kid looks pretty good," called a United parent to Coach Thompson. "Who is he, the one with the wrinkled shirt?"

The United coach had left his players to talk with some of the parents, who stood about ten yards from Brittany. The coach turned and watched Shio trap a high lob with his chest, catch it with his foot, and then toss it up to his back. He smiled.

"No idea, but it doesn't matter. He might have talent, but he lacks a body. He's a toothpick. I could teach him some things, but without a body he has zero chance of being great." He turned back to the father he'd been talking to before. "A lot of kids want to be stars," he said loudly, "but they have to be built for it. That kid has no body."

Brittany frowned. She had the urge to run up and kick the patronizing idiot in the back of his red and gold warm-up pants. Instead, she took a seat on the ground, inwardly seething. All her nervousness had turned to anger at patronizing judgmental grown-ups.

Big Murdock wandered in a circle behind her. Even without all his wild hair, he looked a little crazed with nerves.

"So what happens next?" he asked, finally stopping to stand next to her.

"We wait for the game to start," Brittany told him. "Then we watch, I guess." She breathed out. "I think everything will be okay … I mean, those people from the warehouse aren't here and they'll never think of checking this place. You can relax and just watch the game."

Big Murdock grunted. "I was a football player … never had much use for soccer." He abruptly started pacing again.

The game began with the Sharks kicking off first. They would be attacking the goal on Brittany's right. It was a good thing Shio had shown up for the Sharks. Without him, there would have been no substitute players. The lone sub was a quiet, chubby boy named Eric, who seemed perfectly happy not to be on the field. He'd already thrown up once in the parking lot.

Mason had to resist his own urge to throw up. As the players took the field, Mark made sure to find him and Shio. He glared at both, mostly at Mason.

Shio never looked back, but Mason rubbed his forehead nervously. Before, he'd so wanted to go out and prove he was worthy to be a United player. He thought Shio would help him, but now it looked like everything was unraveling before it even began. If the United players hated him, what chance would he ever have of playing for them?

Craig called his name, getting his attention. As usual, Craig Anderson played center forward with Mason on the right wing. Slender Daniel played on the left and looked lost out there. Shio stood behind them as the center midfielder.

Mason met Craig at the ball. "I'll tap you the ball," Mason said, "And you pass it back to Marco, okay?"

Craig only grunted in response.

"On my whistle, boys," the referee told them. Two linesmen, one on each side of the pitch, would also oversee the game. Both raised their flags to signal everything was ready.

"You Sharks are in for it!" Mark said, glaring across at Shio.

Hands on his hips, Shio stared back from his position and then surveyed the rest of the United players, much like a general overlooking the field before battle.

"Hey, what's he doing?" Tommy asked. "Posing for a magazine cover?"

Then the whistle blew.

Mason touched the ball and Craig immediately took off, straight into the heart of the United defense. Mason groaned and ran to the right wing position.

Shelly smacked her forehead from her right midfield position. She glowered at Shio. Usually she played center and wasn't happy to lose her position to the new kid. Suddenly, she took off from her position and charged after Craig.

"Where are you going?" Shio called to her.

"To get the ball back!" she snapped at him. "Craig is going to lose it!"

A second later, Craig did lose the ball. All at once the United players were on the attack. They swept up the left-hand side with a series of quick passes. With Shelly out of position, Shio was caught covering a wide space. He started to cut off the ball where Shelly should have been when a glancing elbow from Mark, who'd run by, caught him in the back and sent him sprawling to the ground.

Just like that, the Sharks had no midfield. The left midfielder, a boy whose name Shio couldn't remember, had run upfield at the whistle and now stood on the United side with his hands in the air.

Rebecca and Shawna were the right and left backs respectively with Ben and Alec, the team bookworm, covering the middle. Alec looked as if he would rather curl up in a ball and read a horror novel. None of the defenders knew what to do as they stood frozen on the ground while a wave of red built toward them.

Ben tried to charge the ball, by this time at Mark's feet in the center, but a quick fake sent Ben kicking air. Next, Mark went straight at Alec. The tall kid stood there like a beanpole. Just as he reached him, Mark slid the ball to the right, directly in the path to Tommy.

Two dribbles later, Tommy was in the box and sent a hard, low shot into the corner of the net. It took less than two minutes and United had the first goal.

"Come on!" screamed Shelly. "We can do better than this!"

Shio brushed dirt off his shirt and bit his lip as Mark trotted past.

"Nice legs," Mark smirked as he went by. "You should try standing on them."

When Craig positioned the ball in the center again, he looked at Mason. "Touch the ball," he said. "I'll show them."

Mason sighed. Craig was technically the captain of the team. Shrugging helplessly, he complied. All his thoughts of glory had vanished. He wouldn't play for United. This game was already over.

Craig took two touches to his left and then lost the ball. But this time the attack had come from behind—from his own teammate. Shio had learned from Shelly and had immediately started charging up at the whistle. In a flash, he swooped from behind Craig.

Mason gave a start when he saw the midfielder deftly take the ball from his own teammate. He stopped and stared. So did most of the Sharks, mostly in disbelief.

At first, Mark laughed when he saw the steal. But then Shio slashed through the United front line with the ball seemingly attached to his feet.

Tommy was the closest to the ball at first. When he moved in, Shio spun past and cut behind him, the ball never leaving his feet.

Mark's eyes widened in surprise. "Get him!" he shouted, giving chase.

None of the United players were prepared to face Shio's skill. With a series of step-overs, feints, and jukes, Shio danced through the midfield so fast that support from the forwards never reached him.

All of a sudden, he streaked past the last defender with the ball still glued to his feet. Instead of striking the ball on goal, he faked a shot so hard that it sent the United keeper sprawling to the right. Shio then calmly cut left, walking the ball over the goal line. Just like that, the score was tied 1–1.

The United crowd had barely settled in their seats from cheering the first goal. Now they stared in disbelief. The kid with no body had waltzed through their entire team. Nobody had stopped him.

From across the field, the small crowd of Sharks parents screamed with delight. Mason stared with mixed emotions as Shelly and Daniel ran and slapped Shio's back. He had done nothing so far but watch.

Coach Thompson on the United sideline was beside himself with rage.

"You call that defense?" he screamed at his players. "That was a walk in the park! Box him in!"

Then he motioned his defenders in for a brief huddle. "Look," he said in a softer tone. He sounded grim. "That kid is really good. *Really* good. I want you to pressure him, bump him, knock him around like no tomorrow! Got it? Keep it legal of course," he added when the linesman cleared his throat.

The game quickly turned rough after that. Suddenly, the promised exhibition turned into a dogfight. United no longer played to tune up for the next game; they played to survive for the next game.

Inspired by Shio's run, Shelly and Daniel attacked the United players with all-out fury. Mason joined in the attack, but mostly the United players kept the ball away from his side. They were too busy trying to get by Shio.

Shio sat back in the midfield and waited for his chance to pounce like a raptor in the bushes. Whenever Tom or Mark broke free from the first line of Sharks, they ran into Shio. He always seemed to know where to be and always had the quicker foot to poke or sweep the ball free.

Once he crossed into United territory, though, the red jerseys were on him like flies to a pot of honey. The first time, he'd sent a pass to Craig, who immediately misplayed it and it led to a turnover.

The turnover led to a goal when Tommy and Mark, free of Shio, Shelly, and Mason, who were all caught on the attack, easily passed their way through the remaining Sharks. Mark fired a cross from Tommy past Brandon in the upper right corner. United regained the lead. After that, Shio stopped passing.

"Give the ball to Marco!" Coach Smith yelled at the kickoff, pointing emphatically at Shio. "That's our new strategy!"

It seemed to work. The lead didn't last, as Shio took the ball and used another brilliant run to reach the right side of the United penalty box. Three players were on him with a fourth in support. This left center wide open. Seeing the open spot, Shelly looped from her position, racing to the area, screaming for the ball.

Shio faked the pass and then cut in toward the end line. Then he stutter-stepped before sliding the ball between two defenders and giving chase. The third defender tried a sliding tackle, but Shio scooped the ball up with his foot and hopped over the outstretched leg. A single defender was left between Shelly and Shio. Caught in between, the defender, a tall redhead, made no commitment and Shio had time to place a well-aimed shot past the goalkeeper in the lower right corner. Unbelievably the score was tied at two apiece.

The redheaded defender's face matched his hair as his coach screamed at him while the goalie picked the ball out of the net.

On the Sharks' bench, Coach Smith clapped his hands and yelled what a great job his team did. He ignored his lone sub. A gleam had entered his eye, as if all the success belonged to him.

Soon after, the Sharks took the lead. After the kickoff, the United team pushed forward for the third goal, but Brandon made a diving stop on a shot from just outside the box. Instead of booting the ball, he shot to his feet and flung the ball to Shio. Shio wasted no time with a quick counterattack. Catching the United defense trying to retreat, he neatly avoided two sliding tackles, juked a third defender, and outran the rest to the United goal. A hard shot found the back of the net for a third goal.

Now Coach Thompson threw down his clipboard in front of the United bench. "Put a body on him!" he screamed. "A body!"

"I thought you said that kid had no body!" yelled a frustrated father from the stands.

"Yeah," said another parent loudly, and not with a little sarcasm. "Nobody as small as him in this league could *ever* be good."

Coach Thompson bit his lower lip and looked ready to kick his clipboard into the stands.

After that, Shio started getting shoved, elbowed, grabbed, and tripped any time he neared the ball, on offense or defense. He became a team on his own and continued to press, mostly ignoring his teammates.

On defense, he slid fearlessly into hard tackles; on offense, he took the knocks and kept the ball on his feet. When surrounded, he would pass, but then immediately call for the ball. He constantly went after the United goal. He was a one-player storm, bent on wreaking havoc.

Soon, Mason gave up trying on offense and started dropping back to help on defense. Shelly stubbornly kept going forward with Craig and Daniel, but Shio only passed if he had no other option, like when five defenders surrounded him. He became a Craig Anderson with skill. More than a few of his attacks ended with him sprawled on the ground outside the box. The referee called the fouls, but the Sharks couldn't take advantage. As captain, Craig took the kicks and they amounted to turnovers.

Neither team could break through for another goal as the Sharks, with Mason joining the defense, did just enough to keep the ball free of the back of their net.

Then, as the first half neared completion, Shio was pulled down just outside the penalty box and no foul was given.

As the Sharks players protested, the United offense swept forward. A long cross from the wing found Tommy in the center at the top of the box of the Sharks' goal. The skilled forward pushed a shot passed Brandon to tie the game.

Shio's thin chest heaved with anger when the ball returned to the kickoff circle. "Give me the ball," he demanded, running a sleeve across his nose.

Craig, who had pretty much disappeared on the pitch, meekly complied. Immediately Shio took off for another run. This time he had something other than scoring on his mind.

After juking past Tommy, he moved straight toward Mark. Mark had personally sent Shio down four times with hard shoulder barges and more than a little shirt tugging. Shio slowed for an instant and then used a speed move to get past the United player.

Mark met the challenge, racing after Shio with eyes full of determination. Moving close, he reached out and tugged at Shio's jersey, a strategy he and the other United players had been using on Shio for some time. For a moment, the two were sprinting at full speed, but then Mark moved close and pulled on the back of Shio's flapping shorts. That was when Shio suddenly dug in his cleats, jerking to a stop while bending over at the waist.

Mark let out a wild yell. Caught going full speed while holding onto Shio's shorts, he rammed into the crouched smaller player. Suddenly he went airborne, sailing over Shio. He crashed heavily on the grass and rolled several times before coming to a stop. Stunned, he lay still.

Immediately, the referee's whistle shrieked and he charged at where Shio stood.

"Foul right here, going red's way!" he shouted.

Shio stared at him in disbelief and then showed where his shorts had been shredded on the side. "He grabbed me first, I just stopped!" he protested.

"Be thankful I don't give you a yellow, or even a red card," the referee growled. "Body checks are for hockey, son."

Shio turned away in disgust, but not before shooting a grin toward Mark.

Groaning, the United player got to his feet, shaking off any help. Luckily, only his pride was injured.

Brittany watched it all with growing concern on the sideline. "He's going to lose it," she murmured with certainty.

She hurried to where Big Murdock knelt near the end line of the United goal. The large man had finally settled there and watched the game with an intense fascination.

"Murdock," she said. "You have to do something. Shio is about to explode. I can just tell."

Big Murdock blinked and glanced at her. "Me? Why me?" he asked, suddenly sounding small and scared.

"Why? Because you're supposed to be his father!" she said exasperated. "You said you wanted to act like one. Here's your chance!"

Big Murdock swallowed hard. "That boy is pretty good at soccer," he mumbled. "I only know football. Not soccer."

"Where he comes from soccer is called football, okay?" Brittany at least knew that much. "And if you don't do something soon he's going to start playing tackle football and get himself in trouble. Remember, he's supposed to be enjoying this game!"

Big Murdock rubbed his lip nervously. "I don't know what to do," he muttered.

"What a father would do!" Brittany said, exasperated.

Shio had just taken another hard fall on the field and shot to his knees spitting mad. He charged to his feet and took off after the ball.

Murdock got to his feet and headed to the sideline as if in a trance. He watched almost as if in slow motion as Shio caught up with the ball and slid from behind, knocking the ball from the United player. The player went down, tripping over Shio's feet.

Again the referee blew his whistle for a foul. "Next one is a yellow," he told Shio firmly.

Breathing rapidly, Shio sat up and glowered.

"Time!" yelled Big Murdock running on field. "Timeout!"

"What's this?" cried Coach Thompson. "There aren't timeouts in soccer! Get that buffoon off the field!"

The referee turned and glared at Big Murdock. "You can't come on the field! What do you think you're doing?"

"Preventing a problem," Big Murdock muttered. "I'm getting my boy off the field before somebody, including you, gets hurt."

With that, he scooped Shio from the grass and carried him with both arms wrapped around his middle.

"Let go!" Shio cried, trying to kick free. "Put me down!"

"Calm down, boy," muttered Big Murdock. "It's for your own good. Believe me. It's not worth losing your temper over. Then you might do something you regret." He hollered across the field at the Sharks bench. "Coach, put a sub in! My boy is out."

Scowling, Shio stopped fighting.

Coach Smith, scratching his head and looking befuddled, made to say something but then sighed. He waved to the lone Shark player to take the field. "We lose," he muttered.

The poor sub trotted out with his head way down. Suddenly he wanted to be back on the bench.

The United players clapped and their section started cheering at the switch. "Finally!" called a mom. "Carry the baby off. Wait until he grows up before you put him back!"

Big Murdock paused on the field and turned to the cheering section. "This is a kids' game," he bellowed. "They're not supposed to be grown up, you are! So act like it!" Still carrying Shio in front of him, he marched from the field and knelt in the grass near the end line of the United half, away from parents and coaches. He kept his arms around Shio's waist, holding him tightly. Brittany went to join them with a water bottle.

"Do you want water, uh, Marco?" she asked.

Shio glowered at her. "No. I want to be let go and get back on the pitch."

"Not until you calm down, boy," Big Murdock said gruffly. He pulled Shio on his knee and pointed to the pitch. "Look out there. There are eleven players on a team. Not one. Eleven. You can't win this game by yourself. I don't know soccer, but I know math."

"I don't really care," Shio seethed. He gestured with his chin at Mark. "That piece of rubbish stepped on me and tore my shorts to bits!" He fought to get free, but Big Murdock refused to let go.

"Shh! Just sit still, boy!" he barked. He looked over at Brittany. "The kid is right about one thing. You may want to find another pair of shorts before we have any embarrassing incidents. Remember, this kid wets himself."

Brittany wisely said nothing as she hurried off. She did mutter something about hating sports.

"So do you," Shio said, scowling.

"It was supposed to be a joke. To lighten the mood."

"Not working," Shio muttered.

"No? Well, just listen. I played football long ago and faced people like those thugs all the time. They want to be the best, and if they can't do it by playing fair then they play dirty. Trust me. You don't want to become like them. To be great you have to make those around you great. You win on the field, nowhere else."

Out on the field, the United team scored another goal.

Shio blinked back tears of frustration. He beat on his thighs with his fists. "Now we're losing," he moaned.

"Losing a game really doesn't matter, kid. But this one is far from over. Look at your teammates. Are they really that bad? I mean, I don't know soccer, but you act like you have no friends out there. You've been so focused on the other team you've completely forgotten about your *own* team! Mason is out there, and he's pretty good. So are a number of other players. You haven't passed to them once."

Shio glared, but then slumped against Big Murdock's chest. Glumly, he watched as Big Murdock started pointing out his teammates.

"See Craig? Sure, he loses the ball, but just watch him fight to get it back. He'd be great on defense. And the tall blond kid and the girls—they could be a wall out there if they communicated.

And that talkative girl in the middle, she's good too." He pointed at Shelly, who at the moment was shaking her fist at her defense and yelling about stopping the ball instead of watching it. "With her and Mason on offense, you in the middle, you can be unstoppable. But only if you work together." Big Murdock actually sounded excited.

Shio sighed. "Fine, old man, what do I do now?"

"Never call me that again, for starters." He clapped Shio on the back, nearly knocking him to the ground. "Then get out there and take charge! That team never even met you until today and already they look up to you as their leader. Now act like it!"

Big Murdock rubbed Shio's hair as the boy slid from his knee. For a moment, man and boy stared at each other, each finding new respect for the other. Then Brittany raced from around the field waving a pair of athletic pants.

"One of the moms had these in the car!" she called, out of breath. "See if they fit!"

Big Murdock slapped Shio on the backside. "Go on, kid. Get out there and take this game." He stood and banged his hands together. "Let's pull the game together!"

By the time Shio managed to pull the pants over his cleats and torn shorts, the Sharks let in two more goals. And by the time he ran to Coach Smith to ask to go back in, the score was 7–3, United. The halftime whistle blew before Shio returned to the field. The Sharks walked off dejectedly with their heads hung low.

Coach Smith gathered them around, but seemed at a loss for what to say. "Keep fighting," he kept repeating. "Don't give up. We can get back in this." He never did say how or what the team needed to do to change.

The players slumped on the bench or on the ground, sucking on water bottles and sliced oranges. None seemed inspired.

Brittany went over and sat next to Mason. He sat with his head between his knees in the grass away from the rest of the team at the bench.

"You really love this game, don't you?" Brittany said to him.

Mason snorted. "Not this particular game, but yeah. Soccer is the best."

Brittany shook her head. "I'll never understand sports, but I do wish you could beat those other guys. They seem like real jerks … sort of like the girls at my basketball practice."

Mason shrugged. "We can't win. It's over."

"We can win," Shio said, appearing behind them. He took a deep breath and offered a hand down to Mason. "I'm sorry," he muttered. "I should've passed more."

Surprised, Mason looked up and slowly took the hand. "Uh, okay," he said. "Maybe in the second half you still can. You know, like once pass me the ball."

Shio shrugged. "Maybe. We'll see."

Mason grabbed Shio around both ankles and pulled them out from under him. Startled, Shio slammed down on his backside with a thump.

"Now that's a football tackle," Mason said, grinning.

Shio glared. "That's a rubbish move!" He winced and turned to his side to rub his sore area. "I landed there enough already."

Mason laughed. Then he grew serious. "I never did thank you for standing with me earlier … with Mark."

Shio looked at him hard. "What are teammates for?"

"To pass the ball," Mason said, grinning.

"What about just gas?" Shio said.

Brittany just shook her head. "I'll never understand boys," she said.

"Hey, guys!" Shelly suddenly yelled from the bench. "Let's get out there and disunite the United!"

Chapter
13

Coach Smith sent the same starting players out for the second half, but as they went on the field, Shio motioned for them to huddle up. In the huddle, they linked arms and put their heads together.

"All right," Shio said. "Who here knows how to play football?"

"Don't you mean soccer?" Craig said, slightly belligerently. "I don't know where you're from, but here it's called soccer. And we pass."

Shio nodded and looked over at Craig. "You're right. That's why you're moving to sweeper. You're the center back now."

"No way!" protested Craig. "I'm center forward!"

"Not yet," Shio told him flatly. "You're like a brick wall out there and that's what we need. Don't let the ball past you, and when you get it, kick it to the wings." His deep, dark eyes flashed and swept across the faces of the Sharks. "That goes for everyone playing defense. Stop stabbing at the ball. Just stand in front of it and wait for it to come to you."

"Who's on the wings?" Shelly asked.

"Me and you," Mason said, staring at her. "We have to work together now. Marco will be in the center."

Craig barked out a laugh. "You want Shelly on the wing? We're already down by four goals!"

"Shut your face!" Shelly snarled. "I know soccer like your finger knows your nose. You keep the ball out of our net and just watch me put the ball in theirs."

Craig scowled but then nodded. "You're on. But who's playing defense with me?"

Quickly Shio doled out the positions. Shawna and Rebecca remained in their spots and Alec backed up Craig. Daniel, Ben, and the boy Shio still didn't know, actually named Xavier, were the midfielders. Their job was to clog up the center and keep the ball on the other half as much as possible.

The whistle blew, breaking the huddle.

As they started trotting to their positions, Mason went over to Alec. The tall kid had barely moved out there and looked pale.

"Look, Alec," he said seriously, "you read all those Lord of the Rings books, right?"

The boy nodded miserably. "Uh, yeah. Wish I was reading one right now ..."

"Why?" Mason demanded. "This is your chance to live it!" He'd seen the movies at Ben's house and loved them. One day he would read the books ... "Right now you're the last stand at the fortress. The Orcs are coming. You, Craig, Shawna, and Rebecca are the last line of defense. You are the brick wall that can't break to save the day, got it? You can bend, but you can't break! The fate of our team depends on it!"

The boy blinked as if stunned. Then his blue eyes gleamed with a ray of hope. Swallowing, he looked at Mason and nodded. "I ... think I got it. Uh, thanks." For the first time, he looked ready to enjoy the game.

Mason smacked his arm and ran to his position. Shelly nodded at him as he did so.

"That was ... cool," she said, sounding like she meant it.

Coach Smith frowned and watched in befuddlement as all his players moved to positions he'd never assigned them. His son

Brandon just shrugged at him as he headed for his goal. Before he could protest, United kicked off.

After the late first-half barrage of goals, the United team felt they were in cruise control. That quickly proved to be misleading. Craig suddenly found his inner soccer calling and helped form the backbone of the brick wall of defense.

Alec took Mason's words to heart. He could be heard muttering about repelling the invaders and to hold steady until it was time to … unleash! Then he would suddenly step into the approaching United player with the ball, taking it away. The girls followed his example. They stood their ground and if the ball did make it past, Craig was there to boot it away.

Ben led the charge at the midfield level and hindered and hounded any United player crossing into Sharks space. Where there was wide open space in the first half became a terrible quagmire of flailing limbs in the second. Suddenly, United's attack stalled. But where the Sharks really shined was on offense.

Shelly on the left and Mason on the right, with Shio in the center, and the Sharks' attack became a three-headed monster. Whenever the United defense tried to box in the ball, it would shoot to an open area across the field where one of the Sharks attackers always happened to be.

In minutes, Shelly had two shots on goal and Mason had one. Two more shots had sailed over the crossbar. Only good goal keeping kept the score from narrowing.

Then, Shio sent a perfect ball through the center of the United defense, right in the path of a streaking Shelly.

Mason raced down the right side to give her an opportunity to cross, if she so desired.

Shelly caught up with the ball as she reached the edge of the United penalty box, only to be cut off by the right back, who'd charged from his position to challenge her. The girl never hesitated. Raising her foot for a shot, at the last second she sent the ball skittering across to a wide-open Mason.

He was so surprised that he nearly missed the ball completely. He got just enough to send it skipping into an empty net.

So sure of a shot coming from Shelly, both goalie and defender had moved to block the side opposite from Mason. The Sharks had scored.

All at once, the joy of soccer came to Mason in full force. There was no greater feeling in the world than scoring a goal.

At first he stood there staring at the ball. Then his eyes widened and he screamed with joy. Suddenly he was hugging Shelly. Shio brought them both down to earth reminding them they were still down three goals.

A few minutes later, they were down only two. After the United attack faltered with Craig stealing the ball from Mark, he sent a pass to Mason. Mason used a few skills from Shio and actually juked Tommy. Then he sent a pass to Shio, who raced down the right side, drawing three defenders after him. Mason looped from his position to cover the center. Another defender moved to cover him. Shio looked up and saw a streaking Shelly moving down the opposite side of the field. He immediately put his head down and lofted the ball across the field, directly in front of the girl. Shelly trapped the ball down and moved easily on goal. She banged the ball into the far corner before the defense could recover.

After that, the United team started dropping back and no longer focused on scoring. For a while this seemed to work, as the three attackers suddenly faced as many as ten defenders. Then Shio got taken down by a hard foul just outside the box. He'd spotted a pair of defenders and juked the center back. Instead of going for the ball, though, the United player, a large blond with floppy hair and a big nose, went for the player. His shoulder met Shio in the chest and sent the small boy slamming to the ground.

For a moment, Shio lay motionless and didn't look like he could rise.

Mason charged from the wing and slammed into the bigger boy's back, knocking him down. "You want to pick on one of my players?" he cried. "Try me!"

The whistle shrieked and the referee charged in, separating the teams. "Hey, number 10, to me, now!" he yelled, staring at Mason.

Hearing his number, Mason ducked his head and went to the referee for his punishment. He hoped it wouldn't be red.

Shio was in a kneeling position and just getting to his feet. He nodded his thanks as Mason passed. This is what teammates did.

"Look, kid," the referee said to Mason in a low voice, "good job looking out for a teammate, but if you do it again I'm going to have to throw you out. Okay?"

He and the United defender both got yellow cards. The Sharks got a free kick.

Shio by now walked with a limp, but said very clearly, "I'm taking it." His dark eyes allowed no argument. He stood over the ball and stared at the United goal.

Before, Craig had taken all the free kicks. This time everyone knew there was a new captain for the Sharks.

United formed a human wall in front of the goal, but it was for naught. Shio blasted a dipping shot that went up over the wall and then down just below the crossbar. The goalie didn't see it until too late and could only watch helplessly as the ball struck the back of the net. Suddenly, it was a one-goal lead and the crowd got into it. Both sides were yelling like mad.

Many were simply marveling about Shio.

"Who is that kid?" asked more than one fan. "He's like a magician out there!"

"I want to check his cleats for magnets—the ball seems to stick to them," a United father grumbled in admiration.

"Isn't he from Brazil?" another parent asked.

"Have you heard him talk?" scoffed the same United father. "He may look Brazilian, but he's all English. He reminds me of a young Michal Slaydon."

Brittany heard all this and her blood froze. The thrill of the game instantly turned to fear. Looking around for any suspicious people, she only saw parents and spectators, no murderers. Then her gaze fell on a slender, broad-shouldered man in a knee-length black coat.

He stood near the United bleachers behind a group of mothers. What drew her attention was his face. Cold as stone, with bright green eyes staring intently onto the field, his expression was unfeeling hate. Black gloves covered his hands as he sipped coffee. His attention never wavered. Brittany saw that his eyes remained locked on Shio. Instantly she raced to find Big Murdock.

Poor Big Murdock had trouble of his own. Word had gotten around to the United sideline that he was the father of the "Marvelous Marco." He was soon barraged with questions about his wonder son.

When asked about his English-accented son being from Brazil, he stammered a reply. "Uh, he's adopted … from England, but we moved to Brazil … after the marriage."

"Where's his mother?" asked a woman suspiciously.

"We're, uh, divorced," Big Murdock said miserably.

Finally, he ducked his head and moved close to the sideline to get lost in the game.

That was when Coach Thompson sidled up to him. "Get up there!" he screamed to the field. "Box him in—never mind, he's making another long pass! Get back! Get back!"

He sighed with relief when the ball went out of bounds. Then he turned to Big Murdock. "Look," he muttered. "After the game, meet me and we'll discuss getting your son on United. Okay?" He moved away before Big Murdock could think of a reply.

With five minutes left in the game, it looked as if United might squeak out the victory. But then, after another wild run of dribbling through the United defense, drawing several defenders, Shio slid a no-look pass to Shelly, all alone in the United box. A desperate defender panicked and slid at her from behind, clipping her ankles and sending her sprawling.

The referee immediately pointed to the penalty spot. The United section howled in protest as the Sharks' tiny group of fans cheered like mad. They would get a free shot on goal with only the keeper to stop it.

Mason and Shio ran to help Shelly up.

"Good going," Mason told her, grinning like mad. "Now do the honors."

Shelly winced and shook her head. "He got my ankles good with his spikes ... I don't think I can take it properly. Mason, you do it."

Mason gulped. The game was on the line. The ball would be on his foot. "You ... you sure?" he squeaked.

The girl grinned and nodded. "I trust you."

Shio smacked Mason's shoulder. "You can do this."

Swallowing hard, Mason blinked. "Yeah ..."

A hush fell across the field as Mason placed the ball on the spot and surveyed the goal. The goalie, tall for his age, jumped up and down, waving his arms, until the referee told him that he could not move until the ball was struck. Then, for a moment, everything went still.

The fans went quiet, many with clenched fists and faces, as they stared in either hope or despair. Mason never noticed them. He kept his focus solely on the ball in front of him.

After the whistle, Mason took a deep breath and stepped into the kick. Low and hard, it flew from the reach of the keeper, burying itself in the back of the net just inside the left post.

Mason fell to his knees in disbelief. Then he screamed in joy as his teammates swarmed at his back. Playing soccer was great—but scoring in soccer? Nothing matched it. It had to be the greatest feeling in life.

Better yet, the score was now dead even at seven.

Groans and cries of anguish came from the United fans while the delighted Sharks fans went mad.

Right after the kickoff, the United players attacked with a vengeance. They knew a quick goal would win the game. Otherwise, it would go to a ten-minute overtime and then a shootout from the penalty spot if the score remained tied. They didn't want to pin their hopes on a shootout, where anything could happen.

For a while they worked the ball around the Sharks side. Using the brick wall strategy, Craig, Alec, and the rest of the defense held stout. The entire second half, they'd cracked but had never broken.

Then, with a minute left, Tommy found space from Alec and rocketed a shot off the crossbar from just outside the box. The rebound fell right in the path of charging Mark, who leapt forward for the winning goal. Out of nowhere, Ben slid in and knocked the ball out over the end line, just ahead of Mark's foot. The United player sprawled on his belly, tripping over Ben.

Mark screamed in frustration as he slammed his hand in the dirt.

"Like picking spuds from a field," Ben said evenly as he stood up.

Mark only glared.

The signal for a corner was given. It would be the last chance, possibly, for either team to win in regulation. Tommy took the kick. Caught in the moment, he put too much air under it. It fell in front of Shawna on the far side of the field, who, more out of instinct than desire, kicked out her foot and sent the ball flying up the left wing, right in front of a sprinting Shelly. The girl brought the ball down with her stomach and raced toward the United goal. The United team had brought everyone up except the goalie for the corner. Now it was a foot race to see who made it back in time.

Coach Thompson screamed for the whistle to be blown. Then from twenty yards out, Shelly, tiring and feeling the pressure closing in, launched a desperation shot. It rose from her foot, arching and bending toward the goal. For a moment, it looked on target, but then the bend proved too great and the ball veered sharply right toward the top of the penalty box.

Coach Thompson sighed with relief. Just as the referee started to lift his whistle, Shio charged from the center. He'd followed the play all the way down the field, holding back. Now unmarked, he went after the ball like his life depended on it. Nothing else existed.

The boy launched his body into the air, throwing it sideways. Foot met the ball squarely, sending it rocketing toward the goal. As the body crashed to the ground, the ball crashed into the goal. It never touched the ground until it had already buried itself deep in the back of the net.

It was a shocking goal and nobody moved for a full second. Then the referee's whistle sounded, ending the game without even a kickoff. The Sharks screamed as they ran toward the center of the field.

Nobody could believe what they'd just witnessed. A kid had just nailed a volley from on the run on a twisting turning cross, just as time expired.

Even the United side yelled in amazement. For a moment, there was pandemonium. Coach Thompson tried to demand more time, but really he was just unable to admit defeat.

But it had happened. The game was over and the top seed in the tournament had fallen to a lowly rec team. In Biblical terms, David had defeated Goliath.

Chapter
14

Brittany never saw the goal. During her search for Murdock she'd come across her nightmare coming true.

Deputy Donald had never left—his car was parked near the entrance of the field. And standing just outside his car was a large figure of a man. It was the man from the warehouse who'd been looking for Shio when Brittany had found him. She would recognize him anywhere. That meant the two women had to be around. Shio was in grave danger.

Whirling, she heard the roar and screams. And she saw all the people with cell phones, snapping pictures. They'd been doing it all through the game. No doubt pictures of Shio were now plastered all over the internet. Her heart lurched in her throat. This couldn't be happening …

"Murdock!" she shouted. "We need to get out of here! Murdock! Where are you?"

The large man pushed through the crowd wearing a stunned expression. He blinked when he saw Brittany looking distressed and hurried over.

"What's wrong?" he bellowed.

"He has to get out of here!" Brittany screamed. "I mean, Sh— Marco!" She grabbed his arm and whispered. "I saw the guy from the warehouse! They're here, Murdock!" She felt her hands shake. "What do we do?"

Brittany was talking to wind. Murdock was already pushing through the crowds out into the field.

"Out of my way!" he bellowed when parents wouldn't move quickly enough.

Shio stood from his amazing kick and searched the sea of faces streaming onto the field. The rest of the team was dog piling in the center, but he seemed to be searching for somebody. His face lit up when he saw Big Murdock coming toward him. Without thinking, he charged toward the large homeless man and threw himself in his arms.

Big Murdock caught him under the arms and tossed him easily in the air. Then he lifted him up and said gruffly, "We have to go. Now."

Brittany met them on the field still in the midst of parents, players, and spectators. Word had spread about the game and nobody had left early. Instead, more people had shown up during the game. For a moment, Brittany, Big Murdock, and Shio were lost in a crowd. During that time, Big Murdock knelt down and Brittany shoved a knitted hat on Shio's head and wrapped him with a coat. Big Murdock ripped off his turtleneck sweater, revealing a scruffy old pullover. He dug in the back of his pants and produced a dark skull cap that he pulled low over his brow. Suddenly, he looked more like a homeless man. It all happened in moments.

Big Murdock stood and snatched up Shio and fled through the crowd away from the parking lot. Brittany followed in their wake searching for anybody following.

It was nearing dusk and the temperature had started to drop. Clouds were moving in. As the celebration continued on the field, Murdock slipped into the tree line behind the field. He knew all the trails and expertly led the way from the sports-plex, through the trees, over the train tracks, and eventually to the road leading to Brittany's street.

It wasn't until they saw her house that Brittany started to breathe easier.

"I think it's safe," she said.

Big Murdock grunted. "For now. They know he's here."

Shio rested his head on Big Murdock's shoulder, but wore a satisfied smile. "It's okay," he muttered tiredly. "I'm ready now."

Big Murdock hefted him higher. "You know kid, you're not bad at that soccer stuff," he said gruffly.

Shio lifted his head and put both hands on Big Murdock's massive shoulders.

"And you're not bad at this dad stuff," replied Shio, "for an old man."

Big Murdock barked a laugh. "Only for a day, kid," he said. "But call me that again and I'll still put you over my knee."

Brittany shook her head. "Don't you two get it?" she snapped. "There are people hunting for Sh—for us! Murdock, we have to get him out of this town!"

Big Murdock frowned. "How do we do that?"

Brittany grunted. She'd been thinking about just that since they fled the field. "The only way I know is the train station."

There was a small Amtrak station in the downtown area that still ran a line from Burnhurst to New York City. During Burnhurst's heyday it had been a busy place, but now it was near the point of having to close.

"We can get to New York," she muttered. "From there … I'm sure we can find help, or at least hide."

Big Murdock frowned. "We?" he asked. He shook his head and put Shio down. "I'll go with him. You're staying here. That's final. Believe me, I know how to travel and disappear when necessary. Here's the plan. You two kids go get cleaned up. Use the bus and get to the train station at four. I'll meet you there."

"Where are you going?" Brittany asked him, still not really comprehending that Shio would be out of her life in a few short hours.

"Back to the field to make sure nobody is trying to find you— and to tell Mason what's happening. Then I need to get money for tickets. I'll see you at the station. Now scoot!"

On the way, she'd told him about seeing Deputy Donald talking to the bad man. The police could not be trusted.

"Oh," she breathed as Big Murdock left them. "I hope this works out."

Shio patted her arm. "It'll be brilliant," he said, smiling. "You'll see."

It did not start off brilliantly. Not at all. Shio had spent about as much time on the ground as on his feet during the game and looked and smelled like he'd been run over by a herd of elephants. He moved with a slight limp and looked happy but exhausted. He needed a hot shower.

The only problem, Brittany's mom had returned from church by then and would be home. Most likely she would be watching television on the couch.

Brittany had Shio hide in the backyard while she checked out the house. Moving to the side, she peeked through the window into the family room. Sure enough, her mom sat watching a basketball game on mute while reading her Bible.

She bit her lip. Shio really needed a shower. When she'd left him, the poor kid crouched in a shivering ball with the borrowed jacket providing little comfort. Mud marked his borrowed pants. Drying dirty streaks of sweat lined his face. With no other option, Brittany did the unthinkable. She walked in her house and asked her mom if she could borrow the cell phone.

Distracted, her mom barely nodded her consent. She seemed so focused on reading the Bible that she probably didn't know who was even playing on TV.

Running up to Mason's room for privacy, Brittany flopped on her brother's bed. She was able to dial the number from memory.

"*Hello?*" asked Melissa's voice after the third ring.

"Um, Melissa, this is Brittany," she began awkwardly. "I have a huge, huge favor to ask you. I mean huge."

Melissa sighed on the other end of the line. "*What is it?*"

"Well, I have a friend who needs to, uh, take a shower. And, uh, I was wondering if he could do it at your place." The other end of the line went quiet. "Melissa, are you there?"

"Yeah, but are you? You want a stranger to use my shower?"

Brittany took a deep breath. "Melissa … it's Shio Slaydon. He's in big trouble. Melissa, I'm serious. Shio is at my house and needs our help. It's too long to explain. Melissa?"

The silence on the other end was longer. Then Melissa's voice came back. *"Brittany, you're such a jerk. I hate you."*

Brittany dropped her head when hearing the dial tone. So much for that idea. "One day," she mumbled, "I'm getting a best friend." Sighing, she tossed the phone on Mason's bed and went back to find Shio.

The boy's teeth chattered when she found him. "W-well?" he asked, sounding expectant. Brittany had never let him down yet. The deep trust in his eyes made Brittany step back.

"Well, ah, you can use our shower again, but you have to get past my mom first. And you better take off your shoes and socks here. Sorry, but if my mom sees that dirt on the floor she'll go crazy and definitely find you."

Shio smiled. "S-sounds like my mum," he said, ripping off his hat.

He started untying his shoes with frozen fingers and Brittany quickly dropped down to help. She yanked off his shoes and helped pull off his sweaty, stinking socks and the pads from under his pants. She let him take off his own pants.

His ripped shorts still held together, and, barefoot, he followed her to the back door of the house. After a second thought, he pulled off his dirt-encrusted shirt and threw it behind him.

"Would leave a trail," he said, shivering.

"Just run past me up to the shower," she told him, opening the door. "I'll distract my mom and then find more of Mason's clothes that fit. Okay?" She didn't wait for a nod.

Shio followed her in. Covering his bare chest with his arms, he sprinted lightly past as she turned into the family room and went to give her mom a big hug.

She hoped the crazy half-dressed boy would get by unnoticed.

"Brittany, baby, what's wrong?" her mom asked, returning the hug and pulling Brittany on her lap.

For a moment, Brittany let herself relax in the comforting arms of her mother. She'd forgotten how much she missed her mom and missed being just a child with no worries.

"Nothing, Momma," she said. "I just want to tell you I love you."

Mrs. Tiff smiled and squeezed Brittany tight. "I know you do, baby." She sighed. "These past couple of days I've had a tough time. I, I fell a bit, but now I'm okay. Thanks to my children, I'm okay."

Brittany was alarmed to see tears coming from her mother's eyes.

"Mom!" she cried. "What's wrong?"

"Oh, you know about my troubles ... my job at that department store, it ... it probably won't be there for me after the holidays ... I just wish I could do better as a mother. I don't see my own children much. Speaking of which, where's Mason?"

"Oh, he, uh, just returned from his game." Brittany tensed up. The water upstairs started running. "He's in the shower," she said with relief.

"How did he do?" Mrs. Tiff asked. "I need to see him play sometime."

"Oh, uh, well, he did good. They won."

"Did they? Didn't he say last week they'd be killed? Get up, Brittany. Let me go up and congratulate him!"

"Oh, that's okay, Mom," Brittany said quickly. "Don't do that. He's, uh, pretty tired after the game. He, uh, got hurt too."

That only made it worse. "Oh, how badly?" Mrs. Tiff pushed Brittany down and got to her feet. "Mason!" she called. "I'm coming up! You better be decent!"

"Mom, no! He's not hurt that bad! He's fine, just tired!"

"Too tired to answer his own mother? Mason! You hear me?"

The water stopped. Brittany fought past her mom on the stairs and raced to the top. "Mom," she said desperately. "What about supper? He's going to be hungry. I'm starving too!"

Mrs. Tiff frowned up at her. "Brittany Tiff, you're hiding something, aren't you?" She grinned. "No matter. I'll go start supper, then, but, mind you, you go tell Mason that I want to check him over. I haven't practiced my nursing for some time and this is a good chance to do it! Tell him to come down as soon as he's out."

Brittany raced into her mother's room to find clothes for Shio. She left with an old pair of jeans, a T-shirt, boxers, and a Ninja Turtle hoodie. Entering the hall, she was just in time to see Shio emerge from the bathroom soaking wet with a towel wrapped around his waist. He looked stricken.

"Is it safe?" he asked, his eyes wide with fright. Water ran down his skinny form, forming puddles at his feet.

"Are you crazy?" Brittany hissed, averting her eyes. "Quick, get in Mason's room and get dressed! Hurry before my mom comes up!" Eyes down, she chased him into her brother's room and threw the clothes in after him. Door shut, she leaned back against the wall and gasped for a breath. What else could go wrong, she wondered.

She found out as she reached the top of the stairs.

"Mason!" shrieked her mom from the kitchen. "What are you doing in those filthy clothes inside my house? You were just in the shower a second ago!"

"What?" cried Mason's voice. "I just—" Then it came out sickly. "Oh, uh, sorry … I, uh, was only warming the water."

"That's what you said last time—"

Brittany ran back to Mason's room, banging on the door. "Are you dressed yet?" she hissed. "We have to go!"

Shio cracked the door open and stepped back, looking embarrassed. He wore the jeans, but his back and chest were still covered in water droplets. Too large, the jeans kept sliding down his narrow hips.

"What are you doing?" Brittany asked with a scowl.

"N-nothing," Shio stammered guiltily. He pulled up the drooping jeans and reached down to pick up the T-shirt.

Brittany winced at seeing the raw, red burn on his shoulder now joined with dark bruises on his ribs and back. "You look like a mess," she said. "But we're going to be in a bigger one if you don't hurry. Find socks in the drawer. I'll go down and get my, er, your sneakers. We're leaving now."

Brittany and Shio were able to slip out while Mason was undergoing a thorough physical examination in the kitchen.

"But Mom," they heard Mason complain as they left, "I never got hurt that bad! Really! You don't need the iodine!"

"Hush, baby. Just lift up your arms. How you get down from the shower so fast, I'll never know."

Brittany just hoped her mom never checked outside to find the pile of filthy clothing lying there. Poor Mason would have some explaining to do.

Chapter 15

As children, Brittany and Shio were able to ride the Burnhurst public bus free, but unfortunately the bus didn't stop at the train station. They were dropped off in the downtown area just behind Cooligan's Department Store. The trip to the bus stop and subsequent ride had proved uneventful. Shio kept quiet until they stepped off the warm bus into the cold December air. Gray clouds covered the sky like a blanket. It almost felt like snow.

"Brittany," Shio said as the bus pulled from the curb, "I, um, don't think I thanked you for everything you've done for me."

Brittany shrugged, barely hearing him. She stared at the back of Cooligan's. Seeing the store reminded her of what her mom said about soon being fired. A truck was parked outside the loading entrance and a man was taking down boxes, stacking them in a pile by the door. Inside those boxes were clothes her mom would not be selling.

What was the use of helping people when it didn't really change anything? In just a few hours, Shio would be far away on a train with Big Murdock and gone for good. Brittany would be left behind for a crummy Christmas with her overworked, soon underemployed mom. Her face must have looked miserably depressed, because Shio took her by the hand.

The boy wore her pink sneakers, black winter hat, and Ninja Turtles hoodie. Even dressed ridiculously he remained striking. His dark hazel eyes searched her face.

"It's going to be fine," he said. "You'll see."

"Right," Brittany mumbled. She shook off her self-pity. There wasn't time for that yet. "Let's get to the train station," she muttered, pulling her hand free. "It's only a few blocks from here."

"Wait," Shio said. He took a deep breath and peered again at her. "Tell me. What would make you happy right now? I mean really happy?"

Brittany raised her eyebrows. It was a strange question to be asking and for a moment she thought to laugh. But then she saw he was serious.

"I don't know," she said. "I guess seeing you safe. Come on."

Shio seemed disappointed with the answer, but he walked lightly by her side. A change had come over him, as if the soccer game had freed him from a terrible weight. His eyes roved over all the buildings and took in the Christmas decorations.

Downtown Burnhurst was not much to look at. Besides Cooligan's, there were a few restaurants, an old bookstore, a couple of gas stations, and a few other odd businesses, all in little buildings not more than two stories. Main Street only had three traffic lights. Even with Christmas fast approaching, they were the only ones on the street, except for the man unloading the boxes behind Cooligan's.

That was because, Brittany knew, almost all the shops and stores were closed on Sunday—something left over from the county's beginning. Sunday was a day of rest. Tradition died hard in Burnhurst.

Then Brittany saw them. A homeless couple—a man and a woman—trudged from around the corner of the department store, coming in their direction. Each was dressed in a heavy coat and wore a hat with multiple scarves. Brittany couldn't tell if she knew them and only knew their gender due to the black coat on one and pink coat on the other. Both looked like they carried invisible packs of rocks they were so bowed down. Thinking of Fred and Myrtle, she paused at the edge of Cooligan's to watch them. Shio moved to her side and waited.

"Hey, you, kids," the man at the truck said rudely, jerking a thumb behind him. "Scram!"

Brittany blinked and stared at him. A sudden surge of anger ran up her body. "We can stay here if we want," she said.

The man had a new jacket and wore brown leather gloves. He also wore a hardened sneer on a grizzled face. Wisps of gray stuck out from a red hat. "Don't get smart with me, girl," he barked. "I know your type." He jerked his chin at the homeless couple. "You're like them. You'd steal a man blind if you could. Now beat it before I call the cops!"

"Come on," Shio said softly, tugging at her sleeve. "Let's go."

Brittany turned and glared at him. She almost shoved him away, but instead huffed and followed him away from the store. What did the boy know? He was one of the rich. Once he remembered who he was he would be back in his mansion and forget all about Murdock and those who helped him.

She stopped as they reached the front of the store. Whirling on Shio, she poked a finger in his chest.

"Do you know what would make me really happy?" she asked with unfeigned bitterness. She nodded at Cooligan's Department Store. "See that store? If those clothes would be given to the homeless instead of being sold to rich people who don't care about the suffering of others. *That* would make me happy."

Shio's eyes widened. "Really? Is that what you want?"

"Yes," Brittany snapped. "I work with the homeless, almost every week. While we sleep in nice warm beds, they're stuck out here. You saw Murdock's place. He's one of the fortunate ones. Most don't have anything but the clothes on their backs and that often isn't enough. Now let's go."

"One minute. Wait right here."

Brittany made to protest, but Shio shoved Brittany in front of the window display of Cooligan's.

"Hey! What are you doing?" she asked.

"Just wait there!" Shio called, racing around the corner.

Brittany, cold and angry, turned to the window. She figured he needed to go to the bathroom. Like her brother, being a boy, he would slip behind a building. Hopefully the rude man wouldn't catch him.

She eyed the snow scene in Cooligan's with more bitterness. An old-fashioned store, Cooligan's always put up a Christmas village train set in its window at this time of year.

"Have a very merry Christmas firing my mom," she muttered. With the store closed, the village resembled most of Burnhurst. Silent as a grave. Dead.

Then she heard the rattling of a cart coming toward her. Working in a shelter, she knew it was probably a grocery cart pushed by a homeless person with all their belongings. Many brought such carts to the shelter and refused to give them up when told stealing them wasn't allowed. Thankfully, few stores ever cared to get their carts back.

This cart belonged to Cooligan's, but it hadn't been stolen by a homeless person. It had been taken by Shio.

He turned the corner out of breath pushing a cart loaded down with a large cardboard box about the size of Brittany.

Brittany's eyes widened seeing him and cart. "What, are you crazy?" she asked. "What are you doing?"

Shio grinned mischievously. "You'll have to help," he gasped. "I barely got it in here and almost lost it going downhill."

"But-but, what is it?"

"What you wanted. I already checked. These are coats."

"Why would I want a box of coats? Where did you get it from?"

"You said you wanted to help the homeless. We have over thirty minutes before we have to be at the train station. That's plenty of time to pass them out."

Brittany shook her head and stepped back. "No. No way. You stole these from the truck, didn't you?"

"More like borrowed. Come on, we'd better hurry before that guy finds out." Shio glanced worriedly over his shoulder.

"I don't believe this," Brittany groaned. "We can't do this!"

"Why not? Would you rather go back to the truck and give the box back to that guy?"

Still mumbling about them all going to jail, Brittany helped Shio push the heavy cart across the street and down an alley where she knew some of the homeless liked to gather. She could not believe she was now a criminal … with Shio Slaydon.

In all the craziness, she never had the chance, or the courage, to ask if Shio remembered his past. In reality, she didn't want to know—not yet. She didn't want to ruin the strange friendship they had developed—even though it had led them to a life of crime. Worst of all, she found herself enjoying it. She'd never done anything like this before.

In the alley, Shio had jumped into the cart and ripped open the box, spilling out expensive coats for businessmen. These were well made with the finest material and were long enough to cover a man from shoulders to feet. Then he started calling out in high clear voice that coats were here. "Free coats!"

Two men, both from the shelter, actually came from behind a dumpster. Seeing Brittany, they immediately went for a coat. Brittany was sure they thought this was some sort of shelter project.

Shio and Brittany left the alley with the warm thanks of two grateful men ringing in their ears. After the initial success, they started going into more alleys.

In Burnhurst, the homeless liked to huddle in backstreets on cold days and nights, especially the few that ended in stone walls. These walls were built to separate the downtown area from residential zones. Downtown had five streets with narrow alleys, making a total of ten. Only a few of the alleys were open on both ends.

After a while, Brittany and Shio had lost track of time. They laughed and joked as they pushed the increasingly lighter cart from alley to alley passing out coats to any person they met there.

Finally, they were down to the last few coats. Flushed with excitement and cold, they turned down a final backstreet. This one was between a Laundromat and an Italian restaurant.

"Coats!" sang out Brittany. "Anybody there?" It looked deserted. Dumpsters surrounded by trash faced each other in the middle and at the end was a wall covered in graffiti. A pile of crushed cardboard lay at the base of the wall.

Shio suddenly let go of the cart and ran to the blue dumpster by the Laundromat.

"Look at this," he said excitedly. He pulled out a basketball and immediately dropped it to his feet and started dribbling it like a soccer ball.

"Haven't you had enough soccer today?" Brittany groaned. "I thought you were exhausted."

"Not anymore! You try it!" He passed the dirty orange ball to Brittany's feet.

"Gross," she said. Then she gave it a kick and sent it spinning past Shio, striking the Italian restaurant dumpster and rolling to the cardboard.

"Goal!" Shio shouted. "Nice shot!"

"I was trying to pass it to you," Brittany said, trying to keep from laughing. Shio's exuberance was catching. Then they heard a groan from the cardboard boxes.

"Hmmpph," groaned a deep voice.

"Oh my gosh," Brittany said. "There's somebody there!"

She and Shio ran to the boxes.

"Where are you?" Brittany shouted.

"Right here," snarled a man's voice. The top box flipped up and up popped the man from the soccer game. He was the one Brittany had seen watching Shio from behind the moms. In his hand he held a gleaming sharp knife. "Remember me, boy?"

As if shot in the heart, Shio jerked to a stop and stared. He recognized him. All his excitement had drained away, leaving a frightened boy frozen like a statue.

"Wh-who are you?" Brittany asked him.

The man ignored her. He rubbed his rough-shaven jaw and grinned coolly. His green eyes glinted with cold malice. They never left Shio.

"Last time I saw you, I gave you a bit of a shock. This time I think it best to finish the job permanently." He waved the knife menacingly. "You know, you gave us a lot of trouble disappearing like you did. Made my boss very unhappy. Worried a lot of people. A lot of people. But I wasn't one of them. Do you know why, boy?"

"We have to go," Brittany said desperately. But the boy only trembled. His face seemed to be reliving a terrible nightmare.

The man continued, almost purring like a cat. "Because I knew it would end up like this. I knew I would find you. And I did. Not smart, that soccer game, boy. But don't worry, I already knew where you were." He grinned. "I got your text."

Shio's eyes widened. Then the man lunged, ramming his knife at the boy.

"No!" screamed Brittany. She threw herself at Shio, knocking him to the side.

A sharp prick pierced her forearm. Then she was on the man. No thought registered. Her arms flailed, striking the man's face, clawing at his eyes. At the same time, her feet kicked wildly. She just wanted to destroy the person in front of her. One kick landed between the legs and the man fell back. As he did, he dropped the knife but grabbed Brittany's arm, yanking her forward.

She yelped in pain and fear, suddenly realizing what had just happened. She was in the arms of a killer.

"You stupid little—"

"Let her go!" ordered Shio's shrill voice. He sounded terrified, but also angry.

The man wrapped a strong forearm around Brittany's neck, nearly cutting off her air supply. He pressed her close to his side as his other hand clamped over her mouth, squeezing tightly. But he didn't squeeze her life away. Instead, breathing heavily, he stood still.

Brittany's terror slowly diminished enough to see why.

Chapter 16

After Brittany had knocked the knife free, Shio had pounced on it. Now he held it blade out. He stood with one foot slightly ahead of the other. His breaths were slow and steady and his face held shock, fear, and pain. The Ninja Turtle hoodie had an ugly rip on the left shoulder. Blood seeped through the rip and soaked Shio's entire arm. Brittany's lunge had saved Shio's life, but the knife had still found flesh. His hat had come off in the struggle and his hair was a wild mess. Only his eyes were calm. Deadly calm.

Brittany's own eyes went wide. She'd seen those calm eyes earlier that day, just before Shio had taken the free kick that scored a goal. All at once, she knew Shio's plan. The orange basketball rested just in front of Shio's feet.

"Drop the knife, boy," she heard the man say from above her. He smelled of coffee and cologne. There was little fear in him.

Brittany had all the fear. She tried to shake her head, but Shio wasn't looking at her. His eyes were locked on the man's face. His target. Brittany was just a human wall to get over.

"Don't drop it and I'll snap your girlfriend's neck," threatened the man. "Then what will you do? Besides bleed, I mean."

"This," the boy said. Swinging out his bleeding arm for balance, he drew back his foot while tossing the knife away.

The man had just started to laugh and press his arm into Brittany's neck when Shio's foot made contact with the ball.

Brittany shut her eyes and screamed into the man's hand.

A loud thud and an orange blur flew past Brittany, smashing the man's nose, plastering it against his face. Shio couldn't miss at that range.

Grunting, the man's head snapped back and his body crumpled to the ground. Both arms slid from Brittany and covered his injured face.

Brittany stumbled forward, just in time to catch Shio as he sagged to his knees.

His face looked chalky as he tried to grin. "That was my goal," he said faintly.

"No, Shio!" she shouted. "You have to stay awake! We need to go, come on!"

Behind them, the man blinked stupidly from where he lay. Both hands covered his face. Blood seeped through his fingers as he stared dazedly at Brittany. Then his eyes cleared. Growling like a savage dog, he started rising to his feet.

"Let's go!" Brittany shrieked. Grabbing Shio under his good arm, she pulled him up and pushed him back up the alleyway. Gasping in pain, the boy lurched into a stumbling run supported by Brittany.

The man tried to give chase, but the cardboard gave way under him and he fell on his face. His muffled screams chased after the children and were more than enough to spur them to move faster.

At the alleyway's entrance they nearly ran into a large figure waiting for them.

Mason had just escaped his mother's examination when the doorbell rang. Hastily, he yanked on his soccer jersey and went to answer it. As soon as he opened the door he knew he'd made a bad mistake.

A large bull of a man shoved the door open, knocking him to the floor.

"Where is he?" he demanded "Where is he?"

"Hey, get away!" screamed Mason, scared out of his wits. "Nobody is here!"

"Don't lie to me!" the man screamed, his eyes wild with anger. He moved into the house, standing over Mason. "I asked around and they pointed you out. The kid came with you! I followed you here and found this!" He held up a filthy jersey and pants. "I know he's here, so you'd better tell me, or else!" He raised a heavy boot to stomp on Mason. "Tell me!" he screamed.

Mason shut his eyes tight and waited for the pain.

"Get out of my house!" screamed Mrs. Tiff, charging from the kitchen, carrying her purse. "Get out of here!"

"No, Mom!" Mason shouted in alarm, opening his eyes. It was too late.

With a roar of rage, the large man went after Mrs. Tiff. He ran right into a wall of pepper spray. Mrs. Tiff had pulled a canister from her purse and unleashed it full in his face. Then she started beating his head with her purse.

"You leave my children alone, you hear! Get out! Get out, you beast!"

The attacker turned into a cowering defender as he howled in pain, clawing at his eyes. Falling to the ground, he crawled toward the door, bellowing with pain. Once he'd crawled through, bleeding from the head, Mrs. Tiff slammed the door shut. Then she sank to the floor. She weakly tossed her purse to Mason.

"Find my phone and call the police, sweetie," she said, closing her eyes. "Then kindly explain what is going on."

Mason gulped as he sat up gingerly. Taking the purse, he searched for the phone.

Still shaken, he looked up. "Mom, the phone isn't here."

Mrs. Tiff's eyes flashed open. "Where's Brittany?"

Brittany screamed, but then saw Big Murdock's face above her. Panting, she sank her face in his warm jacket.

"What are you two fools doing!" he roared. "Don't you know there're people trying to kill you!"

"We do now," Shio said shakily. He grinned faintly. "It's good to see you again, old man."

Brittany nearly sank to her knees with relief. "It was horrible," she moaned. "One of the men is back there! He … he … stabbed Shio." So shocked, she didn't think about hiding the boy's name. "I think it's bad."

Big Murdock glared into the alley. Then he stooped low. "Get on my back, boy," he growled. "Let's get out of this place."

"I'll stain your shirt," Shio said.

"Doesn't matter," Big Murdock said. "I can always get an old one. Now hop on before I stain your backside for almost getting Brittany hurt. Seems like I'm always carrying your little backside, don't it?"

Grinning, Shio rested his head on the back of Big Murdock's shoulders and let himself be lifted up. His left arm hung limp while he barely held on with his right.

Big Murdock handed Brittany his scarf and she hastily wrapped it around the bleeding arm. She looked once back in the alley, but no pursuit came. Not yet. "I th-think he's passing out," she said, shaken. Blood already saturated the scarf and covered her arm.

"Not yet," muttered Shio.

Big Murdock grunted and smacked the back of Shio's thighs hard to keep him awake. "You two are the stupidest children I've ever met," he snarled. "Giving out coats on the streets when murderers are looking for you."

"My idea," Shio said softly, his eyes shut. "Sorry."

"I think we need to call the police now," Brittany said.

"With what phone?" Big Murdock snapped.

"Back pocket," Shio answered, sounding spacey. His eyes remained closed. "Brittany, your phone … it's there. I, uh, have been using it the last couple of days …"

Brittany's eyes widened. Sure enough, she carefully reached into the back of his jeans and fished out the familiar phone. "You, you mean … You know who you are, don't you?" she said in wonder.

"Shio Slaydon?" muttered the boy. He smiled. "Michal Slaydon is my dad. He's supposed to be coming to meet us at the train station."

"What?" cried Brittany. "Why didn't he come sooner? Why didn't you tell us that?"

Shio turned his head and looked at her. "I … never told him where to find me. You're my first friend who doesn't care about my name," he said sheepishly. "I wasn't ready to leave."

Big Murdock growled. He smacked the boy's pants again, this time harder. "You are one foolish boy."

Shio only smiled.

Muttering about the stupidity of kids, Big Murdock led the way from the alley at a rapid pace. Brittany struggled to keep up as she dialed 911 on the phone.

Then she grunted in frustration. The phone had not fared well during the clash in the alley. At some point Shio had fallen on it and gave it a huge crack in the screen. Nothing happened when she tried dialing. "Great!" she said in disgust. "The phone is busted!" She jammed the useless phone in her pocket.

"Doesn't matter anymore," Big Murdock grumbled over his shoulder. "Let's just find his father." He barked out a short laugh. "That explains the coats."

"What do you mean?" Brittany asked in a small voice. "I mean, how do you know about the coats?"

"When I see my friends on the street wearing coats with price tags in the thousands, I ask questions. Soon as I didn't see you at the train station, I got worried and started searching around town. Then I saw all my comrades with brand-new Slaydon coats. They told me about you two fools passing them out like candy. Of all the stupid things to do …"

Shio chuckled from his back. "Thought it was a little funny," he whispered. "My dad would laugh."

"Not if you don't get back to him alive!" snapped Big Murdock.

Brittany bit her lip. "I'm so sorry," she muttered. "This is my fault. I should have told you your name from the beginning."

"Not as sorry as we're going to be," Big Murdock muttered. He suddenly halted and grew tense. "Look."

They'd come up on the department store. Standing in front of it were two women—the ones from the warehouse. The larger of the two brandished a short rod.

"Well, well," called the one carrying the rod. "Jack texted you were coming this way. We were waiting." She said to Big Murdock, "Give us the boy and you're free to go!"

"Who is she kidding?" Big Murdock said. Grunting, he shifted Shio around and moved him onto his shoulder. The boy appeared mostly unconscious. Big Murdock held up his hands, pinning the boy with his shoulder to keep him from falling.

"I have two injured children here," he bellowed. "Why don't you just back off and go away. The police are on their way."

"We want the boy!" the woman demanded. "The spawn of Slaydon goes with us!"

Brittany peered around Big Murdock. "What for?" she yelled, tears on her cheeks. "Why are you doing this?"

The woman looked possessed.

Big Murdock pushed her back with his hand. "Stay put," he growled. "She's crazy."

But the woman seemed to appreciate the question. She lowered her stick and lifted her head in triumph. Her eyes blazed with self-righteous indignation. "It's for justice!" she cried. "Michal Slaydon represents everything wrong with capitalist, corporate greed. He's a symbol of the downfall of our civilization!"

Big Murdock barked out a laugh. "So you torture his son? You're a loon."

"Sometimes we have to do what is necessary to get what we want!" spat the woman. "You look homeless. You should be on our side."

Old Murdock had ditched his clothes from the soccer game and now wore filthy pants and a large coat that looked as if it had been run over by a truck. A black cap covered his shorter hair. Even without his wild beard he looked like someone living on the streets. The woman appeared to be appealing only to him.

"That body you carry is more filthy in the soul than you will ever be in the body. His father is one of the elitist pigs who flaunt their money, treating the rest of us like pawns in their game to dominate the world. He's the one who caused you to be on the streets!"

"The only person who did that was me," Murdock growled. "Blaming a child is disgusting."

The other woman spoke up, sounding shrill and frightened. "The plan was to hold him for ransom, that's all."

"Or kill him if necessary," the first woman said, licking her bottom lip. The strain of the last two days showed on her haggard face. "And if we have to die in the process to get our message across, then we'll do it! The elitist pigs need to know what it feels like to suffer!"

The other woman, younger and smaller, looked horrified. She wiped her eyes and shook her head bitterly. "This isn't the way it was supposed to happen," she wailed.

"Shut it," snarled her companion. "If you hadn't let him get away so easily it would've worked! And it still will! Michal Slaydon lives like a king. He steps on people without knowing or caring. Now we will show him what it feels like!" She again raised her stick and started across the street. "Give me the boy!"

"No!" wailed the other woman. "I'm not part of this! Come back, Michelle! Think of Mom and Dad!"

Her sister snarled back. "My name is now Mandy! Our parents are elitist pigs. Now stay back, Teresa. Or I'll use this on you first!"

"Wh-what do we do?" Brittany asked, frightened. She peeked around Big Murdock as if watching a horror film. The only problem was the horror was real and coming their way.

"Start moving back and get ready to run," Big Murdock muttered grimly. "I have a feeling we know what burned the boy. That stick is dangerous. We can't face them alone."

"You're not alone, Murdock," an unfriendly sour voice said from behind them. "We're with you."

Brittany jumped and turned with relief. Fred and Myrtle stood in front of a crowd of homeless people—five in all. Many wore brand-new Slaydon coats. All of them looked angry. As one, they moved around Murdock and the children.

The large woman faltered in the road when she saw them. "You all should be with us!" she cried. "Hand over the boy!"

"You get on out of here!" Myrtle cried back at her in a voice husky from too many cigarettes. "You ain't one of anything but a piece of garbage polluting our streets! You get out!"

For a moment Mandy looked stunned. Then her anger returned. "You just don't understand! Get out of my way or you'll regret it!"

"We'll see about that," Fred growled, moving to the front to stand by Myrtle. "Try and get by us."

"If that's the way it has to be," muttered Mandy, pointing her rod and advancing to the crowd.

"No, Mandy!" screamed Teresa. "Stop it!" She charged and jumped on her sister's back. The two crashed to the pavement and started to struggle.

"I called the police!" yelled a voice from behind the women. The man from the truck at Cooligan's stood in front of the department store looking scared. "I don't know who you crazies are, but you better scram!"

"We're going to be arrested!" cried the younger woman, now beneath the other. "Didn't you hear!"

"I don't care!" yelled her sister.

"Thanks, Fred," Big Murdock said. "You too, Myrtle. Thanks to all of you. Now you all better start moving on before the police get here. They may be interested in your coats."

Myrtle laughed and slapped Brittany's back. "We did it for the kids." Then she looked worriedly at Shio. "You'd better get him to a doctor, Murdock. He don't look so good."

"That's the plan," he grunted. With Brittany at his side and Shio now cradled in his arms, he began walking around the tussling women to the man at Cooligan's.

"We have injured kids here," he called. "We need some help."

The man backed away toward the store.

"Those are the kids who stole my coats!" he shouted. "You keep back, you hear? I don't want any of your trash here! The police are coming for you too!"

Then the fighting in the street came to a sudden halt when a loud pop crackled from the rod between them and a blue electrical charge zapped both women. Jerking violently, they both lay still.

Fred, Myrtle, and the others had backed off when they heard about the police. Hearing the pop, they vanished behind the buildings.

Big Murdock and Brittany stared in surprise at the two women. The rod lay between their motionless bodies.

The man in front of the store rubbed his eyes. Then he glared at Big Murdock. "You keep back, you hear? Go away with the other riffraff. Keep the coats, but stay back!"

"The boy needs help!" Big Murdock roared.

For a moment it was a standoff. The man in front of the store glared at the larger man carrying an injured boy with a young girl leaning on his elbow. Two women lay in the street, slumped over like corpses. Sirens screamed in the distance.

Then, tires screeching, a black luxury sedan sped around the corner and slammed to a stop just in front of Big Murdock. At first he flinched, cradling the children with his body. Then he stood in confusion.

The back door flew open and Michal Slaydon tumbled out, his hair askew and eyes wild.

"Shio!" he cried.

Big Murdock instantly went to meet him.

Shio stirred and struggled to get up from Big Murdock's arms. "Dad?" he moaned.

The sirens were getting closer.

Michal Slaydon ran and grabbed his son, carrying him in his arms. He looked grimly at Big Murdock and Brittany. "You two better come with us," he said in a surprisingly soft-spoken voice. Still, it allowed no argument. "It'll save a lot of trouble. Get in the back. Quick!"

Numb, Brittany followed Big Murdock and they climbed in the back with Michal Slaydon and son. They sped from the scene with a screech of tires.

The man stood in front of the store with his mouth hanging open. It closed with a gulp. "Th-that was … that was Michal Slaydon," he told the motionless women. "I'm … so fired."

One of the women groaned.

Chapter 17

Mason and his mother fortunately didn't need to call the police. Neighbors had heard the commotion and called for them first. Deputy Donald arrived with backup to find Jon rolling around the Tiffs' front yard, moaning about being blind for life. When he tried to resist arrest, a taser added to his misery.

Teresa and her sister Mandy were taken into custody, plucked from the streets as they emerged from their shock. Neither received a full dosage, but both seemed to suffer memory loss. They wouldn't tell the police anything. Jack was later arrested when found stumbling from the alleyway with a broken nose, two black eyes, and a nasty scrape on his forehead.

Aside from assault and resisting arrest, no official charges were made public. The victims' identities were protected by order of higher-ups—the governor had called the police station personally and had politely asked for complete cooperation.

Michal Slaydon let Brittany and Big Murdock talk with authorities by cell phone to share their stories and press charges, but only under the condition that the Slaydon family name not be mentioned in any public report. They didn't want the publicity. The only question that remained was who the traitor could be.

Somebody close to Michal Slaydon, somebody in the Slaydon Arc, had orchestrated the entire incident.

This all occurred as the car sped to the Grand Burnhurst Hotel at the edge of the county. Brittany, at first, had been scared out of her wits—what if Shio's dad was part of the plot? But that fizzled quickly. Michal Slaydon held Shio tightly and clearly looked worried about his son's well-being. At the same time, he thanked Big Murdock and her for everything.

Then he had them talk on the phone—he'd been in touch with the authorities by phone the whole time. He listened closely as Brittany and Big Murdock shared their story. Shio looked content as he rested with his father. A peaceful smile spread over his face.

In the car, on the way to the hotel, Michal Slaydon apologized profusely to Brittany for not taking her directly home. He wanted his son looked at without a hospital visit. He did, though, ask for a deputy to be sent to the house with a cell phone and directions to call the Slaydons' number immediately.

The Grand Burnhurst Hotel, built in 1910, had once been busy with businessmen interested in lumber, but had since converted into a conference and resort center. Large weddings, parties, and retreats were regularly scheduled. When Michal Slaydon had first received Shio's text about being in Burnhurst, he'd immediately booked an entire floor in the hotel. The entire family would be arriving to reunite with Shio.

Before their son's text, he and his wife had lived in constant terror, fearing the worst. They hadn't publicly gone to the police but had gone to private friends in the investigation business. They hadn't turned up anything and the text proved to be the tipping point.

As soon as the car arrived at the hotel, coming to a smooth stop at a back entrance, the passenger door was opened by a tall man in a dark suit. Shio had his arm tightly wrapped with his father's coat but had lost a lot of blood. Michal Slaydon still carried him in his arms and hurried out.

"Doc's waiting in the room, Mike," the tall man said brusquely. "He's ready."

Shio's eyes opened for a moment. "Don't forget Brittany," he whispered. "She's cut too."

"Hush, son," Michal Slaydon said. "Just relax. We'll make sure everything is sorted out, yeah?" He walked briskly into the hotel.

Brittany climbed out of the car awkwardly with Big Murdock behind her. Both looked around nervously.

Tom Blazer introduced himself and shook Big Murdock's hand. He gave Brittany a gentle squeeze on the shoulder and told them how grateful he was for all their help. Then, if they would be so kind as to follow him, he would show them their rooms.

"Rooms?" Brittany asked dazedly. Big Murdock looked too surprised to even form words.

"You don't think the heroes of the hour are going to be sent away without proper thanks, do you?" Tom asked in mock surprise. "Come with me, please." Turning, he left no time to argue as he led both Brittany and Big Murdock to the grandest rooms either had ever seen.

They went past the spacious lobby and straight to the elevators. Nobody spoke a word. Everything Brittany saw was startling. A large Christmas tree dominated the lobby in front of the desk. Surrounded by couches and chairs, it shimmered with gold tinsel and colorful lights. Green holly lined shiny white walls and a fire crackled merrily behind the tree.

Santa must live here, she thought.

Then they were through the golden doors of the elevator, operated by a red uniformed kid a few years older than her. He looked at her like he'd seen Santa Claus.

Tom told the kid the floor and up they went.

Big Murdock was given a room around the corner of the elevator on the fifth floor and was left there to shower and change. When he'd asked what to change into since he had no other clothes, he was told politely not to worry. All Tom needed were sizes and a new wardrobe would be sent up before he finished his shower.

Brittany was then taken to a room at the end of the hall. Her weary feet sank into thick red carpet and all the doorknobs had the look of shiny gold.

Tom Blazer coughed. "This will be your room, Miss Tiff, but before I leave you there, you're to come in this one."

"Wh-what for?" Brittany asked in wonder. Her eyes were ready to pop out of her head. She couldn't believe this could be happening. Hours earlier she thought she was going to die. Now she felt as if she was in Christmas heaven. Maybe she did die back there in the alley.

"Young Shio mentioned you may have been cut and you certainly do have enough, er, blood on you. He's in there now being looked over by Doctor Robbard. Don't worry, he's one of the best sports doctors in the world and cut my knee open twice before. He knows what he's doing. You see, we don't want any fuss by going to the public hospital, so Mike called the doctor here."

Brittany nodded slowly. So she hadn't died. For the first time, she was aware of a dull throbbing pain in her arm. Looking down, she saw her sleeve encrusted with dried blood. Earlier, she'd thought it had been from Shio, but then she remembered the prick when she'd dove at the knife.

Tom opened the door across from Brittany's room and ushered her in.

Inside, Michal Slaydon leaned idly against a marble counter talking on his phone. Seeing Brittany, his eyes lit up and he gave her a genuine smile. "You came just in time," he said. "It's your mum on the phone."

Brittany took the phone gingerly. It was a smartphone and the size of a paperback book. "Uh, hello?"

Her mom immediately started balling on the other end.

Michal Slaydon and Tom Blazer graciously moved farther into the room to give her privacy.

Brittany told her mom everything, apologizing for not telling her earlier.

Her mom just cried harder when she'd finished.

"*My baby is a hero,*" she sobbed through the phone. "*I can't believe it … I guess they told you already. They want you to spend two nights there and I said that was fine if you wanted.*"

Brittany's eyes widened. "Uh, I guess …" Why spend two nights, she wondered.

"They're nice people. You know, your dad used to watch Michal Slaydon play a lot on TV. He'd be proud of you."

Mason's voice called out in the background. *"I can't believe you left without me! How come I'm not there?"*

"Be quiet, Mason!" yelled her mom's voice.

Brittany and her mom shared their stories and ended their conversation with Brittany apologizing for hiding a boy in the house the last couple of days. Her mom just said, *"And I thought I met an angel yesterday … I guess I live with one instead. I'm never going to drink anything stronger than coffee from now on. That's a promise."*

Brittany didn't quite know what she was talking about, but it sounded good to her.

After ending the call, she brought the phone shyly back to Michal Slaydon. The room was more like a luxury apartment. Behind the marble counter was a small kitchen and Michal Slaydon and Tom sat in a large carpeted room with couches, soft comfy chairs and a huge television. An open door on the left led to an equally fancy bedroom.

"Wh-where's Shio?" she asked.

Michal Slaydon nodded to a closed door on the right. "The doctor is putting in stitches in the bathroom," he said, grinning. He was surprisingly soft spoken with a gentle voice. His English accent was much stronger than Shio's. "I hear it's thanks to you it's only in his arm." He lost his grin and stood up in front of her. "Truly, I'm grateful. My whole family is grateful."

"And so am I," Tom added. "Anything you need, you let us know, yeah?"

Brittany nodded dumbly, ducking her head in embarrassment.

Michal Slaydon guided her to a chair. "Now let's take a look at your arm, shall we?"

Brittany rolled up her sleeve to uncover an arm sticky with blood. Thankfully it proved to only be a minor cut.

Still, the doctor, a short, portly man with a round face and thinning hair, gave it a good look after finishing with Shio.

"Thirty-six stiches," he announced, leaving the bathroom, "but there should be almost no scar. Poor boy is broken up about it.

He's all set for a shower and then I have pills to help him sleep, just in case. He'll need his rest for tomorrow."

Michal Slaydon nodded his thanks and changed places with the doctor. He went to tend his son, while the doctor looked at Brittany.

"It's not much," Brittany said, embarrassed at the attention.

"Saving a life is never a little thing," the doctor said gently as he washed her arm with stinging soap. "I try my best to do it for a profession, but you've done it for a friend. And you did very nicely tending to his burn, I might add. It's healing well." He winked. "Perhaps when you're older you can become a doctor like me." He saw Brittany's look of disbelief and looked her in the eye. "I mean it. My dear, you are one very special young lady."

Tom smiled. "And a very popular one. You'd better get your rest too. You have a busy day tomorrow."

Brittany looked up at him. "Uh, what do you mean? What's tomorrow?"

"Oh, didn't Mike tell you?" Tom said innocently. "The annual Slaydon Charity Ball has been moved to here and rescheduled for tomorrow night. I believe Shio has you for his date. That is, unless you decide to turn him down. I know he has a couple older brothers dying to meet you. They will be arriving tonight with their mother."

Brittany's jaw dropped. This was most unexpected. Suddenly she felt faint.

After the doctor confirmed she had no need of stitches, he applied ointment and bandaged it tightly. "Keep it clean and dry," he told her, giving her a couple of waterproof bandage covers. "And do talk to me in a few years if you decide you want to be a doctor. We can always use more people with steady nerves."

Promising to return the next day to check on his patients, the doctor said his goodbyes and left. Tom was about to suggest that Brittany go get cleaned up, but the girl, exhausted and bewildered, had her eyes already sliding shut.

She didn't open them again until Michal Slaydon carried Shio out. Shio wore brand-new soccer pajamas and had a blue sling on his left arm. Either the pills were already taking effect or he was exhausted from a long day and blood loss. Still, he managed a grin for Brittany before going off to bed.

Still stunned, Brittany went to her room, which she found just as nice and had all to herself. A plate of two thick ham sandwiches, a salad, and a glass of cold soda sat on the table. In all the excitement, she had completely forgotten about eating. Now ravenous, she scarfed down the food and thought it the best she'd ever eaten.

After, feeling totally exhausted but determined to clean up and change, she went straight through her bedroom to a luxurious bathroom the size of her own bedroom at home. She spent a long time under the hot water in the tub, soaking it all in while making sure to keep her bandage dry.

Leaving the bathroom wrapped in towels, she found a white nightgown and fresh underclothes, somehow just her size, waiting on her bed. It all had been delivered straight to her bed when she'd been in Shio's room.

Changing quickly, she took just enough time to brush her teeth with a brand-new toothbrush she found lying on the sink with complimentary toothpaste. Finally, with heavy eyes, she collapsed on the giant bed, the size of a small swimming pool. She barely touched the soft, soft mattress before floating off to sleep. It had been a long, terrible day, but an amazingly glorious night.

Sunlight just started drifting into the window, announcing the dawn of a new day, when her eyes opened next. For a moment, she'd forgotten where she was, but then she saw the fancy quilt and blankets. It all came back. She was with the Slaydon family in the nicest hotel in the county. And she was supposed to go to a ball that night.

She nearly fell out of bed.

Emerging from the bedroom shortly after, she found a pile of clothes her size stacked on a couch. She guessed her mom had supplied the sizes. Everything was much nicer than anything she'd ever had before. Soon she saw why. They were all from the Natasha Slaydon line.

After a long, hot shower, still being careful of her bandage, she left her room and wondered where to go. From across the hall she heard the sounds of laughter and hooting and hollering. She was about to retreat back into her room when she saw a note taped on the door.

Brittany, if you're reading this, please come in. We want to meet you.
It was signed simply, *the boys.*

Nervous, she tentatively knocked.
"Come in!" called a muffled male voice. "The door is open!"
Brittany hoped she was doing the right thing when she timidly stepped in. The kitchen area was empty, but there were plates on the counter full of crumbs. Glasses of orange juice littered a table behind the couch.
"Uh, hello?" she called out.
"In here!" called the voice.
She went to the bedroom and found what looked to be the remains of a small war.
Two beds had once dominated the room but had been taken over by the Slaydon brothers. One bed was completely bare. Pillows, sheets, and blankets were strewn all over the place. Shio still slept on the other bed. Everyone else was wide awake. One boy, a few years older than Brittany, lay across two pillows focused intently on a flat-screen TV. He was engaged in a fierce match with an older teen, who sat comfortably on the bed in front of Shio's sleeping form. A little kid about five sat on the floor and cheered every move.
Brittany saw they were playing FIFA, a soccer video game, on an Xbox. Everything looked brand new.
Seeing her, the older teen paused the game and gave quick introductions. He was Marcus and his opponent was Zeon. The little guy gave the name of Chris.
"You must be Brittany," Zeon said, getting to his feet. He ran a quick hand through his hair. Chris and Shio still wore pajamas, but the elder Slaydons both wore designer jeans. Zeon had a

collared striped pullover, while Marcus sported a bright red Liverpool hoodie.

Brittany shyly shook Zeon's hand. "Uh, nice to meet you."

"It's the opposite," Zeon said. "Dad told us everything."

Brittany grimaced. "I just wish it didn't have to happen."

"Yeah, but," Marcus said cheerfully, "thanks to you, Shio survived and you brought our family together. I was supposed to spend the holidays in Sweden before all this."

"Yeah, and I didn't want to go near the ball," Zeon added. "Now it should be a blast."

Chris interrupted. "Aren't you guys going to finish the game? I want to see what Dad does next."

"Nothing special, like always," Marcus said.

"We'll see about that!" Zeon shot back. He grabbed his controller and looked up at Brittany. "We like to use Dad's characters in all the games."

"I don't," Marcus said with a huff. "I always try to injure him."

"Are you buffoons done?" growled Shio, glaring from his bed. He sat up tiredly. "Can't sleep with all the shouting."

Zeon laughed. "Whatever! You slept for over eleven hours! We've been here since last night and you never moved until now!"

Shio tossed his pillow at him with his good arm. "That's because I kept hoping you idiots would leave." He grinned when he saw Brittany. "So you met my brothers," he said. "Sorry."

Brittany nodded. She wasn't sure if she should leave or not, but then wasn't given the chance.

"Here," Zeon said, passing his controller to her. "You play."

"I never played before!" she protested.

"Chris will help you," Zeon called, leaving the room. "I have to go get the little invalid his medicine. Mum's orders."

Marcus chuckled. "I'll go easy on you," he promised. He'd scored two goals by the time Zeon returned with pills and a glass of water.

"Here you are," Zeon said, "you big baby."

Shio made a face at him. "Just because they want me to be a model and not you, you're jealous." He took the water and pills.

Zeon laughed. "Just don't start practicing here. I heard they want you to model underwear."

Shio swallowed the pills and drank some water. The remaining water he threw in his brother's face.

"Hey, you punk!" Zeon leapt on the bed and the two brothers started wrestling. "Not fair, you have a bum arm!" he protested. "I can't pin you."

"You're just a bum!" Shio said.

"Knock it off," Marcus said, sounding bored. "Hey, Shio, get off your bum and come help Brittany. Chris is getting her destroyed."

Marcus and Zeon looked very similar, with wider faces, stockier builds, and more relaxed features than Shio. Chris was more like a combination of all three of his older brothers. In any case, all were nice looking and Brittany still had a hard time believing they were being so nice to her.

She kept waiting for one of them to start picking on her and mocking her lack of video game ability. Instead they only offered encouragement.

"This game is so hard," she cried when Marcus scored again.

"You should see Shio with two hands. He's the real pro," Marcus told her. "Let's see how he does with one hand."

"Better than you," Shio assured him. He climbed from his bed and told Chris to scoot.

At first, Brittany and Shio were way out of sync. Using his good hand, Shio controlled the players' movements and told Brittany when she should pass or shoot. She kept getting the buttons mixed up, providing many moments of hilarity. Zeon and Chris became their cheerleaders and offered lots of advice. They'd just managed to get the hang of it enough to get a shot away when Michal Slaydon poked his head in.

"What are my boys doing corrupting this fair maiden?" he asked. He sniffed. "And how does she stand the smell?"

"Ah, Dad, grab a controller and start playing. Let's see how good you really are," Marcus said in a challenge.

The former soccer star needed no further urging, especially when he saw he got to control his own character. Brittany and Shio sat side by side watching.

Everyone laughed when the video-game Slaydon scored on a bicycle volley from thirty yards out.

"How come you never did that in real life?" Chris wanted to know.

His dad grunted. "I don't want to teach my boys to be cheeky, that's why," he answered. "Besides, I always save my best moves for video games. Now, after this half we're all going downstairs for breakfast. Got it?"

"Ahem," said a voice at the door. A slender woman with stunning looks poked her head in. "Dear, I hate to break up your midlife crisis, but it's getting late. I sent you to get everyone fifteen minutes ago. Maria and I are ready for breakfast."

Michal Slaydon looked hurt. "Midlife crisis?" he said. "I'm in my prime! I just scored my fourth of the game!"

"Dear, remember," said his wife with a smile, "we have a lot to do today. You have to make sure the organizers get here and I have to take Brittany shopping." The woman turned her smile at Brittany. "I'm Natasha Slaydon," she said smoothly. "I hope you're ready for a big day. We have lots to do, you and I."

Brittany stared up at the woman and didn't know what to say. According to Melissa, Natasha was cold and aloof. She remembered that there was supposed to be divorce talks and wondered if she was caught in a family squabble.

Michal Slaydon quickly put down the controller and got to his feet. "Sorry, love," he said giving his wife a hug and quick kiss. "I had to show the boys their old man still had the moves."

"You better show them on the dance floor tonight," Natasha said with a smirk. She turned back to Brittany. "Are you ready to come?" she asked her. "Maria is coming too, so the boys will have to fend for themselves. If such a thing is possible."

Zeon pretended to cheer. "Pizza for lunch!"

"Wh-where are we going?" Brittany asked.

Natasha's smile grew wider, showing off sparkling white teeth. Brittany could see where Shio got a lot of his good looks. "Tell me, have you ever been to New York City?"

Chapter
18

Less than an hour later, Brittany, full of eggs, pancakes, and hot chocolate, found herself sitting in the back of a sedan with Natasha Slaydon. Maria Slaydon, a hyper seven-year-old, sat between them in a booster seat and talked nonstop, asking Brittany all sorts of questions. It would be a long trip—hours of driving, but Brittany was grateful for the questions. She didn't feel comfortable talking alone with Shio's mom. Unfortunately, Maria drifted off to sleep after the second hour.

That left only the two of them to talk.

After some silence, Natasha looked over at Brittany and smiled. "I'm sure you think we're all mad," she said with a tight laugh. Her voice was pleasant but slightly throaty, with a tinge of Russian mixed with her English accent. "You must understand. We're all terribly grateful for what you have done and we want to thank you." She held up her hand when Brittany made to protest. "Not only that," she continued, "but we must keep up appearances. Nobody must know how close we came to losing one of our children. It's nobody's business and can only bring more trouble. That is why this ball must go on." She stared pointedly at Brittany. "Already there are these stories about Shio appearing in a local soccer game. And about his mysterious girlfriend. One such story is how they worked together to pass out coats to the homeless."

Brittany gulped and licked her lips nervously. "Oh, uh, I …"

Natasha laughed kindly. "There's no need to be sorry. It's perfectly okay. Those stories bring good publicity. We just don't want the bad stories to leak out. It may inspire other attempts, or even more gossip. Now, this night is to show the world everything is okay in the Slaydon world and also to celebrate Shio's return and the brave girl who saved him. You will look stunning tonight. I promise."

Brittany soon lost all fear of Natasha Slaydon. The reports on her were completely wrong. She'd gone out of her way, without looking for approval and without any ceremony, to donate large sums of money to every red bucket collecting donations for the poor. They went from shop to shop, trying on dresses and mostly talking and laughing. For lunch, Brittany had her first New York pizza. The sun had sunk behind the trees when they'd returned from their trip. The ball would start in a few hours and there was still lots to do.

A hotel worker carried all Brittany's packages to her room and she quickly cleaned up. Then it was time to get ready for the ball.

Brittany had never considered herself pretty. Her spindly arms and legs never seemed to be in sync with the rest of her body and her lips were too big. But all that had changed. After she'd put on her dress, Natasha had come to her room to fix her up. Now she admired the effects in a mirror.

Her dark brown, almost black skin glowed with a rich caramel color. Her thick dark hair had been put up in a dainty fashion, a single curled strand dangling by her right cheek. The teal blue dress wrapped her body in a gentle hug, leaving her shoulders bare except for a pair of sparkly straps. Sleeves with sparkles covered her arms, hiding the bandage. Makeup and eye shadow brought out her high cheekbones and golden brown eyes while making her lips and nose appear delicate and smooth. She could not believe the image in the mirror could be her.

"I'm beautiful," she whispered, almost in disbelief.

"You certainly are," Natasha Slaydon said, standing in the door watching her. "Now let's show the rest of the world."

The charity ball was held at the formal ballroom located in a separate building behind the hotel. Getting there meant crossing a courtyard and walking a long walk to the main doors. The walkway had been covered in a red carpet and on either side were a mob of photographers. Mixed in were autograph seekers and the curious.

Brittany stared out the window across the courtyard at the ballroom and shuddered. She didn't think she could do it. All those people would be looking at her. Judging her. She'd seen at least five news trucks drive past and vaguely wondered if Melissa were watching the event on cable.

Probably, she thought. The local news would certainly be covering it. Her heart beat wildly in her chest.

It was amazing the changes twenty-four hours could bring. Just a day ago, she had arrived at the back of the hotel covered in blood. Now she would leave through the same doors covered in a fairy-tale dress with a prince at her side. Her stomach started to churn.

She was deciding to go back up to her room when the elevator rang behind her and opened to reveal Shio Slaydon. He'd gotten a haircut for the occasion—spiked in the front and cut short on the sides, it highlighted his smooth thin face, dominated by his wide smile. Even his eyes seemed to smile when he saw Brittany. He wore a tailored tuxedo with a black bowtie. Pulling out flowers from behind him, he offered them to Brittany. His sling had been removed, but his left arm hung loosely at his side.

Brittany took the flowers and ducked her head shyly. "Thanks," she said.

"You look fantastic," Shio told her, flashing a smile. "Brilliant."

Brittany hid her face behind the flowers. "Oh, uh, so do you," she stammered. Then she sniffed. "Do these flowers have peppermint?" she asked, making a face.

A strong minty odor hung in the air, threatening to make her eyes water.

Shio pursed his lips and rolled his eyes. "That's my dad's Christmas cologne," he confessed. "Zeon dumped some down my shirt before I came down."

"Oh. Well, it's, uh, nice."

"Yeah? Is that what you really 'mint'?" Shio asked, grinning. "No worries. I sprayed my mum's perfume all over his collar first. He's the one that smells like fruity flowers."

Brittany stifled a laugh. It was hard to be self-conscious around the Slaydons.

"Should we go?" Not waiting for an answer, Shio pushed the door open and gestured toward the bright lights and red carpet. Suddenly, it was time to be self-conscious.

Flashbulbs exploded in front of them like fireworks on a holiday. It felt to Brittany like stepping in front of a firing squad. For a moment, she froze.

Shio's hand gently guided her shoulders forward as he held the door open.

"Don't worry," he whispered as she went by, keeping her head pointed toward the red carpet. "You look smashing. Just pretend they're part of a movie and we're just characters walking by."

She nodded. Natasha had already coached her to smile and say nothing until they made it past the carpet. Once inside, no media were allowed and only invited guests could enter.

Taking a deep breath, she lifted her head and walked on. Shio fell beside her, brushing her arm with his sleeve.

"Having fun yet?" he muttered. Grinning, he kept his gaze pointed forward.

And all at once, Brittany was having fun. The walk across the carpet with Shio linking her arm with his passed by in a blur. She was vaguely aware of the flashes and questions thrown their way, but she held her head high and kept a smile on her face.

Shio guided her calmly through, stopping them once to pose for a picture just before entering the ball. Then it was over.

Leaving the red carpet walk felt like a calm breath of fresh air after stepping out of a hurricane. Gentle music greeted them, as well as a well-dressed young man leading them to the main event.

"Hope you enjoy parties," Shio muttered to her. "Mum puts on the best."

Shio's mom did not disappoint. Brittany had the most magical night of a real Christmas ball, with little expense spared. Shio, unfortunately, couldn't stay long. He only remained long enough for a brief appearance, which included a dance with Brittany, before doctor's orders sent him off to bed. Before he left, he drew Brittany to the side and whispered to her.

"You're a real friend, Brittany. I won't forget that. Thanks for everything." He gave her a quick kiss on the cheek and said goodnight.

Brittany had no time to miss him. The rest of the Slaydons, minus Chris and Maria, who were deemed too young, arrived and Zeon became her new date.

Zeon, looking as handsome as ever in his tux with a red carnation, never left her side. Smelling strongly of flowers, courtesy of Shio and his mom's perfume, he pointed out several actors and actresses in the crowd, many whom Brittany had never heard of before. All were happy to meet her and very curious about the mysterious beauty linked with the Slaydons. She spoke very little and just soaked in the experience.

Mrs. Slaydon had truly worked a miracle. In less than a day, she had everything moved from New York to tiny Burnhurst and turned the ballroom into a Christmas paradise. A live orchestra and singers provided music on a center stage surrounded by about fifty lit Christmas trees. On the edges of the floor were tables full of refreshments and enough food to feed an army. Chairs and smaller tables for eating were on the far side, all decorated with poinsettias and candles. The remaining space was for dancing. Artificial snow dropping during the snow waltz was just one of the many highlights of the evening.

The real highlight, or lowlight, depending upon how you looked at it, came around midnight.

Tom Blazer had pulled Michal Slaydon to the side and whispered something to him. Zeon and Brittany were sharing a small table with cream soda and snacks and saw the exchange.

When Michal Slaydon hastily put down his champagne glass and followed Tom, Zeon stood and offered his hand to Brittany. "Come on," he said grimly. "Let's see what this is about," he said.

Brittany had never yet seen Michal Slaydon look so grim. She allowed herself to be dragged after the two men. They entered a small door on the far wall and went down a short hallway. When Zeon and Brittany arrived, they saw Michal Slaydon pulling off his jacket and loosening his tie. These were tossed aside on a chair. He looked to be readying for a fight.

"This is where the workers are having a party," Zeon whispered. "Something must've happened."

He hurried after his father down a hall that curved around several more rooms before reaching a small office door.

Tom and Michal entered the office and slammed the door. Zeon put his ear on the door and motioned Brittany to do the same.

She shook her head, too afraid. Just then the door was yanked open and Tom glared out. Seeing Zeon and Brittany, his face softened.

"I thought we were being followed by journalists," he said, smiling grimly. "But I think it's okay for you two to come in. Just don't say a word, yeah?"

He ushered Zeon and Brittany inside and shut the door again, locking it. The office was much more spacious than Brittany thought it would be.

Just inside the door were two rows of three chairs each facing a large varnished desk. Behind the desk, eight large stately chairs surrounded a gleaming circular table. At the moment, only one chair was occupied. A man with thinning hair sat with his head bowed low holding a pack of ice to his eye.

An older man loomed over him, shaking with anger. Michal Slaydon stood on the other side of the sitting man, looking ready to send his face through the table. Four uniformed policemen stood on the far wall with two men in suits.

"That's Luke," Zeon whispered in surprise to Brittany, nodding at the man at the table. "He works for my mum and dad as a driver."

They stayed just inside the door by the desk. Tom remained with them.

"He's the one who tried to get Shio," he muttered grimly to the children.

"But why?" Zeon asked, shaking his head in disbelief. "That makes no sense."

Tom motioned them back outside the office and had them sit in comfortable chairs down the hall. Then he proceeded to tell them.

"Turns out there's much more to Luke than we ever knew," Tom began. He sat in an easy chair facing Brittany and Zeon. "You two have the right to know this, but I trust you both to tell nobody. Brittany, like it or not, you have proven yourself to be trustworthy. You're part of the Slaydon Arc now. Luke used to be." He sighed and rubbed his bald head.

"Our investigators discovered something about him we never knew. His father was a big Liverpool fan and Michal Slaydon supporter. But he treated his own son, Luke, pretty badly. Apparently, he used to beat Luke and tell him to be more like Michal Slaydon. Luke didn't play football—or soccer to you, Brittany—too well and grew to hate the game. Especially, he hated Mike Slaydon. His dad kept badgering Luke to be more like Slaydon. Life is sometimes a bugger. Luke spent most of his growing up being compared to Mike and never coming close to living up to his father's expectations. Luke's hatred for Slaydon grew. It got to the point where he started obsessing about revenge. When his father passed away, the only target left for his revenge was Michal Slaydon. He spent most of his adult life planning harm for Mike—fantasizing about it." Tom paused to take a deep breath.

"Then, when he got a job working for the Slaydons, almost by magic, his fantasy revenge started to become real. He finally decided the best way to get payback was through his children. He wanted a Slaydon boy to suffer like he'd suffered as a child. Zeon and Marcus were his first targets, but then he settled on Shio because of his love of football. Getting Shio was like double revenge—it hurt football and Mike.

"Luke slowly built up his trust and started getting others on board for his scheme. He met Mandy, Teresa's sister, online and used her extremist views for his own gain. He even dated both Mandy and Teresa without letting the other know about it. Teresa's sister was easily persuaded to help take down a rich symbol like Slaydon. She was convinced to reconnect with her sister and persuade her to help."

"How could Teresa be so stupid?" Zeon asked. "She was our teacher! She taught us to think stuff through."

Tom shook his head. "Teresa … she was blinded by a false love, I'm afraid. The other men were just guys he found in the gutter and trying to grow drugs on their farm. He bankrolled his crew and scheme using your father's generous salary. He thought that added to the laugh."

"H-how did you find this out?" Zeon asked, shaken.

Tom grunted. "The investigators uncovered some of it. The rest he couldn't wait to tell us." Tom sighed and wiped his face. "He spied on your dad's text messages. That was how he knew where to find you, Brittany. Shio had texted about a soccer game, and then later about meeting up at the train station. Luke went out with his goons to the only soccer tournament in the county, and when that didn't work, he sent his goons to intercept you and Shio on the way to the train station. It almost succeeded."

For a moment nobody spoke.

"What a poor man," Brittany finally said softly. "I feel sorry for him."

Zeon made a face. "Poor man? That guy is a nut!"

Tom grimaced. "He held in a lot of hate for a very long time and never let it out until it destroyed him. He was the one who leaked information about your parents fighting, Zeon. He wanted to create a distraction to move in with taking Shio. The whole thing was orchestrated by him."

"No wonder Granddad wants to destroy him," Zeon muttered, shaking his head in disbelief.

Tom smiled without humor. "Your granddad flew all the way out from California when he heard the news. He wanted to see the man who caused all the harm and to see Shio safe. First thing he did, though, was pop Luke in the face."

Tom stood and stretched his back. "At least you two know it's now over. Nobody else is out there trying to do harm. The family is safe. Let's get you back to the party. Don't worry about Luke. He confessed and the police will take him away. One day the press might find out about it, but not tonight."

Brittany returned to the ball with Zeon feeling a mixture of relief, revulsion, and sadness. The ball lost some of its luster and not long after, she asked to go back to the hotel.

Zeon walked her from the party all the way to her hotel door and gave her a hug. On the way, he'd told her about Luke's conversation in the mall shortly before the kidnapping attempt.

"That was when he chose Shio over me," he'd said, sounding sick. "I … I can't believe it."

After the hug, Brittany squeezed his hand. "Remember what you said to me earlier," she said. "All this terrible stuff … it brought your family together. Don't forget that. It's not your fault."

Zeon grinned tightly. "Yeah. Mum and Dad were fighting just a few days ago and thinking about not doing Christmas together. Now I can't even remember what they were fighting over."

Brittany couldn't help but smile. "Maybe it was over your mom's perfume. It, uh, smells pretty good."

Zeon lost his grin. "That Shio … I'll get him for that." Then he lifted his eyebrows. "Does it really smell good?" He couldn't help but smile when Brittany burst out laughing. "Well, cheers. See you later, right?"

Brittany hated to do it, but she bade Zeon goodnight and closed the door on her fairy tale. As she got ready for bed, the giddy feeling of indescribable happiness never left.

Her dreams didn't come close to topping her magical day and night.

Extra Time

Chapter 19

Early the next morning, a few days before Christmas Eve, a black limo pulled up outside the Tiff house. A black-hatted driver hurried from his seat and opened the far back door. Tom Blazer came out first, pulling a brand-new suitcase packed with new clothes. Brittany followed him, carrying her dress from the ball wrapped in a bag. All the Slaydon children were back in the hotel and she hadn't had a chance to say a proper goodbye, but it was probably better this way. They lived in their world and she had her world.

Michal Slaydon stepped out last. He put his hands on Brittany's shoulders and thanked her again, then said his final goodbyes and returned to the car. Standing with her suitcase and dress in the front of her drive, she watched the limo go to the end of the street and turn slowly around before heading back to the hotel. She waved a final goodbye and then sighed.

A jogging neighbor had come to a complete stop and had watched the whole thing. He stared unabashedly at Brittany.

Ignoring him, she took her things and started for her house. She couldn't ignore the shrieking coming from the house up the road from her. Melissa, in pink pajamas and a bathrobe, wearing bunny slippers on her feet, sprinted toward her.

"I can't believe you didn't tell me!" she screamed. "Y-you were there! I, I saw you on TV." She slipped and fell on the icy dew of Brittany's lawn so it looked as if she had thrown herself at Brittany' feet.

"Oh, you wouldn't believe it," she gushed. "You were on TV!"

Brittany looked away embarrassed. The jogger still hadn't moved on. He looked to be trying to take her picture with a cell phone.

"Get up, Melissa," she nearly growled. "I would believe it. I was there." She ducked her head and covered her face to block any picture.

Melissa grabbed Brittany's arms as she stood. "No," she gasped. "The TV, they didn't know who you were. Some thought you were a princess from Africa, others thought the daughter of somebody famous. Brittany!" she wailed. "The world saw you with Shio!" She looked about to cry. "He was here, wasn't he?"

"I did call yesterday," Brittany told her gently. "But it's okay." She grinned. "If you must know, Shio is really great. He's an awesome friend, but a little young for me." Brittany didn't mention Zeon. He was only a couple of years older …

Melissa only looked more stricken. "I … I just don't believe it … The whole school probably saw you last night. If not yet, they will."

"Goodbye, Melissa. I'm really tired and want to go home and see my mom."

Melissa gave her a funny look. "Why did the police come yesterday and arrest that guy? Was it about Shio?"

Brittany pretended to look puzzled. "Not at all. Shio was long gone when that happened. That guy was just some crazy. Now goodbye."

She could smell pancakes cooking from the house and just wanted to be inside. After spending time with the Slaydons, she longed to be with her own family. Yes, the Tiffs and Slaydons were different, but they had what counted in common. They had family love.

Brittany had called ahead to let her mom know she would be there. Michal Slaydon had let Mrs. Tiff keep the cell phone … and had left a generous compensation for all the time his son spent at her house. It was so generous, in fact, that Mrs. Tiff had called Cooligan's Department Store to let them know, since she was being fired after the holidays, she'd rather leave early, as in now.

This proved unfortunate for the store. After the press reports of Slaydons' ball at the Grand Burnhurst Hotel, and that the store had been the source of clothing for the Slaydon Homeless Giveaway, it had become a hub for business. Shoppers from New York City and all over were flocking to the store for their Christmas shopping. Mrs. Tiff was offered a position as a manger, but only after the holidays. She was granted a week's vacation, all paid of course. She said she would think about it.

When Brittany reached her door, she turned and saw Melissa still standing in her pink slippers.

"What now?" she asked through gritted teeth.

Melissa slowly lifted her eyes and swallowed. "Merry Christmas."

Shio woke up in a soft bed feeling strange. Everything felt hazy … Slowly he became aware of his younger brother Christopher next to him, watching a cartoon on the tele. He lay on his belly, propped up on his elbows, supporting his chin in his hands and looking quite bored.

"You sleep too long," Christopher said accusingly, looking over at Shio. "You missed breakfast."

Shio threw his pillow at him with his good arm, blinking sleepily. He'd taken a pill on doctor's orders and had slept like a log. "Where's Mason?" he asked groggily. Then he remembered he no longer stayed at that house.

Christopher gave him a funny look. "Who?"

"I mean Brittany." He stretched out in the bed, careful to make sure his wounded arm was resting on his chest. It felt stiff and a little sore. His "good" arm still had the burn, but it was just a mark now. Brittany had taken good care of it. "Is she awake?"

"She left with Dad some time ago, Shio. You were sleeping."

"What?" Shio sat up with a start, ignoring the aches in his arm and body. The bruises from the soccer game, mixed with those from the alleyway, left him feeling like a soccer ball after a big match—kicked all over the place. "She left without saying goodbye?"

"Yeah. Dad said she needed to get home because her mum would be mad." Then he grinned. "And guess what? Mum and Dad said we're all going to England for Christmas. All of us. Even Marcus with his girlfriend."

Shio shot out of bed and hastily grabbed jeans and a shirt. A short time later, he emerged from the bathroom fully dressed, but his hair was an unruly mess.

"Where are you going?" Christopher called as he ran from the room.

Shio had no idea. He ended up coming out of the elevator to the hotel lobby. Visitors were just stirring—many were guests from the party the previous night.

Then he saw Granddad sitting at a table in front of the tree with a mug of coffee.

Ignoring the stares, he crossed the lobby and slumped in a seat across from his granddad.

"Good morning, sleepyhead," his grandfather greeted him. "You don't look so happy to be up. Feel okay?"

"Like I've been run over by a center back," Shio admitted. He blinked rapidly, surprised to feel tears. "Granddad, did Dad really take Brittany back?"

Granddad put down the coffee and pushed aside the newspaper he'd been reading. "I take it you became friends with her, yes?"

Shio nodded glumly. "She ... she saved me. And she didn't even know who I was at first."

"Sounds like you found a true friend, Shio." Granddad sighed. "Unfortunately, she is from a different place than us."

"So what?" Shio demanded. "I mean, I ... I think I miss her. Granddad, the whole time I felt scared out of my mind, except when with her. She ... she made everything feel safe." He frowned and wiped his eyes.

Granddad looked at him gently. "She sounds like a good person, Shio. Somebody who thinks about others and doesn't just react to them. Did she play good football with you?"

Shio managed a grin. "Absolute rubbish."

Granddad reached over and rubbed his unruly hair. "Good thing no photographers are here right now. You better go back up and take a hot shower. Then we talk more while you eat."

"Chris says we're going to England," Shio said. "Is that right?"

"Your parents want to have a family Christmas with all of us together, Shio. That is something our family needs right now." Granddad's eyes twinkled. For a moment, he looked a lot like St. Nick. "But you go up and shower. I'll speak to your mum about what we really need. Perhaps before we go we can send a present to your friend, yes?"

Chapter 20

Christmas started for Brittany like any other day. She was the first to rise and so had to turn on the heat and prepare breakfast. Memories of the Slaydon ball would be fresh for her for a long time. Since that Monday, journalists, agents, and even people from TV shows tried stopping by to ask for an interview. They'd all wanted to call, but nobody knew their number. Brittany refused to see them and, after Mrs. Tiff called Deputy Donald a few times, the harassment had stopped. At least it stopped for Christmas. Hopefully it would be for good.

Like usual, they had no tree and no presents. As Brittany gathered materials for oatmeal, she caught herself thinking of the Slaydons again. She wondered if she would ever see Shio again, or Zeon. And she wondered if they ever wanted to see her again.

Melissa had suddenly become her best friend again and provided her with all the latest Slaydon updates. She'd even invited Brittany for a New Year's party the following week. Brittany doubted she would go. But maybe. In any case, the day before Melissa had told Brittany that all the Slaydons had flown out for England, to spend Christmas there. They wouldn't return to California until January.

Perhaps to keep her mind off the ache in her chest, she switched on the radio to Christmas carols. The radio, like a lot of things in the house, was bought with the Slaydon compensation fund. So at least some good had come from helping Shio Slaydon, she thought cynically.

Still, she knew she would do it all over again. She stared out the window and was surprised to see snow falling. Immediately, she thought of the homeless and was glad the shelter was open all day for Christmas. They would all be there, except for one.

Big Murdock, now back to being Derek Murdock, had moved on. He'd been hired by the Slaydon family to replace Luke. He'd skipped the ball but had found Brittany the next morning just before she'd left the hotel. He'd told her how Michal Slaydon had offered the job and he'd accepted. By now, he was probably with the family, or more likely at their home in California.

"I really need to stop thinking about the Slaydons," Brittany muttered to herself as she turned on the water.

From upstairs she heard Mason moving around.

Unfortunately, or perhaps fortunately, the Sharks had to forfeit their game against United since Shio was an improper player. Of course, how the story came out was that it had been a publicity stunt set up by the Slaydons. They wanted free advertising for their charity ball and Shio had appeared as a "guest star" for an exhibition. The paper was very clear: people like the Slaydons would do anything for free publicity. Already many of those who attended the game were claiming to have seen Michal Slaydon there in disguise.

The Sharks players didn't mind—they got to say they'd played with Shio Slaydon. Ben now had the cleats he'd let Shio borrow on a shelf. Shio's borrowed pants were also claimed by Craig's family and reportedly were never washed. Brittany never asked Mason about Shio's underwear he'd shown up with. At least it had never shown up in the wash yet.

Mason also benefited personally from the experience. While the United coach was sorely disappointed he couldn't sign Shio, he did send formal invitations to both Mason and Shelly to join the United team.

With Michal Slaydon's financial help, Mason would be able to afford it—but he declined. After seeing the players up close and personal, he wasn't so thrilled with the team. Instead, he joined a smaller, rival travel team called the Colonials FC. After all, he realized, you didn't get better by playing with the best, but by playing against the best. He'd beaten United once and felt sure he could do it again.

The doorbell rang, interrupting her thoughts so suddenly that she nearly dropped the measuring cup of oats.

Only one person would come around this early. Melissa probably wanted to show off her new gifts ... or to give another Slaydon update. Irritated, Brittany slammed the measuring cup to the counter. At the same time, she felt a little excited. Without cable TV or a newspaper, Melissa provided the only updates on the Slaydon family.

Brittany found herself hurrying to the door. She wore her pajamas, actually hand-me-downs from Mason. They were blue pants with a red robot top.

She opened the door and stopped dead in her tracks. Michal Slaydon, his wife, and all their kids stood grinning at her. Shio stood between his parents, his injured arm in a loose sling, balancing a pile of presents in his free arm. Tom was unloading more presents from a rented luxury sedan. A Christmas tree was tied on top. The old man she knew to be the grandfather was coming around the other side of the car with bags of groceries.

"Happy Christmas," Michal Slaydon said, smiling. "We just got out of church and decided to drop by for a bit. May we come in?"

Brittany stood rooted to the spot, speechless.

"Oh, they're here!" her mother called from the steps. "I didn't tell you, Brittany," she said gleefully, "because you're not the only one who can keep secrets in this house! They called yesterday and I invited them over!"

"England has rubbish weather for Christmas," Shio said sheepishly. His wide smile stretched across his face.

Zeon wore a lopsided grin behind him. Snowflakes stuck to his hair. "We all decided we'd rather spend it here. Hope you don't mind."

Brittany's mouth finally closed. "B-but you flew off to England!" she finally said.

"That was my doing!" Tom called behind a stack of presents. "I pulled some strings and sent some false information to the press. They'll get over it."

Marcus grunted. "Lisle better get over it," he muttered. Then he smiled at Brittany. "She's my girlfriend, and isn't too happy about it all. Don't worry. I'll make it up to her on New Year's."

His father raised his eyebrows. "With my money, of course."

All the men and boys wore similar dark suits with ties. Mrs. Slaydon and Maria had on identical cashmere coats over forest-green dresses. They'd just come from an early Christmas service, so of course they'd be dressed up.

Suddenly Brittany remembered she wore Mason's pajamas. "C-c-come in," she stammered, feeling her face grow warm. Turning with a jerk, she flew up to her room to change.

Christmas had come to her home. It would be a very merry one indeed.

Epilogue

Later that day, as the turkey just finished cooking, Brittany stood with Shio outside to ask a huge favor.

Mason and the other Slaydons were locked in a wild soccer tournament on a new Xbox system. Maria and Chris served as the spectators. All the kids, with Michal Slaydon and Tom Baker, had just finished a freezing game of American football in the snowy backyard—in their church clothes—and were thawing out. Shio, who only wore his sling in private—to keep him from climbing on the walls, so his dad said—had watched the game with Brittany.

The grown-ups were now busy with the food—potatoes, pies, cakes, and stuffing were all being prepared. Christmas music blared from a new stereo system, another gift from the Slaydons. Big Murdock would soon be arriving for supper. He'd spent the day at the shelter for a final Christmas, helping cook the ten turkeys provided by the Slaydons and pass out the numerous gifts, also donated by the Slaydons. Christmas had truly come that year. And finally Brittany had Shio alone.

After the football game had ended, Brittany had asked if Shio could talk in private. They'd wandered to the front yard and stopped at the end of the drive.

"Do you still want to make me happy?" she asked him now, giving him a sideways look while blinking snow from her eyes.

The flakes still fell heavy and there were two inches piled up so far. They did little to hide the anxiety on Brittany's face.

"Sure," Shio said, slightly nervous. "What? The tickets to England with your brother this summer aren't good enough?" He grinned to let her know he was teasing. That had been his present—an all-expense paid trip for three weeks to spend with the Slaydons.

"Oh, no. That is, uh, great. Awesome. But, uh, you see, I have this friend … who really wants to meet you …"

Shio gave a smile as he visibly relaxed. He pulled off his sling and gingerly rotated his injured arm. "Does she live around here?"

A short time later, Brittany led Shio up to Melissa's house. As they climbed the steps they heard a girl's voice call loudly from inside.

"Here, Shio! Here, Shio! Come here, boy! Come here, Shio. Be a good boy! Let me give you some hugs!"

Shio stopped mid-step and lifted his eyebrows at Brittany. "Are you sure about this?" he asked dubiously. His dark eyes looked a little frightened.

Brittany slapped him on the back, sending snow down his collar. "Of course. This is what friends do." She reached over and rang the doorbell.

High above their heads, the clouds parted briefly and a single star peeked through. A bright spot against the darkening sky, it let all below know that Christmas night had arrived. It was time to rejoice.

Snow continued to fall and the star slipped back behind a cloud, much like a soccer ball being slipped into a bag. Christmas remained below.

THE END

Acknowledgments

Writing a book may start as a journey taken alone, but it ends up an adventure with many new and old friends coming to assistance. I would like to especially thank my family and all those close who made it possible to find time to do the writing. Disappearing for long hours, forgetting to shower and eat, and acting rude and surly usually gives cause for alarm. Perhaps they are used to it now, but in my case, the family never panicked and carried on being the wonderful supportive people they are. Of course I could not have done it without the other Saur and Saur & Saur—you know who you are. (Guess what? I have a new cover for you to do.)

I also humbly thank Diana Cox and Kevin Anderson and his excellent editors for their patience and skill. That said, the player of the match goes to Ce-ce Cox of Outside-Eyes Editing & Proofreading. Through her hard work, a rough manuscript has turned into a dream come true. If a yellow card is deserved for any mistakes, it goes to me.

A special shout-out goes to all those who assisted in my "research" of soccer by allowing me to join those pickup games. You made me feel a part of the team from the get-go. And to all the kids and parents of Team 22 Bruins from all those years ago (has it really been that long?), your humble coach gives his thanks for putting up with him. Now that you're grown, I hope you haven't forgotten the joy of the game.

I also thank the countless soccer stars who shared their stories in books, videos, and brilliantly played games. It is an honor to be a fan of such a great sport, great players, and most of all, great people.

And finally I thank you, the reader, for giving me a chance to share this story. I hope you enjoyed it and found something of value. Most of all I hope you see the importance of respecting others, no matter their perceived status. Everybody deserves a chance and nobody deserves ridicule for taking it, no matter where the chance leads them.

Helping others is always better than hurting others.

Now go out there and play soccer!

About the Author

Gregory Saur is the author of several novels for young readers, including *Panterror! The Epic Babysitting Adventures of Rachel Pugsley* and *Royal Pains and Angels in the Outhouse*. From Virginia, he continues on his quest to one day become a soccer star. So far he has achieved this dream playing FIFA '06 on his computer. When he's not playing games, he is usually writing ... which, to him, is the greatest game of all.

www.ingramcontent.com/pod-product-compliance
Lightning Source LLC
Chambersburg PA
CBHW050520190726
48284CB00003B/875